MW01114614

Alone

A Novel

By

Ken Harvey

To Joe
Best Wishes
Ken Harvey #57

Copyright © 2017 Ken Harvey
All rights reserved
First Edition

PAGE PUBLISHING, INC.
New York, NY

First originally published by Page Publishing, Inc. 2017

All rights reserved. Copyright under Berne Copyright Convention,
Universal Copyright Convention, and Pan-American Copyright
Convention. No part of this book may be reproduced, stored in
a retrieval system, or transmitted in any form, or by any means,
electronic, mechanical, photocopying, recording, or otherwise,
without prior permission of the publisher.

ISBN 978-1-64082-535-2 (Paperback)
ISBN 978-1-64082-536-9 (Digital)

Printed in the United States of America

Dedication

I dedicate this book to all the strong women whose faith in God has gotten them through the tough times.

Acknowledgments

I would like to thank all the women who helped me along the way to make this book. I am blessed to have friends and relatives who offered encouragement, praise, and direction . It was a challenge to see if I could write this book, and I often felt like giving up. But like this book, strong women pushed me on.

Preface

I wait until I can't wait anymore. My heart does flip-flops, but so what, it's supposed to do that. It's the classic flight or fight syndrome. This is the moment I've been dreading because I no longer have the control. I can no longer choose my own destiny. It has been such a long time and now this. They said he's changed. They say that he's much better. They say that he's a new man and that what happened in the past really wasn't his fault. The past is the past. All I know is that I hate myself for harboring fear of him. God has not given me a spirit of fear but of peace and of love and sound mind. *God I wish he would have just died!*

Chapter One

I freeze in my tracks as I feel the warm summer air hit my face. I still myself and listened. Beads of sweat form tiny drops on my forehead and my heart begins to race. Everything around me on this God-forsaken island seem to have a unique life force; its own pulse, its own way of being. I know something is out of place. This island that I'm stuck on has become a part of who I am and I a part of it. Now I hope that it would become my ally.

Crouching down, I lower myself to the sand trying to identify the creaking sound off to my right. "Danger," the island whispers. "There is danger."

In the distance, a voice calls my name. It's Frank, he's the danger that the island is warning me about. He's the force that has become so out of line with nature. His low voice heavy with hate floats across the empty blue sky, sending a chill down my spine.

He shouts in anger, "Sherry!" The voice says, "Answer me!" I remained silent!

Each time I hear him speak, my flesh begins to crawl. This was a different Frank than the one I had known, the fourteen-year-old kid is now an eighteen-year-old man. He has become some sort of monster with one thought on his mind, and that thought is my destruction.

A small blue bird flies off suddenly in the background, causing me to jump. My heart beat increases to the point that I feels as though it is going to pop out of my body. God, I hate the feeling of jumping at every little noise. I hate not knowing whether it means my life or death, but that's what I am dealing with. That's the hand that fate set me up with.

I freeze again, hearing the sound of movement off to my left side. Turning quickly, I realize it was only a dead branch falling, but it is enough to force my heart to palpitate at an erratic rate. I've lived on this island for nearly four years, but that was not my choice. Like a castaway from an old TV series, I was stranded. I think it is 1992, but I stopped counting years. This island is now my home, and like it or not, I am stuck with it. If I could just identify the noise, I will be able to locate him. I can find Frank the grown man and turn the tables on him.

I freeze again as I hear him call my name once more. Each time I hear it, my flesh begins to crawl.

"Stop it," I say to myself, hating the feeling of fear that fights to possess my soul. I have to stop thinking like a victim; that's what he wants me to do. He wants me to fear him. He wants me to be frozen with fear. He wants to feel like he's the one in control.

I get down low to the ground and smell the earth beneath my face. Slowly, I crawl out of view. Silently, I thank God that I've kept myself in some sort of shape. My arms feel strong and my body fit. I can feel my shoulders holding up well against my body weight; years in gymnastic as child were paying off.

A small rodent runs past my face and pauses to look at me. It gives me an expression of surprise and then bares its teeth. I bare my teeth, and it returns to the underbrush.

Twigs and branches scrape my arms as I move silently across the damp, dense terrain. I'm not sure where I'm going, but I have to get somewhere, anywhere away from him.

"I'm coming for you, Sherry, and when I do…" I hear Frank's voice.

There is a pause, a sickness that wants to control me, to do bad things to me. He wants me to think of the pain he would cause me and then he wants to let me know that he would do much more.

Suddenly, I remember a Bible verse, "Yea do I walk through the valley of the shadow of death."

I stop. That Bible verse had been planted deep into my conscience, but it did little to comfort me now. My reality is somewhat different than my teachings. What I really want to do is curse. To stand up and shout at the top of my lungs, to tell him that if he comes near me I will cut off his nuts and shove them down his throat. That's what I want to do, it's not too religious, but I call it my Old Testament. An image of my mom shaking her head gets my mind going back to prayer, but like Jesus after he finished fasting, I see a shadow from the devil in front of me. It washes away any memories of my past life. The shadow wasn't there before. I blink, and now it is gone.

Was it him? Was he playing a game with me? A cool shiver runs up my spine and my stomach, which seems to be in a contest to see how tight and knotted it could become. "God help me," I say as I feel tears starting to form in my eyes.

A strong grip suddenly jerks my feet upward, and I'm being pulled along the ground. My body is tossed around like a rag doll; he's strong, stronger than me.

I want to cry, but I will not give him that satisfaction. Crying is for the weak. I can't be weak, not now, not ever!

The sun is behind him and cast a shadow in my sight, so I can't see his face. It doesn't matter, I know who he is and what he wants. His strong musky scent filled my nostrils, and it makes me nauseated. I can't let this happen.

Give in, a voice in my head yells. *Let him have his fun. Separate yourself for the act. He can control your body but not your mind. You are the only two on the island.*

I hate that still small voice in me and push it away to a place deep in my soul. I begin to fight back if only to shut that voice up, to show that voice that I am not a child or any type of person who gives in. No one takes anything from me. Ever!

He put his hand around my throat, and I feel the wind slowly being squeezed out of my body. Grabbing at my shirt, he rips it. Not a problem. I don't think I will be going out tonight anyhow.

Fight, I tell myself. *Hit him where it counts. Remember the year I took a karate class. Remember the chart on the wall that pointed out the areas that could do the most damage, remember the soft spots.*

I pull back my hand and extend the palm upward. I exhale and explode into what I think is his nose. Warm fluid gushes over my body, and for a moment, he let go of my neck, and I can breathe again.

I gasp for air in large gulps, not knowing when his next attack will come. He's still straddling me with his thighs pinned against my body, keeping me from escaping. *God, where is that voice in my head now?*

I know I've hurt him, but I have to focus and remember that when you get your opponent down, don't let up.

In some ways I hated damaging his face. On the island, he had become like a brother to me, a son to all of us, a cute kid with the face of an angel.

My mission now is to do as much damage as possible. If I can hurt him, great, but if I killed him then even better.

My body is a weapon, I say to myself. *Fight like there is no tomorrow*. I curl up my hands like claws and begin to scratch and rip away at his body. I dig in deep into the side of his arm and break several nails, but it was worth it. I hate the fact that I could not dig deeper.

Nevertheless, it is enough to make him scream. *Good*, I think to myself, *let him hurt. Let him feel pain. I'm now the hunter.*

He starts to lift his body off mine, and I only have seconds to get free. I scramble as fast as I can to get away from him. I still can't get a good view of his face, but I know he's hurt. That for the moment is the good news, but the bad news is now he is pissed off.

We both are on our feet now. I maneuver into my kick-boxing stance and ready myself to do some damage. I am tired of running, tired of being fearful, now I will fight. He is leaning over still holding his nose. Blood is flowing freely down his mouth and onto his chin as it pools near the bottom and then drops to the ground

I hope I broke it. I yell to him.

I ball up my fist and swing. He's faster than I thought he would be and ducks it. Then to piss me off, he starts to laugh at me, exposing his mouth that is now filled with blood and then spit it at me. I hate to be laughed at. Everything within me became unglued.

I ball up my fist and swing again, but this time he catches my arm and throws a punch of his own. It's my turn to feel pain. My face explodes as if it is on fire; little darks spots begin to dance around my body and before my eyes.

God, it can't end this way, not now, I think to myself. *I have to stay focused. Don't let him know you're hurt.* He stands and looks at me, not even trying to fight anymore. He just stands there looking. *Do something. Move. Try to come at me. What are you thinking?* I think, trying to figure out what he is up to.

"Sherry, what are you doing?" he says with a grin. "Come on and stop fighting me. It doesn't have to be this way. We can be friends."

He extends his fingers, making the sign of peace. "Sherry, I only want to talk. Can we talk?" His voice is smooth, dripping with honey, full of a false love, a hating lust.

I sense something within me pushing me toward him, trusting him. After all, I knew him as a boy. I helped raise him.

"Trust him," the voice says.

I began to put down my arms and walk toward him as if in some sort of trance. He smiles but that's okay. I am only faking to gain his trust. I move in quickly and kick him between his legs. It's a good solid kick. My instructor would have been proud. I could feel the soft sack between his legs move up into his body. Bingo!

How's that for trust?

His eyes roll to the back of his head as he falls to the ground, shaking and holding himself. He's in pain, and I catch myself now laughing. I've always done that when I was either mad or nervous but know I feel in charge.

Quickly, I look around and find a large stick. I pick it up over my head, inhale, and let it come down with full force across his jaw. I do it several times until I see blood oozing out his ears. "I hope he's dead."

Now what do I do? There really is nowhere to go. I sit there holding myself, trying to weigh my options. We both were stuck, stranded on a deserted island.

A breeze brushes across my face as I inhale salty air. I have been running for what seems like an hour now. I don't really know why I'm running. He's dead. I killed him moments ago, or at least I hoped so.

I can't help wondering if he is truly gone. After all, I didn't check his pulse. I didn't take time to make sure the damage I inflicted was fatal. I guess fear is fear, and fear makes you doubt. It makes you question everything you've already done, changes the outcome, and creates a new result.

Looking at the sun, I can tell it is about high noon. My watch died a long time ago, but I trained myself to tell the time by the position of the sun in the sky. I guess in another life I could have gotten a badge in Girl Scouts.

Just now I begin to feel the pain in my face. I move my tongue around and feel a deep cut in my lip. I taste the blood and spit. No biggie. I have tasted blood before. In a way, it is a good feeling. Like a prizefighter who knows he's been in a fight, it makes the victory that much sweeter. Today reminded me of an old movie, *The Last of the Mohicans*. I feel as though I am the last one left.

It's almost a letdown to have gone through all this and realize the prize is to spend the rest of my life alone.

To be alone by choice is one thing, but alone on an island with nothing but yourself is a whole different beast. I guess that is the hand that I've been dealt.

"Why God?" I say out loud, almost expecting a reply. I feel like shouting at him, but I'm tired of singing that same song. Maybe there is no why, maybe he doesn't care. How could a great and loving God allow everything that's happened to happen? I hesitate and then ask him for forgiveness. I am alive.

I can hear the ocean in the distance. Great, at least I have a better bearing on my surroundings. This island is not that big. One side is protected by a large rocky mountainous cliff. The rest is surrounded by water. This has been my life for the last four years, and I know most of the general surroundings but still there are parts that I have yet to be explored.

The sound of a twig cracks behind me. I jump and prepare myself for battle again. "He has to be dead," I say to myself. "I know he is. I killed him. I saw the blood. He is dead!"

"*Maybe not*," that same little voice says to me again. This time that voice is weak and afraid as if a small girl abandoned by her parents. I wonder whose voice it is, but I didn't have time to investigate. *Did you check the body?* I ask myself. *Did you really kill him?* Maybe this time it was he who is faking.

I hate that little voice I have been hearing lately. I guess it's the first sign of going crazy; but if that's true, I have been crazy a long time. You get used to talking to yourself when there is no one around to answer. All this time on the island and the back and forth conversation that you have only in your mind becomes less abnormal as the years pass and sometimes you even welcome it.

Out of the corner of my eye something runs across my path. Can't tell what it is, don't care, as long as it is not him. I begin to laugh again. "Come on, Sherry, get yourself together. You've done it. You survived and are the victor. This is not some horror movie where the dead comes back to life. You are the survivor."

I look down at my hands and body; I look like bloody hell. Wait, I'm not English, but knew a girl who was. Guess that is where I got the word *bloody* from, and I guess this situation may be the proper use of it.

I can still see pieces of his flesh under what's left of my nails. I need a long hot bubble bath and for a moment a sweet memory of the past drift into my mind. I can see myself soaking in a large tub, bubbles floating gently across my body, the warm water cascading off my back, but reality comes back as I look down. Shirt ripped—damn! I don't have too many clothes left, and I really don't feel like going native. Guess I will have to rip and tear and try to make something to cover myself.

The white sand looks beautiful now, almost peaceful. The small white peaks of the ocean tide flows in gently from parts unknown. I had a life out there once. I had just finished college and received a degree in marketing from Howard University. My parents, although not rich, saved their hard-earned money and sprung for a cruise trip for me. They said that I have been working hard all my life and will probably be working for the rest of my life once I got a job. They wanted me to relax and have some fun.

I hate the thought of them blaming themselves for what they believed was my death. No one could have known what happen. It was no one's fault, or I guess it was someone's fault but not theirs. They were the best parents a girl could have. I mean, they are the best parents; I have to stop myself from talking in the past tense. I am not dead, and I pray to God that they are still alive also.

Chapter Two

I feel myself being pushed from behind, and I tumble to the ground. Bushes, rocks, and sticks push up against my face as I slide down the side of the hill. The good news is that it's not a long fall, the bad news is that I hurt myself pretty bad.

I lay on the ground moaning in pain for what seems a long time. Looking into the glaring sun, I see the birds, clouds, and a shadow. He is standing over me. I thought he was dead, I thought I killed him, but now he is over me. Shit!

I look up at him and feel that this is déjà vu. Matted and dried blood covers most of his face; there is a crazed look in his blue eyes. He smiles as kicks me in the ribs. I feel pain but not so much as fear beginning to build up in me. I know that he will kill me. He will make me pay first and then he will kill me.

The voice in my head tells me to say goodbye. *Shut up,* I tell my voice.

He kicks me again in my ribs more viciously than before. He doesn't say anything, and I don't think he can. His lower jaw seems to be offset from his face. I think I broke his jaw—

my victory. If I die, at least he will live life eating his food through a straw.

He stops for a moment and looks at me, a cold hard stare. I'm really scared now. Pain I can deal with, but him just staring at me freaks me out. What's he thinking? What is he planning?

Slowly he reaches up and grabs the side of his jaw and gives it a sickening jerk. He screams as he doubles over in pain, and then after a minute, he stands. His jaw is back in place. I guess I only dislocated it. Shit!

He starts to kick me again, this time a lot harder and a lot faster. I begin to fade. There is no longer pain. I feel myself slipping away. I guess dying isn't so bad. No pain, no fear, no anything. I don't see a light but that's OK. I know my maker, and I know where I am going.

It's quiet now. Everything is black. Am I dead? I feel peace, and I like this peace and don't want to leave. I guess this is heaven. All I need to do is just wait for my savior. A cool splash of water hits my face, bringing me back. I see light, and I feel sand beneath me and then I feel horrible pain. I don't know if my ribs are broken, but it sure does feel like it.

"I'm glad you're back," he says

"Go to hell," I say, seething with anger.

"You tried to kill me but couldn't, but I just might kill you," he mumbles through a swollen and painful jaw and then tries to laugh but it's sickening. With his mouth swollen and dried blood around his face, he looks like some sort of nightmarish animal or creature in some horror book.

He wants me to be scared; he wants me to be frightened and to react like a little girl. He is feeding on the fear, but I will not allow him the satisfaction

Kneeling down over me, he looks at me with glee in his eyes. Like a kid on Christmas morning, he is being fed by emotions. I decided to flip the script on him.

"Do what you want. I won't fight you."

His face contorts to a frown.

"That's no fun. Come on now. I bet I can make you scream."

I clench my teeth, preparing for the worst, but there is nothing. He gets up and walks away. What type of game is he playing? I'm afraid to move. This is maybe some type of sick adventure of his. Maybe there's a trap, and as soon as I move, he will watch my destruction with glee.

It seems like a long time has gone by, but I know it hasn't. I have to move, have to try; just laying here is driving me crazy. I know something is going to happen. I figured now is as good of time as any to get the ball rolling.

Getting up, I notice that my arm has a long cut on it; there is a mixture of blood and dirt that stopped me from bleeding out. It's weak, but I can still move it.

I see him in the distance looking at me. He's not too far away but out of my reach. Maybe my kick frightened him, maybe not.

Struggling to stand upright, I try to make a bold stance. My body feels funny, but I am not a quitter. There is silence between us but that's OK. I am ready to play this game again.

"What is going on? What do you want with me?" I feel the words blurt out of my mouth. It isn't what I want to say, but what is done is done. I wait for his reply.

"Are you OK?" he said with mock concern.

I stay quiet.

"You really should watch yourself," he says after a while. "Tell you what, I was a little angry and lost my temper and for that I am sorry. Let's start over. We're the only two left on this island. I really don't want to be here alone, do you? Let's call a truce."

Come a little closer, I say to myself. *I will give you another truce between your legs.*

"I know what you are thinking. I must be crazy and I was. Maybe it was the sun, maybe this island. I don't know what got into me. I'm sorry."

The kid is crazy if he thinks that I am going to believe him. The next chance I get, I will stick something straight through his heart, pick up a rock and smash his skull, burn his body, and throw the ashes in the sea and this time he will stay dead.

He starts to hum. I remember the song he is humming. We all used to hum it together around the fire. He enjoyed it so much when he was young, and we loved seeing his big bright smile as our music would become one with his spirit.

What is the name of that song? I think. I can't remember the title, but he knows I liked that song. I guess he is trying to kill me softly with his words.

I begin to laugh.

Even though it is a typical hot day, I feel cold inside. He's just standing there looking at me. "You want some of me, come and get me," I yelled at him, but he does nothing. Time for me to push some buttons.

"You know you look like your sorry -ass mother sitting there," I shout. He tries to act like it means nothing to him, but I see differently. I see the sting. He blinks rapidly and tries to smile.

Yea go ahead and smile. Now it's my turn to get into your head.

"You think your mother would be proud of you? You think you're a man? Your mom was weak, that's why everything around her died because she wasn't worth anything to anyone."

I know they're harsh words, but I have to get him fired up. We need to end this one way or another.

"You want to know the sad part? No one even noticed she was gone."

I notice his hands ball up into a fist. This is a risky game I'm playing, but I have to do something. I can't spend the rest of my time running, and I am tired of playing around.

He starts to take a step toward me but then hesitate.

"She was weak and you're weak. By the way, how's your jaw feel?"

I hit a button. He starts to run toward me. I plant my feet and ready myself for the attack. I bend my knees, but only slightly, just enough to be able to spring into action. Placing my right arm in front with the left in back, I ready myself to throw and block a punch.

Sand is kicking up behind him, and he is moving. He's faster than I thought but that's OK. I will not underestimate him. I narrow my eyes to block out the sun. I focus and see what appears to be the same blue bird that I ran into earlier, maybe a sign from God.

Five…four…three…two—wait, wait. I swing with my right expecting to land a solid punch against his already hurt face, but I miss. That slick little son of a gun dives at my legs, and I feel his powerful shoulders push deep into my midsection. I hear the whoosh of air leaves my body.

Here we go again, I think to myself. As my back hits the ground hard, I somehow manage to hook my arm around his neck. Using his momentum, I flip him over, allowing myself to come up on top of him with some sort of backward head-lock. It was a move I picked up at my old classes, and I hoped it would pay off. I try to squeeze his neck hoping he would pass out. It didn't work. Somehow he managed to grab my arm and pull it free. He's stronger than I expected and pulls my arm and locks it behind my back. I can feel my shoulder and elbow crack as he uses all his force to get me down.

Tasting sand, he pushes my head into the ground. It's hard to breathe, but that is not the worse. I feel his hand feeling on my breast and then moving down to my pants. He is breathing hard; I can feel his heart beating next to me.

Wiggling, I manage to move his hand from out of my pants, but he still has my arm locked. Mind racing, I try to figure what maneuver to use to get free. He has the advantage; he is on top of me with all his weight. I open my mouth and take in as much sand as I can. Rolling my head over my right shoulder, I arch my back to face him. He allows it thinking that he is going to attack me from the front. He wants to see my face, which is to my advantage. I grimace, allowing him to feel like he is in control. He moves closer as if to say something to me. I spit the sand in his eyes with all my force.

Reaction from the sand causes him to let go of my arm. My body falls back to the ground with a thud. It's painful, but I manage to bring my arm back around to the front of my body. It hurts like the dickens, but I push myself to my feet.

He's still trying to get sand out his eyes when I hit him again in his groin. Good old standby. He falls to the ground and begins to cough up blood. I hurt him, but he has fight left in him. He hits me in the stomach, and I join him on the ground. He grabs my hair and begins to throw punches to my face. I feel warm blood ooze out my mouth again. I claw his face, and he lets me go.

He starts to swing wildly, so I guess he is still blinded from the sand. I kick him in the jaw. I hear a *POP* and he screams. I scream also because that kick hurt my foot. I try to ignore the pain, but now I am at a disadvantage. I really can't move that well, but good thing I still got my arms. I throw a punch, hitting the jaw again and this time I fell the sudden give of his bones; it sends him backward. I have only minutes to pounce.

He catches me in midair with a wild elbow to the side of my head. I don't think he knew where I was, but it caught me right in the temple. Stars begin to dance in front of my eyes while darkness tries to overtake them. I lay on the ground right next to him. My body is paralyzed. *Come on, legs, move*, I mentally say to myself. Nothing, there was no response. *Move it, Sherry*, I try to give myself a pep talk, but it doesn't work. Too late, he is on me and he's pissed. What's he going to do? He puts his hand around my throat, and I began to choke. His other hand moves too my pants again. Just like a man. Kicking his butt nearly broke his jaw and he is thinking about one thing.

He pushes my legs apart with his knee; I guess he is going to rape me.

He was like a son to me, to all of us, and now this? I grit my teeth and prepare for the worst. He pulls my pants down, more like ripped them nearly off. Next he lowered himself on top of me and then, then…nothing. He tries, makes the motion on me but nothing. Guess my kicks worked. After a few minutes of struggling to get it up, he settles for beating me. Darkness invades my mind again. I go back to the land of emptiness. Maybe this time I will see that bright light and finally meet Jesus.

Darkness is home for me for a while until I come to. I try to open my eyes, but they hurt to open, I force them anyway. The smell of sea salt burns my nose, causing me to form what appears to be a snarled, "It OK, it doesn't matter." It's something that I would have done anyhow given the situation. My head began pounding, especially near the left temple in which I was hit. I try to move but realize my hand and feet are tied together.

"Wimp," I think, scared of a twenty-six-year-old woman.

Everything is not clear, but I can see him sitting across from me. There's a fire that separate us but that's it. He is sitting on a log, but it's not any log, it's the same log that we use to all sit on while we played games and sang songs. The log was from an old tree that had fallen near the edge of the beach. It took a lot of hard work to move it into place but became our resting place, our sanctuary, and our family table. In a way, I miss everyone. I even missed Cynthia, but only a little.

I moan reflexively as I moved, but I hoped it was quiet enough not to grab his attention; he stirs in his seat. Maybe he sees me, maybe not. I move all my fingers and toes to make sure they were all still there. Yep, still there, that's good. I close my eyes quickly. It's better if he assumes I'm still out, which will give me time to think of what to do next. As the pain increase like the ebbing of the ocean, it becomes hard to focus. Mindlessly, I begin to drift back to the beginning of it all, to where it first started and the events that led me to be alone on the island with Frank.

I remember running to the door on my way to a class, the feeling of butterflies. My stomach is in knots because I had been expecting my parents all day. My mother called me earlier to tell me that she and my dad would be stopping by my apartment later tonight and that they had a surprise for me. Mom was never any good at keeping surprises, but this time she did. She only went so far as to tell me that it was going to be great.

The fact that she didn't spill the beans had me excited. I went through a list of things that I thought it could be. They barely had enough finances to take care of themselves, let alone spend money on me, but they have always been resourceful. I smile, getting my hopes up a bit.

New clothes or maybe that purse that I wanted. Naw, my dad never saw the sense in paying so much for something that you would not use every day.

Maybe it is a homemade meal?

Each possible winner was shot down with a reason why it couldn't happen. No matter, whatever it was, I was ready for it. I had one more class to finish at school before they arrived later that evening. The class was in marketing, which I enjoyed but was not that keen on my instructor Mrs. Harton. She was a tall voluptuous woman in her fifties, silver hair with tough leather skin, at one time in her youth she might have been a knockout but the effects of too much sun and one too many delicacies had taken their toll. A strong raspy voice revealed the hazards of too much smoking yet when she whispered it was like a sexy tempest. She enjoyed having the power in her class and wasn't afraid to use it. Every once in a while, she'd call a student to the center of the classroom and would strip them down with her vast knowledge of marketing expertise. I happen to be that student most of the time.

I figured that if I were to become her victim today, she had better watch out. I was in a good mood and knew nothing could change that. I had been preparing super hard to bring my B in her class to an A and giving the amount of time I had spent studying, she was in for a match.

The class went off without a hitch; no one was called to make an example of, just slides and a few minutes of lectures. I guess things must be going my way. The teacher excused the class, but as I was leaving she called, "Sherry, please stay back for a second." I felt a sickness in my stomach, but at the same time, I was ready to fight. I waited at the back until everyone left the room. It was a large class and took a few minutes, but there we stood, both of us facing each other. She grabbed my hand gently and pulled me to her side.

"Dear, I just wanted to tell you how proud I am of the job you are doing," she said.

I shouted at her not fully realizing that she had paid me a compliment. "I am doing the best I can." I stepped closer to her face. "And I have been working my butt off to get an A in this class, so give me your best shot." I could tell she half-expected my sudden outburst; she laughed.

"I know that I've been hard on you, but you have been my diamond in the rough, and I would like to believe that I have been the pressure to help form you. Continue the good work." She smiled. "You will be getting an A in my class." And she then patted my hand and walked away.

I stood there in a daze for a moment soaking it all in. Could this day get any better?

After a long walk home, I was floating on cloud nine oblivious to the people around me. I unlocked my door and looked around. The place was a mess, but after quickly placing a few items in my closet, running the vacuum, and opening a window to allow the fresh air to replace to the stale smell, the house was as good as new.

My stomach growled but that's OK. I've gone without food before. Besides, I want to be hungry just in case the surprise was my mom's homemade ox tails and greens. Looking at my watch, I noticed it was 6:45 p.m. If my dad had anything to do with it, they should be showing up any moment. He hates being late and would do everything in his power to always be on time, if not early. It was something he learned in the military.

The doorbell rang. That's my dad. I smiled as I think about his punctuality. I rushed to the door and opened it. My mom is all of 5'2", slender and pretty. She has light caramel skin that reminds you of the caramel apple you use to see at amusement parks, thick wavy black hair, and hazel eyes that seem to hold you in place with a gaze.

My father is the exact opposite; he stood over six feet tall with smooth dark skin. Although at one time he was a trim athlete, he has put on quite a bit of weigh giving him a large jolly frame. His clean-shaven head gave him the Michael Jordan look, which sit well with the shape of his head.

"Baby girl, baby girl," my dad said with his arms extended wide for a big hug. My mom knew the routine and moved out the way, waiting for my dad to get his satisfaction.

I ran into his arms, which was the customary greeting for the two of us. Next my mom came up to my side and gave me a kiss on the cheek. That was how we always did it regardless of when or where.

I rushed them in and sat them down, hurrying them through a conversation that merely filled time. I wanted to know what the big surprise was but knew better than to be rude. My mom, sensing my excitement, nearly gave the surprise away at the door had not my father jumped in and changed the subject.

"Baby, we are so proud of you. Everyone is proud of you." By everyone, he meant the whole town in Petersburg, Virginia, where I was from. Everyone knew everyone's business which in some ways was good but bad if you every got into trouble.

"Bet you can't wait to find out what the surprise is?" my dad said, grinning ear to ear.

"Of course she can't," my mom said, unable to hold it in any longer. "The whole church is so proud of you and you know we are. Last Sunday, the pastor requested a special offering for you and the congregation raised enough." My mom paused and moved in a little closer. She was like the kid at Christmas waiting for the surprise instead of me. "We raised enough money to send you on a cruise and a little spending cash before you start off your new career, new life." She began to apologize that it was not the best ship, but I stopped her.

I had always dreamed of going on a cruise since watching reruns of *The Love Boat* on the TV channel when I was a child. I was not much of a partier, but I did love the ocean even though I had really never been out to sea. The gift was perfect, and the look of love in my parent's eyes brought tears rolling down my face.

That was their gift, and for the moment, I knew that I was the luckiest girl in the world.

Chapter Three

A sharp pain radiating in my stomach brings me back to the present. He walks by and kicks me trying to see if I was still out. It took most of my willpower, but I didn't move. I allow my body to become soft and absorb most of the force. The pain was great, but I could take it. I had to take it.

When I trained at my dojo, Grandmaster Kim use to drop medicine balls on my stomach to toughen me up, big points for him, even after all these year my abs are still strong.

I hear him mumbling to himself and walks away. He curses my name under his breath, but as long as I'm still alive, he can curse me all he wants.

I part my lips slightly as I let air out my body. I know he is watching me, and I don't want anything to seem out of place. Even though I feel the aftereffects of the kick, I keep a nice rhythmic beat to my breathing.

I begin to listen to my breaths—inhale, exhale, inhale, and exhale. It becomes soothing after a while, almost hypnotic. I began to drift back to that familiar place of my past.

My parents waved me off as I set sail on my first cruise. I bought along a few swimsuits (although I wasn't much for sitting in the sun with my natural tan and all) and a lot of outfits just to lounge around in. Everyone seemed so friendly and in a way I was a little sad that is was just me going, but I had always been kind of a loner and not really a dater. I did enjoy the company of men, but I figure when the right person showed up, I would know it. Maybe I would meet him on the cruise.

The ship was small and really didn't look that safe, but for the money and because the cruise was bought with love, it was perfect. It began to pull away, and I waved goodbye to my smiling parents. My mother looked childish standing next to my dad as we move slowly toward the ocean. I felt that he should put her on his shoulder like a child at a parade to give her one last look. Others were yelling and waving next to me. Some were couples, some single. The skies looked gorgeous above, clear and only filled by the bright sun. *This is going to be a great cruise*, I thought to myself.

Everyone started to walk away from the railing once the ship pulled out of the harbor. Some waved a finial goodbye to their loved ones and then faded to their rooms or to explore the boat, but I stayed there. I put my arms around myself, soaking in the love that was given to me by my parents and my church. A man in uniform walked by and smiled. He's cute—maybe this will be a great cruise.

After an hour of just walking around, I headed back toward my room. It was small but had a port window to look out of. I see endless water and began to wonder if this would be all I have to look at for a few days. It's great for the moment, but it may get boring after a while so I am thankful that I brought a few romance novels that I had been waiting to dig into. I sit down for a second but can't stay still, so

I decide to get up and take a look around and explore my surroundings some more.

The first thing that comes to mind is how uniquely made the ship was. I was surprise that the ship resembles an old sixties movie hotel with its huge pillars and large billowing curtain in one section. There was one shop to buy gifts from. It was filled with clothes that ranged from dressy outfits to cheap ones and various other highly priced gifts for those who could afford it. Wide stairs also line the walls leading you to each and every floor. A casino was lodge tightly in the corner, and I was sure that by the end of the night, it would be packed to overflowing. A large pools was placed near the middle of the ship; it was accompanied by a small putting range and a rock-climbing wall.

I had just made my way to the upper deck when I met the captain. He was a large man; about six feet tall with broad shoulders and a radiant smile. He spoke with an assurance that you would expect from someone that could captain a ship. In some ways he reminded me of my dad as he took my hand in his and smiled. "Is this your first time?" he said.

"How could you tell?" I replied. He must have noticed the slight trembling in my throat as I stood trying to gain my balance.

"There is nothing to fear. This baby nearly drives herself. I am just here to make your ride is as enjoyable as possible." I smiled trying not to let him see how hard my heart was beating.

"Try not to hit any icebergs along the way," I said. He smiled and tipped his hat and said his goodbyes.

I hit myself in the head realizing how stupid I sounded. *"Don't hit any icebergs."* How idiotic. Way to go you marketing genius. For the rest of the cruise, I figured I would stay out of his way so nothing else stupid came out of my mouth.

I found my way toward the food court and nearly fainted at the amount that was spread about. Everything your mind could imagine was laid out in front of me. Large watermelons cut into the shape of swans filled with different fruits. Chicken cooked several ways, freshly cut steak, hamburgers, hotdog, the display seemed to go on and on; and I ate and ate and ate. The food wasn't as good as Mom's, but it was still very good.

For the next four days, everything was perfect or what I presumed perfection to be. The maid made my bed up every morning and food flowed from every orifice until I began to tire of eating. The sun seemed to follow us, bringing about the perfect temperature to warm our souls and tan those who needed the sun. Everything was perfect until the day I heard a boom.

Have you ever had a day when everything outside was quiet and peaceful, there's not a cloud in the sky and nothing to distract you? No birds, no, animals, no wind, no anything. The day seems almost like a picture printed in a magazine.

That was what this day was like; everything was just right until out of nowhere the once-blue sky becomes gray then dark black. A loud ringing boom rocked the foundation of the ship. A moment before, everything was perfect and stable then in a heartbeat there was swaying back and forth and a powerful wind that began throwing furniture around. We were at once is a powerful superstorm. In a way I was angry with the captain. He had promised me smooth sailing all the way and now this. His strong voice come over the loud speaker as he explained that the storm had rolled up out of nowhere and the only thing they could do was to go right through it. He told everyone that it should be a short display of lights and wind, but it would be over shortly. He lied.

In the beginning that's just what it was, a simple lightning display. I kept telling myself to look at the window and see how awesome Mother Nature was. I tried to convince myself to enjoy it, but I was not much for lightning, especially since it seemed so close to the ship. It also didn't help that an angry rolling ocean was our only foundation.

A few moments after the light show, the rain started, soft at first, a gentle tap on the hull of the ships walls, and then the rhythmic beat of drums, a flash followed by a great boom and then the rain came on in full force. The winds began to pick up, tossing the ship back in forth. I was thankful the captain ordered everyone to back to their cabins because I could easily see someone falling overboard. My heart began to pound, and my legs became wobbly as I started to look for the nearest bag to throw up in.

I moved to close my window, not really wanting to see the sea anymore. A loud buzzer came on telling us to get our life vest on just for safe measures.

For the size of the ship, we felt like a toy in a child's bathtub. Giant waves splashed against the metal hull, causing the ship to rock from side to side and then up and down. Deck chairs were thrown overboard and the things that were not locked down were smashed against each other. In my own twisted sense of humor, I laughed as I thought about the whole bottom deck throwing up.

Holding my stomach, I kept thinking that things couldn't get worse, but I was wrong. Amidst the screams from frightened passengers, I heard a loud bang; and although there was thunder and lightning outside, it sounded different. Chills ran through my spin as I realized that it did not come from outside the steel wall of the ship but from somewhere within.

This was bad news. I closed my eyes in silent prayer and opened them to see there was now water running across my feet; the ship was sinking. "Maybe the ship is not sinking," I tried to tell myself, maybe it is just water from up above or a busted pipe. I held on to whatever lie I could think of but the continued rush of water and the panic screams down the hall told me differently. My head began to be filled with images of me drowning. Although there were no black people on the *Titanic*, I would make up for it by drowning at sea.

The lights began to flicker, and it felt as if my heart was keeping the same rhythmic beat of the out-of-control lights. Flicker on for a second, then darkness, then light again. Deep down, I wished that I had paid more attention to the instructions that were given after we boarded the ship. Now my mind raced trying to remember the exact way to evacuate.

Another flash of lighting and then complete darkness followed. For a moment there was nothing, no lights or sounds, and then red flashing lights, screams, crying, and a loud buzzing sound signaling for everyone to start the evacuation process. Seeing the horror and dread on people's faces gave me a feeling of impending doom as I rushed to get out of my cabin

Take the stairs, not the elevator—at least I remember that much. I ran to the top of the ship just in time to see a huge wave hit its side. The ship rocked back and forth, creaking as though it was going to break apart, but it held or at least for that moment. I started to shiver not from the cold and rain that accompanied the storm but from the fear. I look out beyond the deck to see if there was land nearby. There was nothing but the blackness of the clouds and the sound or roaring water.

The ship's personnel were trying to hurry people into lifeboats. At times like this, they must be the bravest people in the world, I thought. I'm not sure if I could guide someone to safety while my life might be in jeopardy. Again, I thought of the *Titanic* and hoped they still believe in women and children first.

I'm not sure who all were on the boat with me. I've never thought myself as a selfish person, but I pushed and shoved with the rest of them. My church would not have been proud, but this was a time of survival.

The wind and the rain was blinding as I grabbed along the edge of a lifeboat. There were several of them already in the water as they lowered ours with a powerful crash on ocean. I couldn't tell how many people were on board, but I heard their screams. Men, women, children, all of them screaming. I was one of them.

The best roller coaster in the world had nothing on the heights and dips we face as our little boat came crashing back down only to rise up in the air again. An elderly woman next to me lost her grip and tumbled overboard to what I presume was her death. I reached out for her, but there was nothing I could do; she was lost to the blackness that in turn would be waiting for me. What was supposed to be a small storm went on for hours and hours. I remember seeing in the background flickering light as the cruise ship capsized and began to sink.

Funny how perspectives play a large part of your life. The cruise liner seemed as small and distant as a firefly against the darkened skies. We must have appeared as no more than a spec ourselves. I saw a man in front of me screaming words that I could not hear. The rain drowned out his voice, and my heart was beating so loud that it was hard to focus on his mouth and read his lips. I could not tell if he was part of the crew or not, but he seemed to be trying to tell me something amidst the blinding rain

Another huge wave came crashing, sending several more people overboard. I held on for dear life each time the boat came crashing down on the watery surface thinking the lifeboat would split apart, but it survived. Life vest would do little good against the tremendous force of the pounding waves if you fell over. I couldn't tell how long we fought the storm, but in the end after it had calmed down, there were only five of us and a child still left.

I looked across at the group getting a mental picture of those around me. The same man who was trying to yell something at me had survived, but he didn't look well. His name was Stan and he had several large bloody cuts on his body and face, and by the awkward position of his body, it appeared as though some bones might be broken. Soft moans escaped his mouth as he drifted back and forth between consciousness. To my right was a fairly large Caucasian woman who stared at me with haunting dark oval eyes. Her long dark black hair was matted to her head, and she looked as though she would vomit at any time. She said her name was Cynthia. There was no protocol, no handshake, just a slight nod of acknowledgement to recognize that she too was a survivor

Next to her was a petite blond woman, her name is Kathy, and she looked fairly young. Even among the tragedy, I could not help but notice that she had the prettiest blue eyes that now match the calm sea. Even soaking wet, she seemed so photogenic that she could have been a model for life vest. She held her arm around a young child that could have been about thirteen or fourteen. There was no doubt that he was her child. His wavy blond hair had begun to dry in different spots, giving him the pillow head look that you often saw from white kids in college. He also possessed the identical blue eyes of his mother. Frightened, he held her close, squeezing her waist.

The third lady, Rosa, appeared to be of Spanish descent with light olive skin and dark black hair. She was short but shapely and may have been eighteen or a bit older; although she appeared young, judging by her taunt look she has had a hard life. She did not speak, so I figured her English was not that good. I rounded out the rest of the group, and as I cupped my hand in my face, I said a silent prayer and tried not to cry.

We had been in the water for a few days; the nights were the worst because if there was no moon, only darkness comforted us as we drifted around endlessly to a place unknown. On board the small raft was some water left over from the rains, a first aid kit and a small amount of food, but everything else was destroyed. The flares were wet and destroyed. The radio was smashed and at the moment so was our hopes. If there were some sort of beacon, it did not work or at least not that I knew of.

Stan was doing poorly. His cuts had become infected turning black and purple with a tint of yellow. His whole left side seemed to be swollen. The large gashes seem to fuse together with pus and blood, and worst of all they were starting to stink. I tried to ease his pain by talking to him; I wanted

to make him as human to me as possible and not just someone that was waiting to die. He told me his last name, which
accompanied the first name I already knew. Even in pain, he
said it was a sense of pride. Stan, Stan Lawson. He was married to a woman named Julie, and they had two kids. He had
worked on the ship since it had first set sail nearly ten years
ago and said that he had never experienced a storm like what
we went through. "I can't understand why we started taking
on water and all the equipment went dead," he kept saying
over and over during his moment of sanity.

He tried to pass on his knowledge about survival to me,
but his speech was slurred and most of the time he rambled
back and forth about things that made no sense. One of the
few times he was sane he made me promise that I would tell
his family that he loved them. I squeezed his hand and promised. I tried to reassure him that things would be OK, but we
all knew differently. There were limited supplies in the first
aid kit and deep down we knew we had to decide whether
or not to use it all up on him. We did not have to speak, our
looks told the answer, and so my speaking to him was the only
ointment for pain that I could offer.

We all had lost several pounds, but Rosa seemed the
worse. She was already very slim, but now she appeared as a
survivor from a concentration camp. We faced two problems
as I saw it; Stan who was nearly dead and the fact that we
were nearly out of food. The small supplies we had consisted
of crackers, a few candy bars, dried fruit. Water would be the
next problem because it had not rained since the last storm,
and drinking seawater was out the question. We drank spar-
ingly from what we had left over from the storm, but it was
not nearly enough for all of us. Fortunately, Cynthia had self-

ishly taken a bunch of clothes with her as if she had packed for some sort of emergency. I thought of the room it took on our small lifeboat and the extra person that could have replaced it, but then to my shame, I was glad because it we had one less mouth to feed

The sun was a vicious monster pounding down on our heads. The only real protection we had against its blistering heat was the clothes that Cynthia brought with her on the boat. Even with that protection, most of the women had become a shade of red that resembled a fresh steamed lobster.

The sun also continued to cook Stan's poor sick body. The infection on his arm and face had turned his body to a mush of infection. The smell had become so putrid that we used the clothes to cover our noses as protection from the stench. Greenish brown puss oozed from open wounds, dripping into the boat and contaminating the water that was not saved. He was near death but not quite there.

Cynthia decided to take command of the situation and told us to throw him overboard. Everyone else was silent and looked to me for direction since I had been the only one to talk to Stan. I had not wanted to become a leader, but faith sometimes puts you in position to become what you were meant to be.

"He stays," I said, putting my hand on his soft soggy shoulder. The thought of me touching someone like him a few weeks ago would have been out of the question but now it was as if I had to protect a friend.

I could tell Cynthia did not like to be challenged, and she was ready to go to battle over the issue as if Stan were no longer a living person but something akin to a child's sickly pet. Stan spoke up out of nowhere, startling us as we realized that he was conscious. His voice was barely a whisper, but we all leaned in close to listen. "Just one more day, just one more day," he said in a weak plea. It was the only words he spoke, but it said everything. I'm not sure if anyone is prepared to die especially the way he was dying, but one more day may have been his way of making peace with his maker, and I made a vow to myself that we would allow this. Cynthia soften a bit, not out of pity for Stan but out of the fact that he would be dead anyway, and one more day would not make a difference

Chapter Four

Stan lasted longer than a day. It was the second day beyond his plea, and we were out of food and starving and waiting for a man to pass on. We seemed like vultures waiting on it prey to die so that we could dispose of the corpse. I hoped him dying would be easy, but death is never easy. At night, sleep was hard knowing what may happen. I looked at Stan in between my moment of fighting for nocturnal bliss and forcing myself to stay awake to check if he was still alive. Deep down I hoped he died between the night and the next morning. I could not imagine us having to decide what to do by morning if he was still alive. He was already living on borrowed time.

Hunger pains racked my body as I wavered in between sleep, fear, and starvation. Tomorrow would bring a resolution one way or another.

Everyone else dozed off against the gentle waves after giving in to lack of energy. My heart went out to the young boy who still held on to his mother's side. I believe she said his name was Frank. Good name. He looked like a Frank.

Tomorrow, Frank may have to witness a death either naturally or with assistance.

I moved close to Stan and nearly choked on the smell, his decomposing body produce an odor that was similar the rotting fish and shit. "So how are we feeling, champ?" I asked, trying to put on my best face. The moonlight hid most of my discomfort, but I pressed in closer. "You need anything?"

"Maybe a steak with some potatoes," he said, trying to smile. He made a joke, maybe he will get better. That thought soon vanished as he coughed up dark red blood and curled up in pain. I placed my hand once more over his soft body and told him not to speak. We both tried to get some sleep.

I am not sure, but it seemed like he smiled at me. I don't think he died right away, but when I woke up in the morning, Stan's eyes were close and his body limp. We all looked at each other until Cynthia spoke, "I guess he's dead, huh?" she said in a matter-of-fact way. I did not like her. The way she said it brought a chill to my body. It was cold and heartless.

"Should we not say something?" Rosa said in broken English. She had not said much throughout this whole ordeal, but now her statement demanded attention.

"What can you say about a man that you don't know on a boat in the middle of nowhere?" Cynthia said, rolling her eyes, not wanting anything to do with what she felt was a waste of time. Kathy remained quiet holding her son close to her as if to protect him from the unpleasantness at hand, and so I spoke, "Lord take care of Stan. Amen." There was nothing else I could say.

The moment of truth had come; we had to dump his body into the ocean. I clasp my hand together and silently repented for what I was about to do.

We all sat quietly pondering how it would be done. Cynthia began opening and closing an all-purpose knife that had been part of the boat supplies. The noise became almost deafening to my ears. After a few minutes, I put my hand on hers to stop her. She pulled away.

"Don't touch me," she said full of an anger and hatred that I had not seen in her before.

Putting my hand up to show her I meant no malice or harm, I told her to calm down, but I also began to size her up. If I had to knock out that crazy twit, I wanted to know what I was in for.

"Here's what we are going to do," she said. "He's dead and that's a fact, but pushing him over board does no one any good." We all sat kind of puzzled at what she was talking about. "We need to survive, and I can't go any longer without food." She pointed toward the small box that held our first aid. "There're some hooks in there and a line, but we need bait." We all sat looking at each other, and then it hit us what she was talking about.

If I had anything in my stomach, I would have thrown up on the spot, even so I begin to dry heave. She wanted to use Stan as bait. Rosa, already weak, fainted as the morbid image that sunk into her mind. Kathy, as the protective mom, put her hand over Frank's ears. It was me and Cynthia, and now I knew I didn't like her. She was crazy.

"There is no way in the world I am going to let you do that," I told her, looking into her crazed eyes.

"Don't see you got much choice," she retorted. "We've got to eat and he's dead. He won't mind, and I'm sure the fish won't. Win-win for everyone," she replied. I went to reach for the knife, and she cut me. Warm blood oozed out of my hand as I grabbed it in pain. I could see Frank's eyes widen as I curled back.

"Don't ever try that again," she growled in an almost animal-like tone. I wasn't sure what to do. Any move I made would cause a vibration on the raft, and she would swing the knife again.

"I cut, we fish, and we eat. It is that simple. I don't know how much longer we will be out here, and I will not die this way," Cynthia said. I just sat there in horror at what I was hearing. She was willing to cut up a man, use his flesh as bait, and then eat the fish. I am not sure if that classified as cannibalistic, but it was pretty close.

"They're going to rescue us. You don't have to do this," I said, trying to reason with a madwoman. She didn't budge. I try to make Stan seem human instead of the dead corpse that he was. "Remember, Stan," I said pointed to his body. "He has a family like you do. He has a wife and two kids. They would not want their father to go this way." Cynthia's growl started to soften and then she began to cry.

"What about us? What about us out here in the middle of nowhere? What about how we are going to die? You think our family wants us to die of starvation?" she yelled in between her sobs. In her own warp way, she made sense; but if that's living, I would rather die.

"We can't do it," I said, wrapping a piece of cloth around my hand to stop the bleeding, as well preparing myself to make one more strike at her.

She readied her knife sensing what I was planning, but then Kathy slowly put her hand on Cynthia's hand and spoke. "Don't do it." That's all she said. Cynthia looked into her eyes and for some reason lowered her arm. It was a scene right out of *Beauty and the Beast*. She lowered the knife, and as if some veil was lifted from her anger she calmed down, put the knife to her side, and cried. Kathy hugged her as did Frank. If they expected me to do the same, then they had a long wait ahead of them.

Cut a man and fish with his flesh—I wanted to reach over and slap the taste out of her but my hand hurt, and I was feeling weak and tired from lack of blood and food.

I started to fade in and out, but I should have known Cynthia would be the person to step up and do the job. She put her hand under Stan's body and pushed him over. There was a small splash and then his body began to sink. Before he went under, his body flipped over until it was face up.

I think I saw a smile on his face, perhaps he was at peace, and then I faded into blackness.

I felt a burning sensation in my hand as I blinked to see Rosa's face looking down at me. Her deep sunken eyes displayed the sad situation we were in. My first thought was to kick Cynthia, but I held back my anger until I could get a better scope of our predicament

Rosa spoke almost in a whisper. "How are you, senorita?" I didn't say anything but nodded my head to show I was all right. Rosa took my hand out of the water and placed a fresh bandage she had made of torn cloth around my wound. The salt burned, but the attention I was getting made it feel a little better.

I tried to move, but she placed her hand over my shoulder forcing me to stay put. "Stan is gone. I don't want to lose you," Rosa said, trying to smile. Even on the boat, alliances were taking place, and I was glad to have someone on my side.

My head was still throbbing as I lay wondering what next. The "what next" was answered by the grumbling of Cynthia's voice. She leaned over and tried to apologize for the way she acted. She said it must have been the heat or lack of food that caused her to go off the deep end, and that it won't happen again. She pointed out the fact that she gave Kathy the knife, which I assume was supposed to make me feel good.

All through church, I've been taught to forgive, but my mouth could not form the words. I just looked at her and gave her a half-ass smile, which I figure was the same as her half-ass apology.

She didn't say anything more but went back to her side of the lifeboat. Rosa smiled at me and then returned to where she was sitting. I glanced around and looked at Frank. His face was a blank stare. He had seen a lot in a short amount of time. Death was never pretty and then seeing us fighting over Stan's body had to leave some mental marks.

I wanted to hug him, hold him, and tell him that everything would be okay; but I wasn't sure of that. There had been no signs of a plane or any type of rescue effort. We may die out in the middle of nowhere and who knows what his young life could have been.

Maybe God was talking to me, or maybe I felt guilty, but I didn't want his last memories to be of hate. I sucked in a deep breath and then reached out my hand to Cynthia and rubbed her leg. I told her I understood, it was OK, and that I forgave her.

I wondered, is it a sin to tell someone that you forgave them when you don't? God looks at the heart, doesn't he? I knew the answer but wanted to convince myself otherwise.

A small cloud floated past us as we tried to think positive thoughts. Nothing seemed to stand out in my head, and by the looks of everyone else, they felt the same. I almost wanted to laugh because I was so tired of crying.

Cynthia started to make a move toward me, and I ready myself to fight when she stopped short and pointed toward something in the distance. Her words were inaudible as we all turned to look around. In the distance, we saw a small speck. Our hearts collective skipped a beat at the thought that there may be an island out there. We all began to hug each other, and I even hugged Cynthia. Frank did not seem to get too excited, but I assumed he was too weak from lack of food. He just watched us.

After a few minutes of jubilation, we all settled down to a sad realization. We were floating in the middle of nowhere and had no way to control the direction the tides took us. We had no paddles, no motor, no anything.

There also was another problem: my blood and Stan's body brought about an unwelcome visitor—a shark. If this was a movie, I would have been scared because in most movies the black person dies first, but this wasn't a movie, and I had no plans on dying.

There was only one shark that we could see moving around our boat, slowly at first, as if trying to figure what the large object in the water was. It made wide circles around us, and then slowly it began to move closer. I told everyone to freeze and not move. I had seen somewhere on TV that sharks sometimes think that boats are wounded animals, and if we splash around, it would attack.

It came close to the surface, and I could see its dark black eyes. Rosa started to scream, but Cynthia put her hand over her mouth. We just sat there for a good ten minutes watching the shark circle around us and then out of nowhere it disappeared. We no longer saw its fins, there was no longer movement in the water, and it just disappeared.

We all looked at each other holding our breath. Did it leave? Were others going to come and replace it? No one knew, and I wished Stan were here to give us some wisdom. OK, I had to be the leader. We had to do something, and we couldn't just keep sitting out in the ocean waiting, so after about five minutes, I moved toward the edge of the boat. I had to take a look and see if it was still out there.

Putting my hands near the edge, I leaned my head over to take a peek; and as if in slow motion, I saw a faint shadow getting larger toward the surface. It was the shark. I couldn't react fast enough and knew my head would be its next meal, but instead, I felt myself being pulled to safety. It was Cynthia, and she had become my rescuer.

The shark pushed his head out of the water showing its awful rows of teeth and somewhere in between them was an arm and hand with a wedding ring. It had a piece of Stan in his mouth.

There is nothing worse than hearing four women scream hysterically at the same time; the shark swam around some more, jumping out of the water toward the lifeboat. We all screamed and held each other and then the most remarkable thing I had ever seen happened. Frank, nearly tripping into the water, ran to the edge of the boat and hit the shark square in the nose just as it was jumping up. His frail tiny fist hit the large shark's nose with a loud thud. The shark seemed to wiggle in pain before returning to the water and then it swam away.

I sat there with my mouth wide open, exposing my gold caps. I was in a state of shock. We all sat there still and looked at each other and then he spoke, "Sharks have very sensitive noses. I learned that from the Animal Channel." I did not know whether to laugh or cry, but I hugged him. We all hugged him and for a moment we had hope.

Salt water sprayed my face as we all used our hands to paddle toward the island. My shoulders burned with pain, but that was minor inconvenience compared to the joy we felt at possibility of reaching land. We continue to paddle for most of the day, not really making much progress, but God was on our side. Gentle waves continued to push us toward the shore until we finally made land.

Jumping out the boat, we felt the warm sand under our feet as we pulled the lifeboat on dry ground. We all began to dance in a circle, holding each other's hands. Energy that we had not known seemed to spring forward out of our bodies. I was no longer hungry, no longer tired, no longer mad. I was happy. We all were happy and screaming like little schoolgirls.

After we finished and the excitement wore down, we began to realize that we were on an island that we knew nothing about. The island was laced with large trees and dense shrubs in the distance. It was a typical look for what you might expect from a deserted island. A large sheer rock wall stood high in the background to the west of where we stood. I could only assume that this was an island made by a volcano, but I couldn't tell how long it has been around.

The island itself was a beautiful and breathtaking sight, endless white sand that cover the brim of the land like a luxury shag white carpet, trees swaying in the distance, and a feeling of peace. We grouped together and moved in toward to the trees hoping could find some food, which was number one on our list. We all stayed together fearing the unknown but determined to eat, to find salvation. Slowing moving in deeper in the trees, we found numerous types of palm and trees we could not even being to name, but it didn't matter; it was shelter against the heat. Cynthia took over right away and wanted us to go and search for meat. It was not that I wasn't on board and part of the team, but after what she wanted to do to Stan, I was not ready to be under her control. She wasn't my boss, and I remembered why I hated her. "We need to look around and see if there is any food on this island," she said, trying to establish her command. I started to protest, but like it or not, she was right; we needed food. I did, however, bring up the point that we needed to stay together. Call me a chicken, but I have seen too many horror movies and knew splitting up could be dangerous.

Cynthia protested thinking that we could cover more land if we split up, but after the rest of the group agreed with me, she gave in. We set off for the west side of the island for no particular reason except that direction looked like it had the greatest amount of trees.

Trudging through the brush, our legs began to feel heavy with the weight of our journey and the lack of food. We hadn't gone a hundred yards when Frank fell to the ground. His little body had endured as much as it could, and now he laid face-first in the in the dirt and leaves. His mother rushed to his side crying over him, and my heart cried out for her. Every bit of motherly love could only do so much; we had to find food.

Cynthia stopped and went toward Kathy and Frank. She showed a passion and sensitivity that I was not aware she had.

She put her arm around the both of them and promised Kathy that she would find food for them. It was a tender moment but only lasted for a second and then she returned to her drill sergeant self, giving orders and pointing out directions.

After moving deeper in, we heard birds and small animals and figured if they were out there, then there must be food—heck, they were food. Against my better judgment, I took off running. I am not sure but even the thought of food gave me energy to keep going.

Right near the edges of some large trees, attached to some bushes were very red berries and I picked them up and began shoving them into my mouth. Just as I began my second intake, my hand was slapped away. "Those could be poisonous," Cynthia said. "You might die."

That was the second time she may have saved my life, but the second time she pissed me off. "How will we know if they are good?" Rosa asked.

Cynthia was quiet then said, "I guess we will know soon enough." She looked at me and gave a half-smile. God became a distant voice to me as I reached out and struck Cynthia in the face. I amazed myself knocking her to the ground. She seemed surprised but moved quickly back to her feet and into my side. We tumbled to the ground, swinging wildly at each other. "If I die, then I am taking you with me," I shouted.

Rosa tried to break us up but felt the effect of two angry women. She went flying on her backside. I landed a couple of good shots on Cynthia, having been trained in a little self-defense.

My parents felt it necessary for me to take self-defense lessons before I went to college. Their reason being that if I ever said yes to a man, that would be between me and God;

but if I said no, then I would mean what I said and my fist would back it up. I was saying a few things right now and enjoyed hearing Cynthia's answers.

We tumbled for a few more moments. It was a test to see who was going to be the boss of the island. Although she was strong, I believe I could have won, but then it hit me. A sharp pain in my stomach doubled me over. Once I was down, Cynthia hit me with a strong right. I was on my hands and knees and the berries and her strong right made her the new boss of the island.

Chapter Five

A searing pain shot through my body, causing me to throw up the berries. I could only see Cynthia's feet as I threw up what was left of them and then dry-heaved as my belly continued to cramp. My body went from cold to hot in flashes. Rosa ran to my side trying to help me, but there was really nothing she could do. Everything started to go dark. I was blinded, and my body began to convulse. After a moment it ended and then to my horror I couldn't move. I was paralyzed, and there was nothing I could do about it. After what seemed like forever, my sight slowly returned, but my body was frozen. I could see Rosa above me, and with the sun behind her, she almost looked like an angel. She moved out of the way and then the devil appeared. Cynthia looked at me and smiled. Things weren't looking good for me.

After checking my pulse, Cynthia lifted me on her shoulders and took me back to the beach. She threw me one the ground as if I were a sack of potatoes.

I landed next to Kathy and Frank who had already been moved back to the beach. Rosa came to my side and began speaking Spanish over me. I not sure what she was saying, but her passion spoke a universal language. Cynthia stomped off out of sight and was gone for a while. I couldn't tell the time, but it seemed like she was gone and maybe would never come back. With my eyes open, staring at the heavens, I made a silent pray to God. Heck, we all needed a miracle, but I didn't mind if he used it on me for the moment.

Rosa gathered some water and took some clothes and tore them into rags. She did this so she could wash my body. For a while I did not feel anything but slowly her touch felt like warm sparks against my skin. I wanted to scream because of the intense pain as my nerve endings came alive, but I was glad to feel something. I didn't see Kathy but could still hear her crying over her son. I was not sure of anything, but I hoped he had not died.

Huffing and puffing, Cynthia yelled out in a scream. Rosa looked up and seeing her she thanked God for even the sight of her. Good Ol' Cynthia had found some food. She came to us with a shirt full of large bugs, and this being the moment of a miracle, I started to regain my movement. Blinking rapidly, I tried to sit up, but I hadn't fully regained my strength.

Cynthia took something that looked like a roach and put it into her mouth. Its legs were hanging out as she crunched hard against its body, white and green body fluid dripped out. She chewed it for a few moments and then took out a small piece, and moving Kathy to the side, she dropped some in Frank's mouth. I hadn't fully regained my strength, but if it took all I had, she wasn't about to put food from her mouth to mine, especially a chewed up bug.

"He needs some protein," Cynthia said, sensing what we were thinking. She appeared like a mother hen feeding her young chick. Frank coughed a bit, but he swallowed the first bite. His little body moved a bit, trying to get more. It was a funny sight in a way, yet even the little food he received restored some energy. Kathy hugged Cynthia and through her tears said thank you.

I hadn't fully regained my movement but once again had to face Cynthia. We had been through this before, and I think we both were tired. She only handed me a bug, a big dead brightly colored bug, and told me that I should eat. I looked at the bug and figured it was better than the berries.

I am not sure if words can describe the feeling of having something that was once alive in your mouth. I kept imaging it springing to life trying to free itself before I had to bite down on it. Warm blood, scales, and hair all move around in between my teeth as I tried to chew. Sharp claws pinched against the inside of my cheeks and tongue. Killing the bug was hard enough, but having to swallow was the worse. I felt every part of the body, legs, and the head move down my throat. It felt as if it were fighting the whole way down

We all ate and then Cynthia took over again. "We have a choice. We can stay here and hope for the best, or we can get going and try to make shelter." We all looked at each other knowing that we had to get shelter; we didn't know what was out there or if we were alone, but we did know that it was going to be night soon and that if anything we needed to get a fire going to give us some light and protection.

There were plenty of trees and branches to burn, but we needed to have a way to ignite it. The plan was simple: Cynthia and Rosa would gather wood, and I would stay with Frank and Kathy. My body had come back to normal, and I was ready to help and humble enough by everything to follow instruction. It wasn't such a bad job hanging out with them as I got a chance to know them a little better.

Kathy told me that she had Frank when she was sixteen and wasn't married to the guy who helped produce him. She never really told me his name but seemed to want to get away from that subject. I figured it was because Frank was sitting there and so I moved on. She told me that her parents were middle-class suburbanites and both still alive although divorced. She seemed almost childlike when she spoke of her dad and how great he was. She gave me an example of him working all summer to help out the poor, which in my book made her family all that more appealing.

When she spoke about her mother, her voice turned frosty sending chills throughout my body, and she abruptly changed the subject. My parents were still together, but I had friends with divorce parents and felt that maybe I understood her in some way. I quickly changed the subject and drew my focus on Frank. He still didn't say much, and she seemed to be the overly protective mom. I found out that he was fourteen, but looking at his appearance, he was small for his age. His cobalt blue eyes matched his mother, and the thick wavy blond hair made him the all-American good-looking kid in spite of his small thin frame.

I tried to make conversation with him, but he withdrew back to his same quiet shell. "That was very brave," I said to him about the shark. He didn't even look up but only hugged his mother more. It was strange to believe that the once brave kid was now this little insecure momma's boy.

Cynthia and Rosa went looking for shelter and then came back after about a few hours with good news. They had found a cave a couple miles inland and wanted us to take a look. It would be dark soon, and so we needed to get going. I looked at Frank and Kathy and asked if they thought they had enough strength to move. Frank didn't say anything but got up to his feet while helping his mom. I guess my question was answered.

Cynthia moved in close to Kathy, which I thought was strange, but I said nothing. I wondered if they knew each other from the ship. Rosa walked up to me and asked me if I needed any assistance. I thanked her but wanted to walk myself. I didn't want anyone to think that I was weak, especially Cynthia. I purposefully moved up front and told her to lead on. I wanted to give her the acknowledgement that she did something well but also by walking by her side, I wanted her to know that I would always be around. She only gave me a sideward glance and then led the way.

I was pretty sure we didn't have to worry about food as we heard animals making noise. The biggest problem I imaged would be trying to catch them. As we traveled over dead trees, rocks, and other obstacles, I was amazed that Cynthia could find her way back to the cave. I didn't want to show it, but I was impressed. I had never been much on direction and so I was pretty much at her mercy or at least for a while.

Rosa kept patting my hand, and she became more and more excited as we came near the cave. It was as if she had found a long lost diamond, which in a way I guess at the moment did have comparable value. Once there what I saw was truly amazing. It was indeed a cave surrounded by a large dead tree that had somewhat blocked its entrance. Large bushes and other trees surrounded it, giving it a good wall of protection. It was also fairly hidden, which would also be good if we weren't the only ones on the island. My biggest fear came with the thought of walking into it and bats flying out to attack us. I was not scared of much, but I knew what I did not like. Bats had to be at the top of the list. Once we entered it and nothing flew out, I realized that it was larger than it appeared on the outside. It had a flat hard ground that appeared to be made out of smooth stone covered by a thin layer of sand. Thick heavy walls made the cave cool in comparison to the heat outside. There were also large rocks set aside as if they were cubicles for individual space

We all went in, and Rosa went to work cleaning as if it were something she had done all her life. She moved small rocks out the center of the ground and found a small broken branch with leaves to sweep the place clean. The dust lifted up for a moment, and as it settled, we discovered that there was a cross breeze. Finding the cave was good, and we could make a fire in the cave and not worry about chocking to death, but we also had to find out where the breeze was coming from at the other end

My stomach began to bubble again, and I hoped I was not going to go through the same feeling as I had before. I braced myself for pain, but it never really came, the only feeling that came was that I had to go relieve myself. This was a part of stranded life that I knew I would not like. While on the lifeboat, we had to sit over the edge and do our duty taking a rag to clean ourselves, the whole process was disgusting, now it was the island's time

I ran outside the cave and did what I had to do, returning to a worried look from Rosa. "You feel better?" Rosa asked. I nodded and got back to business. "Did you guys check to see where this cave went to?" I directed all my questions to

Cynthia. I could hear my voice echo off the wall in front of me; there was no reply.

"I'll find out," I finally said. Rosa moved in close to me and said that she would go with me. It felt good to have her next to me. I trusted few people, but I felt a kinship between us.

Cynthia grunted about us doing it later and said that we needed to take care of a few things first. She said that we needed to get food and to get a fire going. Frank interrupted and spoke in his little weak voice. "I will start the fire," he said. We all stopped and looked at him. Kathy put her arm around her son proudly. "He used to be a Boy Scout. Trust him if he says he can do it, he will. The kid was becoming more and more amazing as time went on. I figured even if he couldn't do it, it would give them something to do until we returned.

Cynthia looked at him and smiled; it was the first time I had ever seen her smile. She actually had a pretty smile, but I would never tell her that. She gave him a thumbs-up and rubbed his little head. I guess she had really taken to him.

It's funny, we had only been on the island for a short time and our roles were defined. Cynthia tried to be the leader, and she would be the hunter. I also fought for leadership, but I would be the explorer. Rosa in her own cute way was my sidekick and friend. I was not sure of Kathy's place, but she was the mother of our little genius.

We all set out to do our task, which in a way felt good. If we were to survive, we would all have to work together in some form or another. I remembered Cynthia's right cross and figured if anyone was out there, they may have the problem instead of her.

My exploration took me to the back of the cave, which continued to go back a great distance. The lights from the opening of the cave had faded to dim glow. It was quiet now as Rosa and I leaned against the damp cool walls; the only noise heard was us breathing. I started to regret my decision to explore, but Rosa stood up to her title as a sidekick and began to rub on my back as she told me little about herself. There was much that I didn't know about this young lady that seemed so meek.

Rosa began to tell me about her life in Mexico. Her father was a diplomat and the favorite of their people. She said that they had wealth and position in their country, but like most countries, there are those who have and those who have not. The people that did not have money had crime. Drugs were the biggest problem, and her father would often speak against it. "That was very bad," she said in her broken English. She went on to tell me that when she was young, she and her mother were kidnapped by men who ordered her father to stop making trouble for their drug trade and that the people who kidnapped her were part of a drug cartel that had been rising in power.

Her father had always told them that he had to do what was right regardless of the price. Rosa lowered her head as she explained that the price was part of her family. Her mother was tortured and killed in front of her, and she was to be next. The death of her mother was enough to drive her father over the edge and so he gave up his political ties and used all his money as ransom to get her back. She said that all this happened when she was very young and the memory is faded a bit, but she still sometimes has nightmares. I moved in to comfort her, but she pulled away. She did not want pity for all that they had suffered, but it was her way of letting me know that no matter how bad things may be, things could be worse.

After she was released, they escaped to America and her father worked the rest of his life as a migrant worker even though he was a highly educated man. I could see tears well up in her eyes, but I gave her space and allowed her to continue to talk. "He never hated anyone, for all that happened and even in America where he was treated like a second-class citizen he taught me how to love." She turned and looked at me. "Do you think he was a weak man because of this?"

I stood there stunned for a moment and then gave her a hug. "I think your father was a saint."

She smiled and continued to tell me more of her life. "My father died in his sleep holding a picture of my mother. The night before he asked me if I hated him for allowing them to hurt and kill my mother. I told him no, but deep in my heart, I did. Although he died with a smile on his face, he let my mother die and at the end it did not stop the drugs. Men sold the same drugs he tried to fight against and you tell me was it right to let my mother die?" Her words came out as matter-of-fact, there was a hint of anger as if she had suppressed her feeling, but in the end, it was just the voice of a child longing for answers.

There was really nothing that I could say. I wondered what words of wisdom my mother would have used in a situation like this. She could always speak things in such a loving and God-fearing way that a person always left her feeling at peace. I tried my best to imitate her as I clumsily struggle to find the right words. "It's not wrong to feel the way you do, but if that feeling affects the rest of your life, it will eat you up and then the drug people and all the people against everything your father stood for would have won. Your mother died for a cause. She died so that somewhere down the line, people can live better and your father, I am afraid, sacrificed the most. You have to give up your anger, turn it over to Jesus, and allow peace to flow in you."

I listened to myself and nearly hurled because my words were empty and hollow. I'm not even sure if I believed them myself, but I figured it was a good thing to say. Rosa smiled at me and said that she found peace in serving others. She said that after her father died, she was left without money but ended up working as a nanny for a wealthy couple helping to raise their kids. She said that she was on the ship with them when it sank.

We were quiet for a while, and I silently said a prayer for her. *We need some good news*, I thought to myself as I search for something to lighten up the situation. I tried to whistle in an attempt to get our minds on a different track, but it did little to change the situation.

Moving farther along in the cave, it started to get brighter on the other end as we made our way toward what appeared to be an opening. We looked at each other and increased our pace. Like two kids on an adventure, curiosity got the best of us. Once at the opening we saw something truly amazing. The opening led to a cliff about fifteen feet above a beautiful huge lagoon with a variety of blue, green, and purple plants. The water was crystal clear, appearing to be only a few feet deep, but as Rosa threw a rock, you could tell that it was much deeper than it appears. A waterfall was constantly feeding the water as mist sprayed our entire bodies. I assume this was fresh water, as I did not feel the heavy weight of the salt on my body as I normally did when the ocean sprayed me.

Rosa squeezed my hand and said, "See, I have made my peace and we are blessed." I smiled at her, and we both looked for a way down.

We were sliding and laughing as we grabbed vines and tree limbs to the bottom, which was right near the edge of the waters. I looked at Rosa, and she looked back at me. This seemed too good to be true; I leaned over and dipped my cupped hands into the cool waters below. I figured I had already gotten sick from eating the berries, and so I might as well become the official taster. I put the water in my mouth and was in heaven. The finest of bottle water had nothing on the delight that was now trickling down my throat. It was cool, refreshing, and sweet; and I felt my body being renewed.

Rosa was a little more cautious and waited a few moments to see if I had any ill effects. I couldn't blame her, as I probably would have done the same. Once I waved her on to taste it, she did; and I could tell by the look on her face she experienced the same as me.

I didn't think it would rain a lot on the island, and we had no way of purifying salt water so this was a gift from heaven; and we, like the days of the Old Testament, drank to our fill. Looking over at my reflection, I nearly laughed at how bad I looked. A black woman with rain and sun on a new perm was not a good combination. My hair was straight in some places, matted in other, and I knew my breath stank. My skin was starting to break out with small bumps and peel in places where the sun had become too strong.

As I moved the water to destroy my reflection, I saw fish, not only one but schools of them. They were swimming so close to the surface that I felt I could reach in and pull one out.

We had found our little paradise and everything seemed to be going great. I enjoyed our find even more because I could go back to the cave and rub what I found down Cynthia's throat. I caught myself for a moment not liking what I was becoming. I prayed for God to help me not to become a monster on the island.

We both looked at each other and smiled like two schoolgirls about to get into trouble. "It would be great for all of us if we could bring some fish back to eat," I said. My motives were not pure as I wanted to do it more than for food but so that I would move ahead in the position of leadership. Bugs were OK, but we wanted something more familiar.

Rosa looked around and found a sharp stick that was perfect for what we wanted to do. She handed it to me, and I waited for the right moment. Inhaling, I went for it and missed but maybe this was the pond of stupid fish because they swam back around near the surface. I tried a few more times not having any luck. Rosa tried to hold back her laugher until it got the better of her.

We laughed for a moment and then she took the stick from me. She walked over with confidence, and on her first try, she stuck one. She looked at me and said, "When you are poor, you learn how to survive." I could not help marvel at the lady next to me.

After a few more tries, we had enough for everyone to get a fish even some leftovers. This was truly Jesus feeding his flock. I even got a fish for Cynthia, *a small one but enough*. We took the fish back up to the cave. The good news was that it would be a hike for anyone to come up through the back entrance, which was also fairly hidden by trees and branches as well. We felt safe that if anyone were on the island, they wouldn't go through the trouble of coming up from that direction.

Entering the cave, we also saw that we would have a good vantage point from where Frank and Kathy were sitting at. As we moved closer to the front, we saw a small fire surrounded by some of the rocks we threw to the side. I wondered how it got started but then saw Frank standing over it smiling broadly. I remembered he said he was a Boy Scout, and I guess he lived up to his training. If I ever get off this island and have kids, they will all be in the Boy Scouts

Although it was still hot outside, the fire felt good against the clamminess of my skin. It was warm and in a way felt like being home in my parent's house near their large fireplace. Throwing the fish to the ground, we felt like warriors coming back with a kill. Cynthia returned also with different fruits and berries. That night we feasted like royalty. We repeated this process for several weeks, taking care not to overfish the pond. Most days we stayed on a fruit only diet, and it was enough to sustain us, plus I was able to lose some of those unwanted pounds that I had been trying to lose.

Over the weeks, we found out that we were alone on the island; but with a supply of food and fresh water, we felt confident that we could survive. Although there were some things we did not like about each other, we made the best of it figuring that the island was too small and life too short to become enemies. Some of us gravitated to others more, but that was normal as we became like kids on a playground choosing our friends. We stayed in the cave because it was the perfect place for shelter and also it was near the beach and had the lagoon out back. If I were a real estate agent, I could have sold this location for millions.

Frank turned out to be our little superstar. I didn't realize that he was so smart, but thanks to TV and the Boy Scouts, he proved himself very helpful. We all found out little things about each other although Cynthia still did not tell us much about herself.

Each morning I would walk to the edge of the beach hoping for a plane, a boat, or something to rescue us, but it never came. In the Bible, I think it was Hebrews 11:1 it said that faith is the substance of things hoped for, the evidence of things not seen. I was becoming content with the fact that the five of us would be on this island until we died, but I still had hope.

We had become a family, and at night sitting around our campfire on our beach, Kathy stood and began to speak. We all became silent and looked at her as she had our full attention. "I have been thinking about Frank and raising him, and if you ladies will accept this, I would like for you to help me raise my son and make him the man he is supposed to become. The way I see it is that we all have qualities that makes us strong, and we should teach him since we all know what our perfect man would be like."

I didn't know about anybody else, but I was honored. It had been something that had been on my mind for a while. "I would too," Cynthia and Rosa in unison, so it began with us raising Frank.

Cynthia began self-defense training for Frank and tried to teach him how to shake hands as a man because a handshake, she said, is a man's bond. A person should make his mark in the world by making money and being successful, plus you should be able to take care of your family, she would say. She was also the disciplinarian and at times she was very abusive toward Frank, but she said it would toughen him up; his mother agreed. Cynthia also implemented a physical training program for us all, which I had a mixed reaction to. On one hand, I felt that we got enough exercise on the island just by living; but on the other hand, I knew that exercising helped keep my sanity, and I wanted to be in shape if they ever rescued me.

Rosa taught him about sensitivity, how to treat a woman and how to pay attention to women's need. She also gave him grooming skills on how to be immaculate and clean shaven using the knife Cynthia had brought with her. They had daily lesson on his emotions. She also said that he needed to treat all of the women on the island with ultimate respect because when the time comes and they get off the island, women will judge him on how he treated us.

As for myself, the first thing I taught him is to be God fearing and to place the Lord first above everything else. I believed that everything else would fall into place if he had a solid foundation. I also was the teacher and continue his education as best as I could without books. I believe without knowledge that you could not go far, and I still had hope that we would be rescued. I also taught him to be articulated, to be self-assured, and independent.

Kathy, his mother, gave him affection and love as she tried to spoil him as best she could on the island. A habit, which I had grown to hate, was the way she would whisper in his ear about things while keeping it a secret from the rest of the group. It was something that she used to make sure that we knew he was still her son.

Relationships started to form as I noticed Cynthia and Kathy had become really chummy. It wasn't that we didn't all have friendships with each other, but theirs seemed to be something more. I was not sure what was going on, so I started to watch. I thought we had gotten through the era of trying to establish position of dominance and alliances, but maybe I was wrong.

Over time, Frank also was starting to mature and his voice was starting to crack. We made a big deal of the fact that our little man is growing up.

Cynthia, to my surprise, kidded with him the most, but it seemed more hurtful than playful. She walked around mocking his newfound bass as if she were trying to challenge his manhood. I looked at her and then Kathy waiting for her to say something, but she only laughed and followed Cynthia's lead. I started to say something a few times but then figured that I really had no authority to interfere.

Rosa, who is the closest to his age, only four years his senior would often take him by the arms and dance as we whistled or sung songs. That was our entertainment, dancing and singing; Rosa would sing songs in Spanish and would often teach Frank the language. He was a quick study, and soon he and Rosa would have conversation between themselves without us knowing what they were saying. Cynthia would be so disturbed at the bond that she once walked up to Frank and slap him across his ear and pulled him away from Rosa.

Kathy seemed to know soul songs, which gave me the impression that either she was raised by very soulful parents or that she dated a black man.

Cynthia tried to sing, but it still came out as more of a loud grunt. I had to admit that I was the best singer and felt like his good old black auntie that would show him the other side of the world.

It was a beautiful day and the temperature had to be about the midseventies. The fruits were in full bloom along with the flowers of the island causing a sweet aroma that tantalized all of our senses. Everything was going well until Cynthia and Kathy shocked us.

Cynthia stood as she made her big announcement and my mouth drop opened as I heard what she saying. Cynthia told us that she and Kathy were in love. I figured something was going on between them, but I only thought it was an alliance. Now I realized that it was an alliance all right and much more.

I looked at Frank wondering how he would react; he said nothing but only walked up to Kathy and hugged her. Cynthia grabbed him around the neck like a proud father hugging his son. It was weird to see what had just happened, but there it was, a reality I had seen countless times in my old neighborhood. Not necessarily the relationship of two women in love with each other but the role of fathers being taken over my mother because the fathers just weren't there. I was raised to believe that being gay was not right, but who was I to preach to her? Plus this was not the time nor place. It would wait.

Rosa stood silent looking perplexed. She said a few words in Spanish, and I think one of them was pig, which I'm sure was directed toward Cynthia. Cynthia frowned at her and began to lay the new law as to the way things would be from now on. First, she stated, "Kathy, Frank, and I will be living in our own area. I have found a spot for us, and Frank will help me build it. Frank is now my child, and if there are any problems, you should come to me." She also said that we are no longer to instruct him anymore and that she was is taking over the rest of his training. She capped off her comment with a deep throaty kiss to Kathy as if the cement their deal.

I guess something like this was bound to happen, and looking back, I should have seen it forming. I eventually told Cynthia that what they were doing was not right and that even though there were no men on the island, two women together was wrong. But in defense of her newly chosen mate, Kathy spoke up and said that she loved Cynthia and that she had treated her better than any man had ever done. She continued to say that together they would raise Frank and that they didn't need a man to make him the right.

I threw up my hands not wanting to hear anymore. We all had a part in raising him, we all felt a kinship to him, and the way Cynthia talked about their relationship it somehow dishonored the entire race of men. Cynthia spoke as if God somehow made a mistake by putting men on the face of the earth, and I guess that is what I took offense at. Men represented my father, and although he was not perfect, he was perfect in my eyes.

After taking a deep breath, I exhaled and looked at all of them. It was not my place to judge regardless of my belief. God would do that, but he would want me to show love. Hell, at the end, judgment comes to us all; and I was not sure if I was standing in the right line. If they were a couple, then I guess I had no choice but to deal with it. I apologized for my words and my behavior. Walking slowly over to the both of them, I gave Frank a big hug and shook Kathy's hand. I still couldn't bring myself to hug Cynthia but reached out and shook her hand also.

Rosa, following my lead, did the same thing although she gave her love and acceptance more freely. She said some more words to Frank in Spanish and a big smile came across his face. I had to make a mental note to myself to learn some more Spanish.

After the news there was an awkward period for a while. I did my best not let my opinion get in the way, but it did. I made it a point to walk away from Cynthia, and she did her best to do the same with me. Rosa went on being friends with Frank, which I suspected she would. She had the kindest heart, and it wouldn't be in her nature to do anything else.

Time passed and things pretty much went on as they did before with the only exception being the outward physical affection shown by Cynthia and Kathy. One day Kathy came up to me and pulled me to the side. I really had no beef with her, but still it felt uneasy. She led me to a large log that was on the beach and sat me down. Cynthia, Rosa, and Frank had gone on a camping expedition, and so it was just me and her.

"You hate me for loving Cynthia, don't you?" Kathy said. Her tone threw me off a bit because we had not really talked that much and for her to be concerned about my opinion was a surprise. I tried to deny what she said, but we both knew I was lying.

She looked in my eyes and told me there was a lot I didn't know about her, a lot she had never told anyone. I had to admit I was puzzled as to what this was and why it was coming out now. Maybe it was her way of cleansing her soul.

Using communication skills I had learned in college, I tried to ease her into the conversation. People often want to be heard, and if you give them enough room, they will talk. I took her hand and said that whatever she wanted to talk about I would listen, and she didn't have to say anything she didn't want to.

She smiled at me and in an instant I realized where Frank got his charm. "My parents were very wealthy people." She paused, as this was a painful experience. "We had everything money could buy, even the things money couldn't. There was love in the house but not like the shows that you see on TV. My father worked a lot but also made a point to spend time with us. My mother was there with me as I grew up showing us as much love as a mother could give." Her words began to trail off into silence. I put my hand on hers trying to give comfort.

She smiled and forced herself to continue. "I guess all the trouble started when Steve moved in." My eyebrow moved up a notch. I had never heard of a Steve, and now I wondered what the heck happened in her life. Maybe he was in a gay relationship with her dad, which would explain a lot. I tried to put snap judgments out of my mind and just listen as she continued, "Steve was a distant cousin of mine, and my mom allowed him to stay with us. At first he was very nice, almost like he was a big brother to me."

I hoped she was not going to say what I thought she was. I guess she saw the look on my face and stopped me before it could go any further.

"No, he did not do anything to me physically. In fact, he would always try to protect me, but there was something about him that brought trouble. The more he stayed around, the more things seemed to change. First, my dad quit his job, saying that wanted to spend more time with the family but instead he spent more time away with Steve working on business deals and that's when my mother started to feel like she was being left out of the picture and began to see other men. I became very angry at her, angry at my dad, angry at the world." She pulled me in closer. "You should never have a child out of anger." Her words were cold and to the point. "I began sleeping around with any and everybody, people I didn't know, people I did. You'd be surprised how evil people can be." Her voice was now ghostlike, void of emotions. "Men can be evil."

Chapter Six

Men can be evil—those words stayed in my head for the moment. I figured that explained why she hit it off with Cynthia. I squeezed her hand not only because of what she may have went through but also the fact that I had hoped to get married one day, and if this was the outlook for men, then I was in deep trouble.

Kathy continued, "I was hurt in so many ways, made to do things that were unspeakable. I'm not even sure who Frank's father is." I tried not to show my emotions but that one threw me off guard as I now tried to form a picture in mind of Frank to see if there were any differences that I may have missed. I continued to listen as her eyes began to water. "The thing that hurt the most was that my parents didn't even care." There was a hint of anger but not a consuming anger like I expected from her. She moved closer to me, her voice now faint. "I don't know why I kept going back, but I did— back to anyone that seemed like they cared. I just wanted to feel loved."

I didn't have words for her at that moment. Spoiled little rich white girl was the one of the thing that came to my mind, but hurt and pain goes deeper than skin color and wealth. Hurt and pain is what it is, and no matter why, she was hurting. The devil comes to kill, steal, and destroy. It all made sense now as to why she would go with Cynthia. She wanted to be loved and protected, but I also knew that she was a victim talking. She had a family and what ever happened at least she had a good start.

She continued, but I wanted her to stop; any more bad news and I felt as though I would scream. "After Frank was born, they kind of left us to ourselves," she said. "My dad's old friends would come by to check up on him, but he wasn't the only one they wanted to check up on. They were filthy old men who took advantage of me. My family finally fell apart, my cousin Steve convinced my dad to do some illegal things, and they both ended up in jail where they both were murdered. My mom left with another man and disappeared, and I have not seen or heard from her since, and I was left alone to fend for my child and myself."

I looked at her perplexed wondering where this whole thing was going. Why had she chosen me as the person to confess her soul to? Maybe this is what Mama meant when she said that I had a calling on my life? Whatever it was, I really didn't want it. Knowing this about her served me no purpose, and if we got off the island, I'm sure I would never see her again.

"I had money," she continued, "and if I ever needed more, all I had to do was bring Frank around and people would pay to keep me and their nasty little secrets quiet." She turned and looked up toward the sky as tears began to stream down her face "We took this cruise to get away from it all. Get away from the looks and stares and everything else." Inhaling deeply and then exhaling, she looked into my eyes, searching to see if she could trust me. I tried to let her know that she could by squeezing her hand once more.

"You don't understand," she said, "I was mad." Her whole continence changed. She moved her hand away from mine and hugged herself. "I was mad at everyone and everything. We both were." I assume she meant Frank but was not sure anymore. "I wanted to get even with them all, show them that they would miss us and so we—"

She was interrupted by Frank's laughter as they came toward the beach. At once, she changed and smiled. She put her hand on my shoulders and said thanks. Giving me a hug, she left and caught up with the returning group.

I could see Cynthia giving me a jealous glance, but I was not worried about her. It was now Kathy who was a concern. I wondered if she was crazy. Just my luck, I was on the island with a crazy woman. In a way, I felt sorry for her but at the same time I wanted to slap some sense into her head. People are evil, mean, and wrong; but not everyone is like that. If you feel sorry for yourself, you will always feel like a victim, I knew Jesus died to give us strength, but you give an open door for bad thing to happen if you do not trust in him. When you draw a line in the ground and fight, bad things still happen, but now you win some battles. I wanted to continue our talk later; there was more that Kathy wanted to say, but for now I was content with just having Cynthia jealous. I paused felling like such a hypocrite. *What's wrong with me and my dislike for Cynthia? Please help me, God*, I prayed.

I made it my mission to hang out with Frank as much as possible. Poor kid had been through a lot, and now with Cynthia as his new dad, I wanted to try to put some stability in his life. I also wanted to try to talk some more to Kathy. We seemed to stop halfway in her life story and now each time I tried to resurface the issue, she acted as if we never talked.

Frank was becoming the perfect young man, and in a way, I think that is what we were all trying to do, *"make him the perfect man."*

I caught Cynthia beating him once, and I don't mean spanking him lightly. Although he was a strong young man, this could have classified as abuse. Kathy just sat by and watched, and I guess I was no better because I didn't do anything. I figured I could be the anti-Cynthia and show him love and peace, possibly offsetting the beatings he received. It almost became creepy as he adjusted to the intensity of the punishments Cynthia dealt out. He would just sit there and look out into space as Cynthia would hit him with a branch or stick. He would not move, not scream out, just endure it all, just taking it and holding it in. It became a weird cycle. The more he didn't show emotions, the harder she would swing until eventually she would wear herself out, yet he would not give her the satisfaction of breaking.

I had reached my limit once after one of his beatings and walked over to confront her but that turned into a big fiasco. Both Cynthia and Kathy began to yell at me about it being their responsibility to raise their own child. Cynthia's yells I expected, but to have Kathy yelling at me threw me off. I took as much as I could, but my reactions took over and I swung at her, So much for our new relationship. She went down hard, and before I knew it, they all were on me; Cynthia and Frank began to kick and punch me. Cynthia was tough enough, but Frank was strong, stronger than I expect. The only thing that saved me was Rosa stepping in to calm them.

I sat there battered, bruised, and alone. Betrayal hurt worse than a bruise, and I guess that instead of teaching love I only taught division and hate. I still try to befriend Frank, but I figured if they wanted to beat him and he didn't mind, more power to them. Later I even began to justify what was happening saying that he's strong enough to take it, or he must have done something worth his punishment or even feeling that he would be old enough in a few years and then he would get back at her. I became blind to what was going on in order to heal my hurt.

Frank learned to endure, and over time, he grew into a young man. He stood about 6'2", and I am sure weighed around 200 pounds. Good looking, well versed, sensitive but strong, and his biggest gift was his laughter; he had a lovely laugh, which to me was essential to any normality. I had pretty much become the loner of the clan other than Rosa keeping me company every once in a while. I still talked to Frank every now and then, but I also knew where my boundaries were. Cynthia and Kathy were like parents who had a neighbor they didn't want their kid to associate with. I had to admit, loneliness is a tough thing to deal with and being there with people around but no one to talk to made me think of all the people in the world who just exist but have no one to call a friend. I made a mental note to myself if I ever get off this island to stop and say hello to people, make friends, shine a light for others.

Life itself had become a lesson for me. Watching everyone and how they lived their lives was like a classroom. Over the years, I had a chance to analyze myself and think back to where I came from. I had a chance to look deep in myself and had come to peace with the fact that I would most likely die on this island.

The biggest problem with our situation was not so much the abuse that Frank took at the hands of the others but the fact that he may not get off the island, and there was a whole world that he had not ever had the chance to experience. What does a young man on an island full of women do? There was only so much that could be taught by us. It is one thing to be taught manners, but they did little good if you had no place to display them. Also as Frank had become a young man, the thought occurred to me about what he would do sexually. He wasn't gay as far as I knew, and by all accounts had succeeded in our little experiment of becoming the perfect man, but the question remained of what he would do for a relationship. I had no interest in him, and the only person that seemed to be anywhere close to his age was Rosa. That question was answered the day I went fishing for food by the lagoon.

I heard a grunt in the bushes and thought it was an animal. By now my hunting skills had become pretty good, and I had learned how to silently sneak upon unsuspecting prey. Every once in a while, a wild animal would show up; and if we caught one, we would feast for days.

The hunt was now on for me, and I crouched down low and began to move slowly through the bushes. I stopped for a moment to feel the breeze flow gently against my skin. It was good news in the fact that it was blowing away from the direction I was coming. One thing for sure was that animals could pick up your sent in a heartbeat; and if they got it, they would take off running long before you got close enough to do any damage. Another point I also had to take in account was picking the right fight. Although the animals were good eating, they also were mean and could rip a hole in your body with their claws or take a chunk of meat from you with a bite. I hoped it was a young, which would make it easier to kill, but I was ready for anything. Holding a spear that I had made, I crept slowly toward my prey. I couldn't recognize the sound the animal was making and mistakenly assumed that it must be wounded. Tall grass moving ever so slightly, I lifted my spear to kill, and to my surprise, it wasn't an animal. It was Frank and Rosa making love. Looks like Rosa was teaching Frank more than Spanish.

Can't say I was shocked, but seeing Rosa and Frank didn't sit right with me. Nothing wrong with an older woman getting a younger man, but since we all treated Frank like our son and seeing them as they made love make me sick. It almost seemed incestuous.

This was going to get interesting once the other ladies found out. I wondered how Cynthia would take the news. How long had this been going on? I tried to creep away not letting them know that I was there, but Frank heard my movement. He jumped up and chased after me. I ran as fast as I could, but he was fast, faster than me, and in a moment I was caught. "Please don't tell, please." He seems like a little kid begging not to get in trouble. Fear was all across his face.

"I won't tell," I promised him.

In truth, they didn't do anything wrong. I guess it's natural that a woman and man should get together, but I had to wonder: Did Rosa seduce him, or did he seduce her?

As I made my back way toward the beach, I saw Cynthia and wanted to go over to her and tell her what I knew. In some ways, we all revert to schoolgirls at the playground playing metal games of gossip

"I got a secret, and I won't tell ya."

That's what I wanted to say, but I made a promise and I intended to keep it. Cynthia gave me a sideward glance, as usual treating me like a redhead stepchild but then asked me if I had seen Frank. I swallowed and tried not to give an impression of knowing, but my body language may have given it away.

"I think I saw him near the lagoon. Why?" One thing I learned about Cynthia was that she did not like to be questioned. She was ex-military, a businesswoman, and independent to the bone. From what I gathered from the other girls, she was a divorcée. I am not sure if she had been gay all her life or if it was through some dramatic event, but after her divorce, she started going out with women; and from there on, the rest was history.

In her relationship with Kathy, there was no doubt that she took on the role of the man. She looked the part with a stocky body and muscular frame, and as if to accentuate the point more, she would often chop her hair short.

"Is there something going on?" she said as I walked past her. She put her hand on my shoulder. It wasn't the placement of her hand but the fact that she touched me as to control me. I turned and stared her dead in the eyes. "I said he was at the lagoon, and that was it."

She had to settle for what I told her, and I walked away. Frank followed shortly after my confrontation with Cynthia. He was a grown man, but she ran up to him and slapped him across the head. "Where have you been?" Frank just took it like usual and said nothing. Peace is a funny word—one minute you have it, and the next it is gone.

Rosa followed up behind Frank a few minutes later; she didn't look at me as she passed me. I stayed silent, but Kathy was watching; I guess she had been watching for a long time. She noticed the way Frank would glow whenever Rosa showed up. He even seemed to have a little more backbone with Cynthia if Rosa was nearby. Kathy was watching the situation unfold and decided to walk over to Frank to get information. She began to stroke his hair at the same time stroking his soul.

He was still a mama's boy and gave into her ways. "Baby, there something I've been meaning to ask you," she said. He looked at her as an innocent kid would look at his mom when he knew he was in trouble but was trying to worm his way out of it. "Is there anything you want to say to me?"

"There's nothing, Mom," he replied quickly, almost too quickly. "I was just out by the lagoon trying to get some fish for dinner. I'm sorry I didn't tell you where I was." I nearly laughed as the drama unfolded right before my eyes.

"What do you have to tell me about Rosa?" she said. Franks eyes went wide, and he turned and looked directly at me. I shrugged my shoulder to let him know I didn't say anything but like most kids his emotions took over instead of his mind.

"Rosa is my girlfriend," he blurted out.

The look of horror on Cynthia's face was priceless as her reddish-brown skin became engorged with blood, making her face near purplish red in color. "You and what...who—" Her words were tripping over each other.

Rosa stepped up and put her hand in Frank's hand. "He and I are one," she said, hoping that his plea would be enough to appease everyone.

"My boy will not be sleeping with a Spanish whore," Cynthia jumped back into the mix.

I stood there with my mouth open. She said Spanish like the word itself was dirty and beneath her. Frank wasn't even her boy, and she had the nerves to say something like that. Frank started to say something to her, but she slapped him across the face. He went quiet again. I couldn't take it anymore and felt it my duty to defend the two.

"Leave them alone," I said. "What did you expect? They're both young and alone. What are they supposed to do? You two got together and that wasn't right." Kathy gave me an evil look. Frank hung his head and held on to Rosa's hand. Kathy was now becoming irate.

"Look at me when I talk to you," she said, taking his head into her hand.

She asked for it, and she got it. "Rosa and I are together, and that is it. There is nothing you can do about it," he said, this time sounding like a man.

He took Rosa by the arm and walked away. I guess mama's little prefect boy just grew up.

Things on the island were crazy now. I didn't speak with Cynthia and Kathy, and they didn't speak with Rosa and Frank; and to top it off, Frank was mad at me. Though I didn't like it, I figured I would have to become the peacemaker. My first thought was not to go directly to Frank and plead my case but to go to Rosa. She was still my friend, and if anyone could get through to Frank, it would be her. I caught her alone one day, and so we began to talk.

"Rosa," I said, "I didn't say a word to Cynthia or Kathy about you guys. Think about it, you had been missing a lot and common sense prevailed." I myself had begun to wonder about Frank's sexuality. I mean a young man his age is nothing but raging hormones, and we're a bunch of half-naked women running around. Rosa and I had built up enough friendship over our time for her to tell that I was being truthful. She paused and then said. "It's stupid, I know, but I have grown to love him." She gave me a smile of relief and then we walked and talked some more. I tried to apologize for Cynthia and Kathy's comments about calling her names as if something was wrong with her. It was just ignorance, I said. She told me she was used to it and that she understood. She was way more forgiving that I would have been. After agreeing to let the past be the past, we made plans on how to get son and mother back together again.

Cynthia and Kathy were at the beach talking when I walked up to them with my hands raised as a sign of sur-render. I took Kathy by the hands and apologized to her directly for hurting her feelings in any way. I then moved to Cynthia and told her the same. I made a speech about how us all needed to be together on this island and how we were a family whether we liked it or not. I guess the simplest way to stop strife is just say you are sorry, *another mental note I made for myself.*

Frank and Rosa walked up to us, and as sappy as it sounded, we all had a group hug. I knew this was just a start, but the truth was we all had to start somewhere. There was still some tension, but after all the drama, things were starting to look good. We had a big party that night and really got to know each other even better. Hard to believe it had been nearly four years, but it was, and there was still so much more that we did not know about each other.

Deep down, I was a little jealous that everyone on the island had someone except me. I had to question God and ask why he was punishing me. I hadn't done anything wrong in my life. I tried to be a good person, and I know that my parents always prayed for me. Why, even on this island was I the only one to be alone?

To add more insult to injury, Cynthia knew I was lonely. She did not say it, but she knew. I could tell the way she would look at me or some of the comments she would throughout that were meant just to hurt me. I knew she was a racist and I tried to look past it, but her comments were getting on my nerves.

One day I saw her alone and decided to approach her. I told her as politely as I could how I felt about things, and I guess she felt the same way because she swung at me. For a big woman, she was fast, but I was faster. I ducked and pushed her. She stumbled backward struggling to keep her balance and then fell on the ground. Her head hit a rock. I heard the thud and then saw blood gushing out the back where it struck. She lay still on the ground not moving. I started praying to God as I ran over to her hoping she would be OK. Looking down, I saw her eyes rolling to the back of her head and body convulsing. She took in several deep breaths and then stopped.

I didn't know any CPR, and I am not sure if I did it would have done any good. Judging by the blood she lost, I was pretty sure she was gone. My mind began to race. I had murdered a woman. Accident or not, she was dead and it was my fault. I was already the loner on the island, and with this, I was a good as dead myself.

I looked around praying that no one saw us. Part of me said that I needed to come clean with everyone; the other part of me said not to tell them everything, to say there must have been an accident, and I found her that way. I wasn't sure what I should do. I sat there alone in the grass for a moment and cried with a devil and angel on each shoulder.

Get it together, girl, I told myself. *Run and find someone. You're not a nurse. Maybe she is still alive.* I had to keep thinking about this despite wanting to run and hide. The worst thing would be to know that she was still alive and died because I did nothing. I had to find someone; Rosa would know what to do. She had seen death so many times before. I forced myself off the ground and ran toward the beach. I had seen her there last and prayed she was still there.

I began thinking about Frank and nearly tumbled to the ground. My god, if he is still there also, I will have to tell him that I may have killed his mother's lover. Regaining my footing and running to the beach, my prayers were answered. Rosa was there, and she was alone. "Rosa, help, help," I shouted loud enough for her to hear me but not loud enough for anyone else.

The moment she saw me, she ran toward me concerned that something had happened to me. In another time, I would have been touched at her concern, but I didn't have time. She tried to speak, but I grabbed her arm and pulled her toward the inner part of the jungle. We moved as fast, she tried to ask me what happened, but I just told her that Cynthia was in trouble and nothing else. She didn't need to know the rest of the story; I just needed to know whether Cynthia was alive.

We reached Cynthia and things didn't look good. Her face was now a pale bluish white. I knew enough to know that wasn't a good sign. Rosa went to work right away, not asking questions but immediately rushing to Cynthia's side, placing her ear next to her chest. She looked up at me for a brief second and then returned to work. Feeling the wound on the back of Cynthia's head, she ripped off part of her clothing and placed it on the wound to stop the blood. *Why didn't I think of that?*

She began calling out Cynthia's name gently and rubbing her hand. There was no response, and then she leaned over to listen to her heart again. I wasn't sure if that was a good or bad sign, but it looked bad. She began to give her mouth to mouth as I watched her chest began to be filled with Rosa's breath. All the things she did, I knew I should have done but then didn't think about. *Maybe I wanted Cynthia dead, maybe I could have saved her, but subconsciously I ran for help so that she would bleed to death.* My mind started to play tricks on me making me feel like a monster.

I'm not a monster, I had to kept saying to myself to stay the storm. Seconds seem like hours as I waged a battle in my head. In the distance, I heard someone yelling my name, but it seemed so faint, so far away until I felt Rosa grab my hand.

"She is breathing," she said, "but just barely. We can't move her like this. Go and get Frank and Kathy."

My heart dropped another notch as the thought of seeing their faces when I told them Cynthia was near death.

"Go now," Rosa said, her Spanish accent becoming stronger the more she was in control. I took off running screaming for Kathy and Frank. Between screams, I prayed that Cynthia would be OK. I hated her, but I didn't want to see her dead.

She came at me. I protected only myself. It was as if I were two people, one running and screaming like a madwoman for help, the other planning my defense for when it all hit the fan.

Frank and Kathy met me halfway, which was good. My legs were burning, and my lungs hurt. I wasn't sure I even had the energy to return, but I didn't have to. Once I told them that Cynthia was hurt and pointed in the direction, they both took off. As small as Kathy was, she took the lead racing like a madwoman though the bushes with Frank close behind her.

After regaining my breath for a moment, I caught up with them standing around Cynthia. Kathy was crying as Frank was holding her. I stayed back in the dense jungle for a moment bracing myself for the hate that I knew would come at me. I inhaled and took a step forward; everyone turned and looked at me.

"She's..." Kathy voice tailed off for a moment, but Rosa finished off.

"She's gone," she said, holding back her own tears. I felt my eyes water up also. I wanted to cry like a baby, but first things first. I had to tell them what happen. It was the right thing. I had to let them know.

Kathy spoke up before I could say a word. "Cynthia said she fell, right before she died, she spoke with us." Fell? She said she fell? Maybe I didn't hear right, maybe the punch line was coming next. Why would she say she fell? How could she speak? She looked dead when I left her. How was this possible?

Frank walked over to me and asked me what happened and how I found her.

The God in me was telling me to confess, set things straight, but my other voice told me to let it go. "Don't cause more trouble than you have to. It's only the four of us now, and the island is too big to be alone."

I listened to the other voice. "I heard her scream and found her like that. She's dead?" I started to cry.

There, it was done. Cynthia was dead and I was a liar.
I prayed for God to forgive my soul. That night we buried
her, and no one questioned what happened. We just said our
goodbyes. Kathy was an emotional mess after losing someone
that she had been with all those year. She leaned on her son
for strength. No more beatings for him. He was now mom's
little boy again, but at the same time also had to become a
man. Rosa felt that someone should say something, and they
all looked at. I killed her. She lied to protect me, and now
I had to speak words at her funeral. Oh how tangle my life
had become for not being honest the way God wanted me to.

I looked down at her body, and she looked peaceful. We
tried to make the funeral as close to the real thing as possible. Rosa colored Cynthia's cheek with a rose-colored plant
that she had been using for herself. Kathy took her necklace
that she had always worn around her neck and placed it over
Cynthia's. She began crying as she kissed her lover goodbye.
Frank placed a beautiful dark green flower with the prettiest orange streaks running down the middle of its stalk on
Cynthia's closed hands. The flower brought a beauty and
peace to the woman who was once my enemy.

I had no gifts but only came over and stroked her hair.
I said a silent thank you to her and began my sermon. I did the
best I could to imitate the words I had once heard at church.
I began with the scripture about death, but it had been a long
time since I had read a Bible. What I didn't know I ad-libbed.
"Yea though I walk to the shadow of death, I will fear no evil."
I went on to talk about the joy and good times we had on the
island. I closed with asking God to accept her into his home
and to pray for forgiveness for us.

Maybe the forgiveness was too much to ask for guilt was already digging into my soul. I was a murderer. As I spoke, it felt as if everyone were looking at me, seeing the guilt in my eyes, cocking their heads to the side wondering why. I turned my head and buried my face in my hands crying. I couldn't hold back anymore; tears flooded down to the ground.

Feeling a warm hand on my shoulder gave me comfort as if my savior was saying it was OK. It was Frank. He was the one telling me that it was all right. He said deep down Cynthia respected me as a strong woman and that's why she opposed me so much. He couldn't have known, but his words were killing me inside.

We buried her near a large tree that had been her favorite. It was where she first found the bugs and fruit we ate when we first came onto the island. It was hard to see Frank push the soft dirt over her body. I turned and walked away just wanting to be by myself. I think we all did in some way, but Frank stayed with Rosa, and Kathy just sat by the tree. What else was there to do?

Hours later, I saw Frank and Rosa by the beach; Frank was cooking freshly caught fish while Rosa laid out fruit. This had been their custom since coming out about their relationship. There was not the usual distraction of the world to taint their relationship, and it was only pure love.

I walked up to them still not knowing what to say. I expected sadness but to my surprise there was none, there only seemed to be a relief for the both of them. *Ding-dong the witch is dead, the witch is dead.* Maybe I didn't have to confess, and maybe God was protecting me.

Rosa looked up to me with a big smile. "You will join us?" she said as she walked over and took my hand and pulled me near the food. I looked around for Kathy, but she was nowhere to be seen. "Where's Kathy? I asked not wanting to enjoy myself in front of a grieving spouse. I guess I hadn't really thought of it that way. She was a grieving spouse, and despite my personal feelings, her pain was real.

"Mom is still at the tree," Frank said. He lowered his head, almost ashamed that he was getting ready to eat. He knew what I was thinking and quickly followed by saying that he wanted to give her some space. Rosa said, "In my county we celebrate death. They say it is not the end but the beginning, that is why we should eat and celebrate." I guess she was right, but I still felt funny about eating. I declined the meal and went to comfort Kathy.

Seeing her bent over on one knee grasping the dirt that buried her lover ripped my soul from my heart. I walked up to her and knelt down beside her. Her body shook at my touch. "I'm so, so sorry." My words were truer than she could have ever known. She looked at me, her eyes red. "It's my fault," she said.

"It's not your fault," I said, stroking her hair. I wanted to say that it was my fault and confess right at that moment, but I held back.

She continued to rock on her knees holding the dirt in her hand and saying that it was her fault. I didn't understand what she was talking about. The more she said it, the more I wanted to confess. It was as if her words were hot coals burning on my body each time she said it. *It's my fault, my fault. I killed her. Please stop blaming yourself. It was me*, I thought. I tried to get her to stop, stop blaming herself, and in a way release me of my pain. "You didn't do anything," I said. "It was an accident."

She grabbed me by the shoulder. "God is getting back at me, that's why she died. He is getting back at me."

Her face became stoned, and she looked at me deeply for a moment and then she said that it was her fault the ship sank. "It's because of me, and I killed all those people."

I wanted to hug the poor woman. She had obviously lost her mind yet the sincerity in which she spoke caused me to dig deeper into her statement. "What do you mean you killed all those people on the ship?" I asked, trying to at least offer comfort by letting her talk. Still looking stoic, she started to speak as if she were reliving everything.

"I tried so often to tell you," she said. "I told you about my past life and the way men treated me and my son." I nodded my head remembering her past with her. "Frank was a little bastard son whose father I didn't know," she blurted out of nowhere.

This was starting to get a little weird. She called her son a bastard. I had never heard her talk like that about him. "You know men are so stupid," she said, "if you sleep with them a couple times, make them feel as if they are the best, they'll do anything." I shook my head agreeing, knowing that I had never been with another man in that way. "Before we went on the cruise, I slept with a lot of people just to get what I wanted." She paused and looked at me. "They didn't care. I was just a good lay for them." I was now officially hooked. What in the hell was she talking about?

"I brought many suitcases on the ship, and since John was the head of security, he got them through. He was the first one, kind of liked him, a bit freaky in bed but generally a good lover. Then on the ship I was allowed to go below to the engine room. While Frank was up in his cabin, I was down below with Steve the engineer." At first I didn't know what the hell she was talking about but the more she talked, the more I did not like the direction the conversation was going. God, I hate to think what priests have to go through listening to all the junk in people's lives. "Steve was like everyone else— rough, fast, and nasty. He wanted me to be his little quick fantasy." I started trying to put pieces together. *Let's see, so far you are a freaky mixed-up rich girl, is that correct?* I just stayed quiet.

"When he finished with me, he left me alone, and that is when I hid the explosives near the engine and communication. The storm was an added bonus, but I wanted the ship to go down. I wanted to die and make everyone pay. I wanted to be free." She looked at me as if I should understand. I didn't understand her kind of freedom was craziness. I couldn't believe what I was hearing, explosives? That's why the ship took on so much water so fast. That was the loud bang I heard. It was all starting to make sense. Everything except why she was still alive.

Like a mind reader, she filled in the blank. "At the time I wanted to die. I wanted to end it all and to let everyone know how much I hurt. Guess I wanted to go out in a bang, but when I saw Frank's face, my poor little baby frightened and afraid, I couldn't go through with it. I couldn't kill my son." I felt an anger roll up within me. God, she killed all those people; I moved away from her. Half afraid of what I might do to her, half-repulsed by the mere sight of her. I wanted to slap her, take out my anger on her, but then again we were two of a kind, murderers on an island.

"That's why it's my fault," she said, calmly smoothing the dirt back over Cynthia's grave. "You know, she was the only one who treated me with respect, the only one to really care about me and now she had to go and die." She began to cry again, but I really didn't care anymore. I was numb. "I understand if you tell, but I am asking you not to," she said between her tears. "God is already punishing me."

My head was spinning and my stomach hurt. *Don't tell that you killed over a hundreds of people? We are stuck on this island, and you don't want me to tell. Cynthia is dead and you... Damn, don't tell.* It was as if I were looking in a fun house mirror seeing my sin magnified a thousand times. How could I tell her that we all had our secrets?

I could do nothing now; it was time to face facts. We were on an island, and there were only four of us left. Who could I tell and what good would it do? Repulsion and anger dominated me but also pity, poor little rich white girl, so lonely, so sad.

I told her I wouldn't say anything. She made me promise and I did. Guess I was her new girlfriend. *Why not? I just killed her first one.*

I told her it was time to go; she needed to eat something. I told her that Frank and Rosa were waiting for her. Truth was that I didn't want to be alone with her. She was crazy and that may be an understatement. We got up to walk back to the beach; this time I made sure I stayed behind her.

Chapter Seven

Frank and Rosa had already started eating as we approached the beach. They both stood up and watched as we walked up toward them. Rosa smiled and offered for us to join them. I wasn't sure what to expect from Kathy, but she smiled and accepted the offer. I followed still trying to figure out her next move. Maybe she would tell everyone; maybe this was her purification process. I held my breath to see what happened.

Kathy sat down next to Frank and began to rub his head. "It's just you and me now, son, just you and me." I could feel the uneasiness that Rosa felt with that statement. She gave a sideward glance at Kathy but kept her mouth shut. I noticed that she put her hand on his and squeezed it gently. There was a war brewing, and I was a witness to it.

Rosa looked at Kathy and said that she was sorry again for her lost. Kathy did not respond but pulled Frank closer. So much had happened in such a short time I wasn't ready for anything else. I looked at everyone and told them that I was tired, and while the food was tempting, sleep was more important, and I would go back to the cave.

Kathy gave me a concerned look but figured as long as I was not with them, there would be no risk of me telling her secret.

As nighttime came, I wondered how Kathy was feeling. This would be the first time in a while that she was alone. I guess it was stupid, but I wondered if two women in love were the same as husband and wife. I also wonder after telling me about the ship and the chain of events did it placed my life in jeopardy, the person whom I thought wouldn't be a threat could turn out to be the deadliest.

That morning I went back to the beach. Day one without Cynthia, and it seemed to be a bit strange not to hear her strong husky voice calling everyone to breakfast. I looked around at the familiar surroundings seeking comfort in them like a child seeking comfort in his favorite blanket. The log we all sat on was still there; the trees lined the coast as they always have. Everything was the same, yet it seemed as if everything were different.

Rosa sat alone on the beach looking out at the waves. It puzzled me, but I figured there were many things that puzzled me lately. Walking up to her, she seemed startled by my presence but still kept her head down. The same bubbly person that once was my friend seemed gone and replaced by a shell.

"You OK?" I asked, wondering where Frank was. She told me that he was with his mom at Cynthia's grave. She still didn't look up at me. I could feel that something was wrong, but I was still tired. The lapping of the waves and the birds in the air calmed me down enough to feel sorry for her. I sat down; she was my friend after all, and despite how I felt, friends took care of friends. There was a moment of silence and then she looked up at me. Her right eye was swollen and had begun to blacken.

I wanted to ask her what happened, but she answered before I could form the words. "I fell," she said. I could tell it was a bold-faced lie. Over time you get to know a person, know things about them and how they react. I could tell she was lying by the way the right corner of her mouth curled up as she spoke. She would have made a lousy poker player, but now my biggest issue was to try to get the truth from her.

"How did you fall?" I asked, trying to sound concerned instead of accusing. She didn't reply, which I figured might be the case. Obviously Frank did it, but I didn't understand why. They had been lovers, and he had never hit her before.

It was a fall she said again, and I knew that was my hint to let it go. I figured I would find out soon enough, and it probably had something to do with Kathy. The whole idea of her blowing up the ship was still freaking me out. I wondered if it was a temporary lapse of judgment or if she were just crazy and had been fooling us continually.

Laughter erupted from behind us, as I turned around shocked to see Kathy and Frank holding hands. She seemed jolly and carefree, not like someone who just lost her lover. "Oh, Rosa, how's your eye?" She started laughing again as if it were a joke. Even more unsettling was that Frank joined in. Rosa looked up almost in fear and replied that she was OK.

A lot has happened, lots of weird things, but Rosa was my friend and I didn't care what type of weird alliance Kathy and Frank had; no one would hurt her. I walked up to Frank and stared him in the eyes, "Did you hit Rosa?" I asked him point-blank. He looked at his mom and then back at me, "A woman needs to be put in her place."

Cynthia died, Kathy killed everyone on the ship, and now Frank was beating his girlfriend. Guess that idea about creating the perfect man was gone out the window. He was as crazy as his mom and so was Rosa for letting it happen.

"Frank," I said, "you don't hit women, ever!" Before my voice carried some authority with him but now he just stared at me, and I felt the coldest chill of my life with the sun still shining on my back. It was frightening how much hate he had, but I had my own. *What if I told you that your mom was a killer? Bet that would take that stupid look off your face kid.* Kathy stepped up between us. "Frank and I are mother and son again, just as it was supposed to be. He no longer needs Rosa, so if you don't mind, we'll be getting something to eat." She pushed me out the way, and they continued walking hand and hand down the beach.

Rosa looked at me and asked why. I saw in her eyes a dream that was shattered. She had been through abuse before, and now it was coming back to hunt her. I really didn't have the answer to her question; I was asking the same thing. The only thing I could think of was to make a promise to her. I told her that Frank would never hit her again. I would protect her. With the comfort of my promise, she broke down and started crying.

Frank and Kathy were gone for most of the day; no doubt she was twisting his mind to align with her warped way of thinking. I spent time with Rosa trying to understand what happened. How did Frank go from the sweet loving man we all knew to hitting her? I began to ask her tons of questions, and looking back, I guess that was wrong of me; often we blame the victim instead of the person who commits the crime. "Did you do anything to get him upset?" I said.

I listened to my question and wanted to kick myself. Maybe he is a psycho like his mom.

Rosa looked at me. "I only told him that I loved him, and he went crazy," I wanted to say that he may have been crazy long before that but wouldn't have done any good.

"You must have told him you loved him before now?" I questioned her but then I stopped myself; it was time to help if I could. Rosa's eyes widened with a look of fright as Frank came back toward us. He was alone, which was a good thing, but I had to wonder where Kathy was.

He walked past me and directly in front of Rosa. He kneeled down to her height and took her hand. "I am so sorry for what happened. I guess the loss of Cynthia and everything else caused me to lose my temper. Please forgive me." Rosa jumped into his arms and began to kiss him all over. I may not have had sex in my life, but I could smell bull a mile away, and this kid was laying it on thick.

"Please go get a room," I told them, not really wanting to see Rosa make a fool of herself. Frank gave me an evil look, and to be honest, it broke my heart. He, in a way, was my little boy also. I tried to teach him what was right, but I guess I must not have been a good teacher. "You're right, maybe we do need a room," he said and then kissed Rosa hard against the lips. She moaned for a moment and then caught herself.

She said a few words to him in Spanish, and they both looked at me. He smiled and then came the chills, and then they both got up and walked away.

I sat there alone for a while wondering what else would happen. I was also wondering where Kathy was. I officially felt that she was crazy, but it seemed as if everyone else was crazy also. Maybe this was some sort of bizarre world where I was the crazy one and everyone else was sane.

Kathy walked up to me, pulling me out of my trance. "Did you tell Rosa about the bomb?" I really did not like being confronted like that but answered her anyway. I told Kathy that her secret was safe with me and she smiled. "Good, then your secret is safe with me." Puzzled, I asked her what was my secret. "You think you can kill a woman, my lover, and she would not tell me?"

I stood there with my mouth open. Kathy started to laugh. She moved in close, close enough to whisper in my ear. "Before Cynthia died, she told me you pushed her, but you know what, I am glad she's gone. Her dying was more like a gift for me, so push, fall, either way, I am happy. Now stay out of my way, Little Miss Religion, or everyone on this island will know that you are murderer."

I guess she had me, but now I realized I did not kill the beast. I killed only the monster and let the anti-Christ come to the surface. Kathy started whistling our favorite song as she skipped away.

Things were rapidly spiraling out of control, and now I knew what I had to do. I had to come clean. I tried to get away with murder, and now God was getting back at me. That's the problem with lying; you spend most of your time trying to cover up things and are always scared someone will find out the truth. I now heard my mother's voice in my ear telling me to come clean; God will forgive you. *I miss my mother*. I found myself no longer the strong warrior but a little frightened girl. I closed my eyes imaging my dad hugging me and telling me that it would be OK. It was a good feeling; one that made me want to stay in that special place for the rest of my life, but reality knocked and I had to answer.

I couldn't let Kathy have the upper hand. I had to find the others, confess my sin, and pray for forgiveness. I think Rosa will understand, but it's Frank that I am worried about. He is like his mom but more dangerous. He is strong, and right now, he's on her side. If he stays there, I might be in trouble.

I found my way back to where Rosa and Frank were. I found them asleep in each other's arms. No doubt they made up, and sleep was the natural aftermath. The thought of them together sickened me once I found out that Frank beat her, but the thought of Kathy having control over him sickened me more.

I moved over to Rosa first and tried to wake her without waking Frank. It didn't work. They both stirred and then got up together. I blurted what I had to say out as quickly as I could. It was like a valve being released, but I am not sure if they got it all. "Cynthia didn't fall, I pushed her, and she fell against the rock and died. I ran to get help, but it was my fault. I pushed her because she swung at me. I am not a murderer. I was just protecting myself. Please forgive me, please." They looked at me stunned for a moment. Rosa had a disappointed look on her face that cut me to the bone. Frank's face started to turn red as his anger began to rise. Someone once told me, "The truth hurts right before it sets you free." I was free, but now what?

Rosa began to cry, but what surprised me the most was the way Frank reacted; he stood up and pushed me. It was a hard push that nearly knocked me off my feet. His face turned red as he began to yell, "Murder, killer, liar! I hate you! I hate you!" He was a spoiled kid throwing a temper tantrum, and in a way, I couldn't blame him. The only problem was that he was stronger than a kid and his push hurt.

"I'm sorry," I said, trying to control my own temper. I didn't like being pushed when I was a kid, and I didn't like it now. He stood over me, fist balled and breathing hard. I told him to get away from me. I am not sure if it were reactions or self-defense, but when he raised his hand to hit me, he must have mistook me for Rosa. I lifted my foot as hard as I could and kicked him. He went over like a ton of brick.

I was now standing over him. I told him to never, ever try to lay a hand on me. He lay on the ground balled up crying like a little baby, but I felt nothing. Rosa ran to his side and hugged him. I was angry but more than anything I pitied her. He's hitting her, and she runs to him like an idiot. "Leave us alone," she screamed, looking up at me. Her words stuck and buried themselves deep in my core.

I wanted to say something, but words couldn't form in my mouth. Tears nearly blinded me as I turned to walk away. I was now a lone warrior on a big island. Somewhere in the distance as I turned to walk away, I could have sworn I heard Kathy's voice laughing.

Several months passed by and the loneliness was driving me crazy. I couldn't go back to them that much they made clear. So I sat, watch, tried to remember things that I read in the Bible, things my mother told me, things my dad told me, anything to keep me sane. I felt sorry for prisoners on lockdown. Whatever crime they committed would be nothing compared to the punishment of being around people but not being able to speak with them.

Time seemed as if it stood still. I often hid out and looked at the three of them laughing and talking together. It was if they just forgot me, and I had become some type of animal. Sometimes, perhaps out of pity, Rosa would visit me alone. She covered her tracks and made sure no one knew we were together. I tried to minister to her, but my words were hollow and after everything, I was starting to wonder if I even believed in God anymore.

I asked her whether Frank still beat her; she would not reply but her face told the story. I tried to convince her to leave him, but she told me that she loved him and then gave me a shock. She told me she was pregnant. My mouth dropped open, not really knowing what to say—a baby on the island. What once seemed like a beautiful paradise now seemed like an island of hell.

"Does Frank know?" I asked her, really concerned for her well-being. Although she betrayed me, she was still the only person on the island that talked to me. I often thought about telling her and Frank about Kathy destroying the ship, but I didn't have the heart. It wouldn't have done any good anyway. Who knows, perhaps a baby will bring order back to everything.

Rosa smiled and touched her stomach. "My little bambino." I smiled at her. I couldn't help think about scripture. Maybe this child would be our savior.

Rosa stopped visiting, and I became worried. She was so happy with the fact that she would have a baby, but I worried what Frank and Kathy had to say. It had only been a week since she told me, but a week is a long time on this island when you are alone.

I decided to go and face them to make sure Rosa was all right. As much as I hated being alone, I hated not knowing more. If they didn't want me there, that was OK, but Rosa's well-being was more important than my pride.

I heard talking near our favorite spot on the beach and made my way toward the commotion. The moment they saw me, the talking stopped, and they just looked at me. I went over in my mind what I would say, but like usual, I began to speak before my mind could catch up. "Where's Rosa?" I spoke quickly but straight to the point. Kathy and Frank still sat at the log pretending as if they didn't see me.

I moved over to Kathy and asked her again, "Where is Rosa?"

She rolled her eyes at me and then said I should ask her husband, pointing toward Frank.

Husband. That's what they are calling themselves now? "Whatever." I turned to Frank and looked at him in his eyes. It had been a while since I had really gotten up close to him and realized that he had hair on his face. He looked like a beach bum, but then I guess we all did. Rubbing my own legs, it felt as though I could start a fire rubbing against the thick fur I accumulated. "Where is Rosa?" I said again, this time more forceful. He looked down and then up at me.

"It's good to see you." His statement threw me off guard. I had not expected that from him but still kept alert.

"Tell me where Rosa is," I said once more. He told me that she went to vomit; she had been sick lately. That was a good sign. Morning sickness meant the baby was starting to grow, but now I wondered if Kathy figured it out. She was a woman after all, and with them going at it, always the logical

106

conclusion would lead to pregnancy. "Do you know why she's sick?" I asked him, trying to feel things out.

"How in the world am I supposed to know?" he said annoyed. "She's been sick a lot lately. Maybe she ate something."

OK, good news was that he did not know yet, but I would bet everything I owned that Kathy figured it out. She interrupted me before I could say anything else. "I am sure it is just something she ate."

"You mind if I wait until she comes back?" I said. "I just want to make sure she's OK and then I will leave again."

Kathy started to say something, but Frank interrupted her. "Not a problem, stay as long as you like. We missed you," he said again.

I'm not sure what game he was playing, but he seemed sincere in his offer, but why? For the longest I sat out in the woods like an animal, not welcomed by the tribe and now he missed me. This had to be some sort of game or trap. I tightened up my senses, waiting for an attack. Kathy was near my right side, but I figured I could take her; he was the one I had to worry about. The whole time she stayed quiet only smiling as we talked. Frank dusted off the log next to him and offered me a place to sit. I passed on the offer looking out into the distance trying to find Rosa.

"Are you sure she is OK?" My question was answered as Rosa reappeared around the corner. Seeing me, she quickened her pace. There was a look of fright on her face, which told me she hadn't told Frank yet. I was OK with that. It was her baby, her choice, but I still wanted to talk to her. "Sherry," she said, and she ran up and gave me a hug. There was no doubt that she had been throwing up by the still rancid smell of her breath. She looked around at everyone wondering what our conversation had been about.

Frank stood up, but this time not as loving as he had been in the past. Something had changed between them. She reached over to give him a hug, and he pulled away. It wasn't an abrupt pull away, but just enough to let me know there was trouble in paradise. Kathy made a point to tell her that Frank told me that he missed me. It seemed like a dagger in Rosa's heart, but I had done nothing.

I didn't want to become the middle person in a fight between two lovers. "I am getting used to being by myself," I said, trying to diffuse the situation. Kathy jumped in as usually trying to make a bad situation worse.

"We have been so wrong, Sherry, you out there all by yourself and us here as family. Please forgive us. We were so wrong." It was bull and she knew it, but Rosa was so excited to have me among them so I agreed to stay. I rationalized that at least I could keep a closer eye on how things were going.

We all sat and talked that night. I have to admit it felt strange to be around the three of them again but also good. Everything was going well until Rosa began to look sick. She got up and ran down the beach, and in the quietness of the night, we heard the sound of her throwing up.

I sat around uncomfortable, waiting for Frank to get up and go check on Rosa. He didn't move other than to slide closer to me. This was getting weird. It seemed to me as though he was trying to put moves on me. I tried to adjust myself so that we kept the same amount of distance. I hoped he got the hint, but it didn't work. He started complimenting me on how well I looked and how I kept my body in shape after all these years. I pictured Rosa in my mind, and she had packed on a few pounds no doubt because of the pregnancy, but this sudden interest in me was frightening.

Kathy kept quiet, looking at her son as if it were an experiment to see how well he could pick up a woman. I had bad news for her. I wasn't that woman! I mentioned Rosa again now starting to worry; I hadn't heard her anymore, and she had not returned. Frank ignored what I was saying and continued to try to seduce me. I sickened that he was coming on to me. I wanted to pick up something and throw it into his face. I looked back over to Kathy pleading with my eyes for her to call off her son, but she never said a word.

"I got to go check on Rosa," I said, standing up, no longer able to wait anymore. Frank grabbed my hand. I tried to pull away, but he had a strong grip, stronger than I would have thought.

"She will be OK," he said. His voice was smooth and almost hypnotic.

I pulled away with more force this time. He let go but made sure that I knew my freedom was only because he let me go. That pretty much pissed me off, but my concern for Rosa was greater than my need to punch him in the face. I started to walk away but then couldn't hold it in anymore. I moved close to Frank and told him that if he ever grabbed my arm like that again, I would kill him. He had a hurt look on his face as if he did nothing wrong. Kathy shrugged her shoulder and told Frank to come to her. He got up and walked up to her, sat down, and snuggled his head on her breast like an obedient dog.

I walked away mad and wanting to yell, but I held it in. They were not worth it. Looking down the beach about a hundred yards from where we were sitting, I saw a dark lump near the sand. It was not a full moon, and so I couldn't clearly see more than ten yards in front of me. I called out to Rosa, but there was no movement. Not sure if it were a body or a rock I moved in closer. "Rosa, is that you?" There was still no reply, but then I saw her leg and knew it was her.

Rosa arms closed around her stomach, but she was not moving. There was puke around her, and the smell was awful. I called out her name again, this time more softly as fear covered my soul. I reached over and tried to find a pulse. There was nothing.

I had to make sure I did things right this time. Turning her over, I listened for a heartbeat, checked her pulse, and tried every way to see whether I might be able to detect anything. There was nothing. I began to do as I had seen before. I started pushing her chest and breathing in her mouth. *I always wondered what I would do if someone needed help and had vomit and other things were being released?* It was a no-brainer, you do what you have to, to save a friend.

After what seemed like an hour but was less than ten minutes, I gave up. She was dead. I had lost the only person that was a friend to me. How could she die? Why? Was this because of her pregnancy? Questions flooded my mind and then it hit. I remembered what Frank had said, "Maybe it was something she ate." I wasn't a detective, but I had to know, did they poison her? Was that why he was trying to come on to me? My mind was going crazy when I heard footsteps behind me.

It was them. They were walking toward me, and I was scared. For the first time in my life, I didn't know what to do. No voices in my mind, no words of comfort, nothing but fear. I tried to pray, but prayers didn't seem to give any comfort. My parents would have been disappointed, but it was the truth. They saw me looking at them and then they started to run toward me. It was no doubt an act. It was as if they were talking a leisurely walk in the park until they saw me looking at them. Now they came running full force. *And the Oscar goes to…*

"What happened? Is she OK?" I had to admit Kathy's voice did sound concerned, but it was a lie; everything about her was a lie. Frank looked over Rosa's body and then asked if she was dead. I wanted to take a swing at him so bad. *Dead, does she look dead?* I bit my lip trying to figure out if I should play along or confront them. Right now, I was outnumbered so I chose to wait. I was a pretty good actor myself and began to break down in tear. "Oh my god, she's dead. She's dead." I held my head between my hands but still kept an eye open just in case.

Frank lifted her up in his arms. He started to cry, and I believe his tears were real, but I imagined they flowed because of some twisted loss, not the loss of a life. Kathy walked over to him to comfort him. It was an act; she could care less. In fact, she may have been the one who killed her. Frank looked at me suspiciously. "What happened?"

"WHAT *THE HELL YOU THINK HAPPENED!*" What was I to say? Your mom is crazy, you're crazy, and oh by the way, I think she poisoned the woman that was carrying your child. Better yet, she is the woman who killed all those people on the ship.

I tried to act calm. "I don't know. She was dead when I got over here." He had a look of mistrust. "*Screw you!* I didn't do anything. Rosa was my friend, what you need to do is ask your crazy mother" is what I wanted to say, but I decided to play my hand. "She was pregnant and now she's dead, both of them gone. How could this happen?" Frank turned around with a truly honest look of surprise on his face. He knew nothing about her being pregnant. Kathy hadn't told him.

Didn't know where things were going but I wanted to press my advantage. It was hard to play this game with him holding Rosa's body in his arms, but there had been two deaths on this island, and one was an accident. Rosa's was a different story. Maybe Frank is innocent in all this, but his crazy mom had to be pointed out. "What do you mean Rosa was pregnant?" he asked.

"She told me over a week ago that she thought she might be pregnant that is why she had put on weight and was sick continually. I'm sure Kathy must have noticed." The seed was planted, and I wondered what would happen next.

Frank's face turned red, and his anger was no act; he was mad. He looked at his mom and yelled at her, "Did you know?" She was quiet, but quietness sometime speaks as a words. "You did, didn't you?" He held Rosa's limp body up toward her as if it were some sort of sacrifice. "You killed her?" She started to smile and tried to ease his tension, moving in close she started to rub his arm. He moved away, not being under her spell anymore. "Why, Mom, why?" His voice now sounding like a little kid again, tears began to flow down his face. "You killed my baby, my child." Rosa was not his concern, but the unborn child that she held? He would have just as soon thrown her body out of the way if there were a chance to save his unborn child.

"Son, she was no good for you, and you know it. I saw the way she treated you. She didn't love you." Now I knew Kathy was crazy. Rosa treated Frank like a king. If he said jump, she would say how high. Everything she did was in service to him, and even after he beat her, she still stayed. "But my baby…She was pregnant with my baby."

Kathy began to rub his arm again. "I am sorry, but she was not fit to have your child."

I grabbed Kathy. "You bitch." I hate cursing, but those words seem to fit the moment. "Why did you kill her? Why?"

Kathy stood her ground and looked at me. "My son will not have a bastard child, that by that Spanish piece of trash." Those words said it all; she was crazy, a racist, and a piece of trash. All these year and everything now came to light.

I looked at Frank and asked him what he was going to do. "Your mother is crazy. She killed Rosa. What are you going to do?" I said repeatedly. He stood there like an idiot. Holding Rosa in his arms like a rag doll, he started toward me. Good, he was coming to his senses, and now it would be the two of us against a crazy lady. I wonder what would be our next move. How do you keep a crazy lady at bay? There were no jail cells, no mental institutions; nothing that could protect us from her.

Frank took one more step and then handed me Rosa's body. I reached out for her and then he walked back to his mother's side. "She's my mother" was all he said. I wanted to spit in his face, but I was tired. My only friend was dead, and I was on the island with two crazy people. Kathy smiled at me and took Frank by the hand. They turned and walked away.

Rosa was heavy even with her small frame. I couldn't hold her any longer, and I really didn't want to. Her body was starting to get cold and the realization of what just happened was hitting me with full force. I didn't want to bury a friend, not alone, not by myself. I broke down and cried. I cried long and hard, and at the end, I cried some more.

"Get up," a voice said. "Don't quit fighting." It was a voice I hadn't heard in a long time, a voice that had been my friend and comforter when I was a child, a voice that was a mixture of my mother, grandmother, father, and me. It was also the voice in my head. I didn't want to listen; I just wanted to lay right next to Rosa's body and die. "You are stronger than they are. Fight, fight." As quickly as the voice came, it left.

I found myself yelling for that voice to come back. It felt so good, so right. It was like being reunited with a long lost friend, but in the end, there was only the silence and the waves washing against the shore.

Shaking the sand off my body, I looked at Rosa again. She was as beautiful in death as she was in life. I hated the fact that she was gone, but it was time to move, time to get up. They say God speaks with you in whispers, maybe the voice I heard was him all rolled up with the voices of those I loved.

I really wasn't sure what to do next; I didn't want to bury her. I only wanted to keep her company for a little longer and tell her a little about myself. I wanted to tell her that it would be OK, that we would get off the island and that she would be free. A gentle breeze blew past my face, and I saw my answer. There was a small decaying piece of wood just big enough to place Rosa inside it. As if a message from God, I knew what I would do; she would be free.

There wasn't really much to say, not much to do either. Rosa and her unborn child deserved much better than the way they died. I lifted her lifeless body and placed her on the hollowed out piece of wood, which seemed to be made just for her.

I would send her to sea where she could be free from this island and all the evil that was a part of it. In a way, it didn't feel right having her dead body curled up in a wooden coffin, but maybe this was more for me than it was for her, maybe with her being free I too would be free. I whispered out loud to God figuring that he would understand my anger and rage; he would understand why I hated him so much but also needed him. I figured he would take Rosa home and in doing so take me also.

It was a hard struggle pushing the wooden grave out to sea. For a while, I dug hard into the ground trying to push it to move from its resting place. I fought hard for a short amount of time and then it began to move, a little first and then more. The more the waves pushed up to the shore, the more the ocean came to claim her soul.

I watch as the undercurrents took her body out to sea. Her wooden coffin drifted slowly, quietly, and peacefully out until she was nothing more than a small dot in the great beyond. I guess if I had to die that's the way I would want it to happen, just let me drift floating on the ocean as I imagined I floated in my mother's womb.

I waited there for most of the night talking to God. Maybe talking isn't quite the word I was looking for, yelling screaming, shouting—it didn't matter because in the end I found peace. I found comfort in knowing that I had survived this long. Maybe there was a purpose for me after all. I inhaled deeply trying to renew my strength. The realization that I was alone hit me again, but that was OK. Strange how when you hit rock bottom you can choose to either to give up or look up and rely on your faith.

Now I had to figure out what to do next. Maybe I would just leave those two alone. They deserve each other. Maybe I should just go off into the wilderness and let sleeping dogs lie. Who knows? With any luck, maybe they will kill each other. I looked out at the sea and then to where Kathy and Frank had left and chose to go the opposite way. Maybe my life alone wouldn't be so bad.

Chapter Eight

He was angry, really angry. He walked over to me and sat me up. I couldn't pretend that I'm unconscious anymore. I was back to the land of the living and not the land of memories. He looked at me and then began to yell. "It's your fault that everything is the way it is." I opened my eyes and looked at him. I tried to stare him down, but his anger was greater than my strength. I turned away.

"It's not my fault," I whispered back. "You're the monster." He hit me hard across the face. I felt blood, but that's nothing new.

I tried to reason with him. "Look, I know you hate me, and maybe you have a right to, but I didn't hurt your mom." He grabbed me hard by the arm and lifted me to my feet. "Why don't you want to be with me? It's only you and I left, man and woman. Can't you see we need each other?" His voice was almost like a little child again. He was pleading with me, and I needed to make him feel like I cared.

"You're right. We need to be with each other, but not the way you want to. Don't you remember what we taught you? Don't you remember what I taught you?" I said this in as kind of a voice as I could muster. He held on to me, and then as if his anger had been released, he sat me down gently. He was listening. Good. I continued to talk.

"Think about what Cynthia—" His nose began to flare at the mention of her name, so I knew that was my cue to back off and change the subject. "Don't you remember when you were young? We played games and talk, remember? You would tell me things, you and I were friends."

I could see the tightness starting to be released from his shoulder. That was a good sign. I needed to keep pressing the issue. "Remember when I told you about my family? I told you that you were part of my new family." His face was still hard, but I could see in his eyes that he was starting to trust again. That was good, I wanted him to trust. He was dangerous when he didn't trust.

I decided to try my biggest gamble. "I love you," I said, trying to do my best acting job. For a kid who was super smart, he was stupid.

He cocked his head to the side and repeated what I said as a question, "You love me?"

I was reaching him and that was what I wanted. "I do love you, and I'm so sorry for hurting you," I said, feeling him let his guard down.

"Why don't you untie me?" I said, trying to be polite. He looked at me and then to my surprise he said no. It was not harsh tone but in a matter-of-fact tone. I tried another angle. "Well, can you at least loosen the rope up a bit?" He did not say anything but looked at my wrist.

"Do you really love me? I'm a bad boy," he said, sounding regretful for his actions.

"*Yea, I'd love to cut your bad boy head off*" was my thought, but I told him that I forgave him and that we could be friends. "You have to trust me. We only have each other." He made a move toward me, and I moved back. The hits had made me gun shy. He softly put his hands on mine. "I'm not going to hurt you," he said. "I just want to loosen these up." He grabbed my wrist and loosened the binds that tied me. "I love you," he said and then leaned in to kiss me.

The only thing I could do was take it and act like I enjoyed it. He pulled away.

"We didn't have to go through all of this," he said. "You know I like you." He sounded like a teenager out on his first date.

My mind began to race back trying to remember my childhood. *What is he expecting to hear?* I replied to what I thought he wanted to hear. "Listen. Think about Rosa. She was your friend, right?" Once I mentioned her name, his whole demeanor changed and I knew I had him. "Remember how you and Rosa had a secret and I try to keep it from your mom? She was really mad when she figured it out, but I was your friend. I never told."

Frank smiled; he had a great smile, one that if he weren't on the island and half-crazy, it would drive young ladies wild. "That's right, you never told, did you?" he said. I felt I was gaining points. "I loved Rosa," he said. I just nodded my head and agreed.

It was strange how he and Rosa hit it off. When Kathy found out about it, she blew a gasket.

I asked him to untie my feet; he looked down at them almost in fear. Had to admit I was proud of that fact. A few good kicks in the sack and you gain some respect. "I promise

I won't kick you again," I said, smiling. He hesitated at first and then untied my feet.

Everything inside of me wanted to kick him so hard he would be spitting out toenails, but this was not the time. I wanted to talk to him, keep him calm, and plan out my next attack.

He looked at me and smiled. There was a confidence about him that at times seem to battle with the little boy inside of him as well. I had to keep him talking. "Remember when we first landed on the island?" He withdrew and went back to that same kid from way back when.

I wondered what could be going on in the mind of an eighteen-year-old that was now in control and had been on the island for four years. He had me right where he wanted, and there was very little I could do about it. He moved in close to me almost as if he were asking for permission. I was in no position to fight, so I pretended to welcome him. If I could keep him talking, it may give me a chance to escape.

"Frank, it doesn't have to be like this. I like you, really I do. If you untie me, I will be yours." Frank smiled at me. He was letting his defenses down. *Great for me.* "Frank, I am sorry for kicking you. I just didn't want my first time to be so rough. Didn't Rosa show you how to be gentle?" I could see what I said hit a nerve. Maybe he really did love Rosa. Maybe he didn't know how to be gentle. "Frank, we can have a baby, you and I. I just want it to start off right."

Frank was a smart young kid; we just screwed up his head trying to make him perfect. "You want a child with me? Mom said she didn't want mixed blood. She wanted me perfect," he said. That was a laugh. I hated to be the one to burst his bubble.

"Your mom was a whore. She screwed around with every-one in her neighborhood. You might be mixed yourself, and maybe that's why you went for Rosa in the first place." He stood up, angered. I braced myself for another hit across the face.

"That's not true. My mom is perfect, and she was the only one on this island who loved me."

I told him that Rosa loved him and in fact we all loved him. He stared at me coldly and said that Rosa was only a play-thing. Kathy told him that it was natural to want a woman, but getting her pregnant was wrong. I kind of felt sorry for this screwed-up kid. His mom really did a job on him, but still I needed to get into his head. "Please don't hit me," I said, acting scared of him. "I just wanted you to know the truth." Frank was still angry, but he didn't hit me so that was a good sign. I just had to get him to trust me.

"Frank, I will be good to you. All you have to do is let me go." I told him I was sorry for everything and that I would be his. He started to smile. His walls were coming down, which was a good sign, but still I was playing a dangerous game.

This once smart, bright kid had now become an ani-mal, only living to eat and fulfill his own desire. "You really want me?" he said, looking for my approval. I told him that of course I wanted him, which made him smile. He leaned over and kissed me in the mouth. It was a hard aggressive kiss. I felt his tongue pushing deep into my mouth, moving it all around. It sickened me, but I had to put up a good front. I had to pretend I enjoyed it, make him think I wanted him as much as he wanted me.

I moaned acting as if I enjoyed it. He reacted by pull-ing me closer. I could feel his heart beat against my chest.

His hands began to roam everywhere. Even on an island, my dates seem to be the same. *Why do men grope?* OK, now he was hooked. I had to slow him down before anything else happened. Pulling away, I told him that I wanted to hold him also. I wanted to be next to him. I said the words he wanted to hear: "Frank, I am ready for you." I know you can't taste words, but if you could, my words would be full of poop.

He looked at me. It was a confused but wanting look. He began to stroke my cheek, forgetting that I had kneed him twice. He took my hands and pulled out his little pocketknife and cut me free. I rubbed my wrist, feeling the blood circulating back into them. Raw skin against the heat of the fire brought about pain, but freedom was the ointment.

This was going to be the showdown. I knew I couldn't spend the rest of my life being chased by him, but I also knew I couldn't give myself to him, no matter what; if he won, he would have to rape a dead body.

I put my arm around Frank and began to blow in his ear. I wanted him to let his guard down completely. Moving around his back, I began to massage his shoulder. "There, isn't this better?" He rolled his head a little and sighed. "You know, this will be my first time," I told him. Maybe those words would mean something to him. When he was younger, I taught him about keeping himself pure. I tried to teach him everything my parents taught me, but judging by his blank look, he forgot.

I looked around as I talked to him, trying to see whether there was anything I could use as a weapon. Smooth sand, small chunks of rock, a fire, and then out of the right corner of my eye, I saw his knife. The knife he used to cut branches for the fire. He laid it to the side in his rush to get with me.

I couldn't make a move right away. It was too far, and he was too fast. But it was there, and if there were an opening, I would take it.

It's strange to think that this was the same little kid I once knew on the island. I wanted to blame Cynthia and say that she was the reason or maybe Kathy, maybe there was some genetic issue that hunts her family and he just inherited it, but the truth was that we were all to blame. I stood by and did nothing while Cynthia beat him, and as my dad would say, "To do nothing when you know wrong is the same as doing the crime itself." Rosa slept with a minor, and Kathy was just plain crazy. That was the sum of all our sins. I almost laughed thinking about how in the beginning we would sit around trying to figure out what the perfect man should be like and thinking that we could mold Frank that way.

I guess we got our wish; he was perfectly crazy. Now he looked at me wanting to control me. I started to rub his chest, and he heaved deeply. His shoulders went limp, and he was relaxed; I counted to three. *ONE, TWO, THREE!* I made my move for the knife and had it in my hand before he knew what happened. I had the upper hand. He sat there with a daze and confused look on his face. It took a while for him to compute what happened but then his face became dark red. To him, it was the ultimate betrayal. He lounged at me, and I defended myself. A look of shock and horror swept his face as his body rolled off mine. Blood was pouring out of his shoulder where the knife went in. He flopped on the ground like a fish for a while, struggling to get his breath, and then he stopped facedown in the sand. I did it; he was dead. I killed the monster.

This time it wasn't an accident. I wanted him dead. I would be no one's prize on the island. There was a feeling of exhilaration flowing through my body. I was the victor, and he was the loser. I almost felt sorry from him, but I did what I had to do. In his death, he looked like the little innocent boy that I first saw when we were lost at sea. He looked just like Kat—Oh my god, I forgot all about Kathy. Where was she? During this whole event, she was not around. I am not sure where she was, and now that her son was dead, she became my next worry.

Looking at his body again, I turned to walk away and then I saw her. She stood against the backdrop of the trees, timid like a deer, not sure if she should step out or not. I looked at her still holding the knife ready for a fight. We seemed to be at a standstill and then she started to walk toward me. I readied myself holding my breath. She walked almost as if floating, moving on air, and coming for me.

I could kill again, I told myself. I tried to mentally place where I would stab her but then as I readied myself to strike she walked past me and to the body of her son. She didn't say anything but kneeled over him and kissed him softly on the cheek as she rolled him over. It was as if I was invisible and this was a private goodbye to a loved one. Somehow I knew the battle was over. There would be no more fighting, no more bloodshed.

I turned and walked away, back into the jungle that I came from. I was free, but I was alone.

Chapter Nine

It has been about a month now and no sign of Kathy. I went back to our old stomping grounds and tried to find her, tried to put an end to the mess we both made. Maybe we could somehow learn to coexist. I know it sounded crazy, I even laughed at it—*us working together after I killed her son.* I have to admit it's been troubling not being able to find her. I often wonder what she did with Frank's body. I wondered if she buried him next to Cynthia. It just seemed as if she vanished off the face of the earth. The island was big but not that big.

Journeying back to the spot where Cynthia was buried brought back strange memories. I wondered if maybe I could have tried harder to make friend with her. Maybe all this mess was my fault. Several small plants Frank buried with Cynthia now populated the area where she laid. Her grave had become a beautiful garden full of vibrant colors and that gave me pause. Is this what life is about? We die only to give life. I prayed that there is a heaven, but in some ways, I hope not. After all I've done, I wasn't sure if God would forgive me. I bent over and silently asked Cynthia for forgiveness, not because I needed it but somehow I thought if I could ask her for forgiveness then maybe God will forgive me.

I don't know why I did it, but I stood up and yelled for Kathy. My cry came back void. There was no reply. Maybe this was her way of getting back at me. Maybe one day when I'm alone and my guard is down, she will sneak up on me and take my life. I guess that is why I am trying to make peace. Maybe I am waiting or even expecting my death.

Birds flew by, animals moved about, but no Kathy and then I hear it. Distant at first but nevertheless I hear it. I shook my head thinking that I had finally lost my mind. Maybe I was imagining things, but then I heard it again. I looked up to the heavens, and I saw for the first time in all these long many years a plane. My heart began to beat quickly. What to do? How to get their attention? I ran to the beach, thinking it was the clearest place. If I heard correctly, then maybe they would be able to see me from there.

There was silence for a long moment, and I wondered if maybe my mind had been playing tricks on me. Maybe I heard something, either way I had to assume the best. I tried to think about the plan we had made to attract a plan if it came. Maybe it would be up too far for them to see me? Maybe they were only going to pass by once? I had to do all I could to fight against the negative thoughts that kept trying to flood my mind. I looked around trying to remember where we placed it; it being a small piece of reflective metal that we kept from the lifeboat just in case a plane did fly by. We had given up that thought many years ago, and now it was hard to remember where it was.

Suddenly I remembered, the log, our old meeting place, the place where I stabbed Frank is where we kept it. I started running hoping that it was not too late. I really wished Frank were alive now with him being a Boy Scout and all. Wasn't there some way to signal SOS, the universal sign for help? Depending their distance, I didn't want them to think that it was some reflection off a rock.

I heard the faint sound of the engine again and began to panic. Digging in the sand, I retrieved it. I tried to remember how it went. *Short long short*—that's not right. I tried to find the best angle to get the optimum reflection, but more than anything, I wanted someone, anyone to see me.

The sound of the plane started getting stronger and then I saw it at a distance. It was a small double-engine plane, and it was flying low. The pilot dipped its wing to let me know that he saw me and then flew away. I wasn't sure what that meant, but he saw me; I would be free. *God, I would be free.* But the feeling of joy and excitement was soon washed away to fear. I would be free, but would my freedom just be long enough for me to stand trial for the murder of two people? Would my freedom lead to me being alone in a jail cell?

I now really wanted to know where Kathy was. Maybe she heard the plane, and if so, what would she tell them? I murdered both people in self-defense, but would they believe me? You would think that this would be the happiest moment of my life, but instead I got on my knees and began to cry.

I cried for a short period of time, and then after feeling sorry for myself, I got up and waited. I couldn't run and really didn't care too. I would be rescued, and I had to keep telling myself that. Whatever happens, happens. I would get off the island. Several hours went by and then I saw a small boat in the distance. It took several minutes and then three men with life jackets landed on our island.

One man, a big middle-aged man with small gruff growing on his face began to bark orders and the other two followed. They ran toward me concerned but cautious.

"Are you OK?" the young one to the left of me barked in a military tone. He couldn't have been more than thirty. He's tall, has bronze skin, and is slightly muscular. I stood looking at him for a moment dazed and then jumped into his arms.

The other young man, slightly smaller with a roundish face ran to my side and grabbed me by the waist. He handled me rough, rougher than I expected from the people who were supposed to rescue me. "Get away from him," he said as he pulled his gun and pointed it toward my head. "Don't force me to shoot you."

"Put that gun away, boy," the older man yelled. He was the one in charge, and what he said, they followed. He jumped off the boat and looked at me. "I am sorry for the way he acted. This is his first mission," he spoke quickly and directly. Although he apologized, he still seemed guarded. "Are you alone on this island?" You could tell that when he asked and he wanted and expected a quick answer. I hesitated for a moment, and I could tell he did not like my hesitation.

"I, no, I am not alone. I mean I am, but…," I stuttered over my words, trying to get them out but also scared about the murders. *Note to myself, got to stop saying that I murdered. I defended myself.*

"Which is it, are you alone or is there someone else?" he said, looking me dead in the face. I noticed the other two young men still stood their ground ready to react at the slightest motion. "There is another person, but I don't know where she is at." They all had a puzzled look on their face.

"You are telling me that there is someone else on the island, and you don't know where she is at?"

Guilt and pain swept over my body. I didn't know what to do or where to begin but the little voice that was speaking with me spoke up, "The truth shall set you free." Truth, it was time to be truthful, time to let it go. I went through everything that happened on the island in the last four years, but selectively leaving out the parts that I did not want them to know about. Once finished, they all stood there with a dumb look on their face. It was silent for a moment, and so I figured it was time for me to start asking questions.

"How did you guys find me?"

"Miss," the older one said, "you're one lucky person, and if all you've told me is true—"

I interrupted, "It is true."

"That may be, miss, but from all that you have told me you have Rosa—I believe that's what you said her name was—to thank for your rescue."

Now it was my turn to look dumbfounded. How's that possible? Rosa was dead. My question was answered, "At 0500 hours, we found a decomposed body in a log floating. We phone it in and the neighboring country did a flyby and spotted you. We were giving permission to perform a search-and-rescue mission."

I didn't know what to say. Even in death Rosa saved my life. I started to cry. I wanted a shoulder to lean on, but the men kept their distance. To them I was a murderer and they had to be safe. I sobbed for a moment and then stopped. I needed to get a hold of myself.

"Are you ill or injured in any way?" the younger one said. I told him I was OK, and then they helped me on board the boat. "We will take you to the main ship," the large man said. Once there, we will get you some clothes and food. The ride to the boat seem slow and agonizing, but the closer we came to the main ship, the more my heart leapt with joy. As I got into the boat, the captain looked at me and said again that I was one lucky person. It was the same thing that everyone had been saying. I only bowed my head and told him I was blessed.

They took me to section where I changed and shower. It had been a long time since I had hot water cascading down my body. I was in heaven and hell. I didn't know what would happen to me, but I figured I might as well enjoy the moment. The captain informed me that he would send more men out to the island to search for Kathy. More than likely they would find her, and after she gave her side of the story, I would be locked in whatever prison they had aboard.

Several hours went by, and I had to admit, other than the treatment I received when they first landed on the island, I was treated like a queen. I could hear whispers from some of the men as they looked and pointed.

The ship wasn't large but functional, what you might expect from that some sort of military ship. I wasn't sure if it was the Coast Guard, but they obviously knew what they were doing. Each man moved around effortlessly as they attended their duties. They asked me whether I needed anything to eat and jokingly I said anything but fish. Some of the younger people laughed, but generally everyone had stone faces.

The older man who met me at the island came over to the table I was sitting at. He sat still not saying a word for a moment and looked me into my eyes. "I know this seems like a lot, but imagine my point of view. We get word of a body floating in the water. Finding it, we trace it back to you. You tell us that you accidentally killed two people. We are checking for a woman whom we can't seem to find, so forgive me if I seem a little guarded."

He made a good point, one that I understood. I tried to put his mind at ease and let him know that I would cooperate with him in any way. He smiled for the first time, showing a pretty row of the whitest teeth I had seen in a long time. Instead of the stern look he once had, he now looked fatherly and caring. In some way, he reminded me of my dad. I took a deep breath trying to hold back the tears, thinking about the people I would see again.

"I have neglected to inform you who I am and for that I apologize. My name is Captain Roberts," the older man said. "We are part of a treasure hunting ship looking for lost bounty at sea. I apologize for the guns again, but you understand the business we are in and the fact that there are undesirable out there who would love nothing more than to steal our finds. Once we received the message from the fishing boat, we responded as fast as we could. You said you were aboard *The Lord IV*?" It was the name of the cruise ship that sank. I nodded my head in agreement. "That ship has been lost for over four years," he said, scratching his head for a moment, putting the pieces together.

"That's very strange?" I was curious by his comment but decided to let him continue to speak without being interrupted.

"They gave up on that ship after a few years back. Big lawsuit and the company went under," he said. I wondered how they would feel if they knew it wasn't the ship's fault but a bomb. I held on to that information for later. "They thought everyone was dead, even sent out a rescue ship. Do you realize how far off course you were?" I looked at him with a lost look on my face. He must have read my reaction and began to backtrack.

"Of course you don't know how far off you were, but it is amazing that you survived so long. The island you were on has never been mapped before, pretty amazing considering the technology we have. He stopped talking for a moment and then became serious. "Can I ask you a question?" I raised my shoulder to show that I did not care either way. He continued, "All those years on the island and the few people that were there died, weren't you afraid you would have to live the rest of your life alone?"

The answer was, I told him that you just do what you have to do. He looked understanding; I guess we both were simple people.

He was quietly studying me when one of his men came in; it was one of the same young men who rescued me. He leaned over and whispered in the captain's ear and then they both looked at me. I might have been on an island for a long time, but that look wasn't good. They whispered to each other again and the captain turned toward me. "They found Kathy." A brief burst of joy swept over my body; although I thought she was crazy, I did not want her to be left alone. My joy was short-lived as he continued. "She's dead. They found her body. Apparently, she starved to death." I couldn't believe what he was saying. Starved to death? She knew the island as well as I did; there was no way she starved to death. I became nervous; this was becoming a sure sign of doom for me.

There was more news, which I really didn't want to hear. "They also found the young man you told us about, and he wasn't dead." My mouth dropped open. He had to have been dead. I killed him. I remembered putting the knife in his body and watching the blood flood out. "He's not dead?" My voice was shaky but I kept my composure.

The captain tilted his head to the side. "Aren't you happy?" His question was strictly to see how I would react.

I told him that I was happy, but my body began to shake. I thought about all that I went through and now he was alive. I asked whether he was all right. The captain did not answer but merely got up and walked out of the room. I sat there alone staring at the walls. Frank was alive? My god, what was I going to do? I almost started hyperventilating. I couldn't help wonder what he was telling them.

I got up not being able to sit still any longer. I walked to the door and opened it, but there was a guard stationed in front. He motioned for me to go back into the room. He also let me know that he had a gun. I replied of course and felt sick to my stomach. At least on the island I had the freedom to roam around. Being enclosed in the small room was driving me crazy.

Pacing up and down, I started going through the different compartments. I guess this must have been one of the young men's room or even the captains. It seemed pretty big, and although sparely decorated, it had some comforts that I did not see in other.

I went to one of the desk draws and opened it. It was empty except for a writing pad, a pen, and a Bible. I picked the Bible up and held it close to my body. I don't know why I did it, wasn't sure if I were going to open it, but it felt right. All those year on the island battling with God, it just felt right. I closed my eyes and began to pray. It was a simple prayer but to the point, "Lord, help me."

Putting it down, I returned to the chair I was sitting on and waited. It must have been about thirty minutes of nothingness and then the door opened. The captain walked in; his demeanor seemed different this time, as if a weight had been lifted off his shoulder. He smiled at me and extended his hand to help me up. "Frank collaborated with your story. He agreed with everything you said." I had been ready to defend myself, and this nearly knocked me off my feet.

Chapter Ten

"Frank agreed with me?" I know it sounded like a question, but I couldn't believe what I was hearing. The captain, now friendly, put his hand on my shoulder.

"He said the stabbing was an accident. He said it was a misunderstanding." That was good news to me, but how do I say that he was crazy also and that he was trying to rape me? Staying quiet, I felt as if I were making a deal with the devil.

"His wound was near his heart, but I think it must have been more blood than anything. He survived, but unfortunately, his mom didn't. He's in stable condition right now. We will ask him some more question later." He looked at me again. "Are you OK? You look a little sick?"

Sick? That was an understatement. Of course I was sick, but who do you tell? What do you say? The captain turned to leave and then stopped. "By the way, he asked to see you."

My heart began to pound at the thought of seeing him again. I tried to plan one step ahead if he wanted to see me and had to figure out what he would want. I looked at the captain trying not to show my fear. Saying OK, I allowed him to take me by the arm and gently lead me down the narrow hallways. We spoke along the way more about the changes that had occurred since I had been away. It seemed like a lot but going to see Frank overshadowed everything else.

I soon realize that a short walk could seem very long if you are not sure what is at the other end. I tried to control my breathing, but my heart kept racing. We made our way to the end of the hallway and turned to the right. I expected to see Frank lying up on a table, but he was sitting up and looked in pretty good shape. His shirt was off exposing the bandages across the spot where the knife went in but other than that he looked good. He flashed a bright smile as I entered and jumped off the table to greet me. "Sherry," he said, extending his arms to give me a hug. He seemed so much different than he did on the island.

I walked toward him, guarded but not wanting to seem as if I weren't happy. He wrapped his arms around me and gave me a big hug. It seemed genuine as he pressed himself close to me. His arms were strong, and he rubbed my back for a moment. I pulled away from him, and he did not resist. "I am so glad you are safe." His voice was smooth. Everyone waited for my normal reply, which was to say that I was glad he was OK, but I could not bring myself to say it. The captain gave a suspicious look in my direction but then turned to look straight ahead.

"It has been a long time and a lot happened on the island. I've already told these men that nothing was your fault. I just want to go home," Frank said as he looked around the room almost as if he were giving a speech. "Sherry and I have been through so much together. I prayed every night for a rescue." He put his hand over his eyes as if he were fighting to hold back tears. It was good acting, but I knew better. Looking directly at the captain, he asked whether he could have a few moments alone with me. Everything in my body wanted to protest, but I had to hold my tongue. I need to play this out and see what he is up to.

The captain hesitated for a moment and then ordered everyone out; he said he would give us five minutes. That seemed like five minutes too long, but now he had the upper hand. Frank waited until everyone was out and then looked at me. His whole demeanor changed going from the angelic man who was happy to be rescued to the face of a demon. He grabbed me by my arm hard. It hurt as I could feel his grip tearing into my flesh. His voice became more of animalistic snarl instead of the honey-dipped voice he displayed before.

"I hate you," he said, his voice was cold and hard. "Do you know what it was like to be too weak to move and to have your mother starving herself to death to feed you? Do you? His voice raised a level and then he brought it back down. "You thought you could kill me? You know that place you used to tell me about, was it heaven? That's right, heaven. When I was on the ground dying, I heard voices calling me, telling me to let go and come to God, but I told them to go to hell. I couldn't die yet. I had to come back and get you."

A chill ran up my body. He was cold, heartless and, angry and wanted me dead. I tried to pull away, but his grip was firm. He pulled me even closer. "You belong to me." He leaned over and kissed me hard in my mouth. I struggled to get free, but he kept forcing himself against me. A knock at the door interrupted him, and he let me go. The captain walked in and looked at the both of us. He excused himself, eyeing us as if he walked in on two lovers getting reunited. It didn't help that I was wiping my mouth, hating the taste of his lips against mine.

"I hope I am not interrupting anything." He was a typical man, thinking sex first instead of anything else. He gave a knowing glance at Frank like an old friend. "We will be traveling for about five days before we come to the nearest island. I already informed the Coast Guard, and they will meet up with us and take you the rest of the way home." He seemed to get a little excited. "There is already a huge buzz about this, and you two will get us much press." He smiled again, not because of caring, but the thought of all the free publicity that he would get.

"Great," Frank said, putting on the old charm again. "Sherry and I can't wait." He spoke for me as if I were not there or, worse yet, as if he owned me. I prayed for that little voice that has been guiding me all this time to speak up again and tell me what to do.

I tried to keep my distance from Frank for the five days we were on the ship, but it was impossible. We often were the hot topic of the boat many times. They wanted to talk with us together. Frank would smile and do most of the talking while also grabbing my leg under the table. I was between a rock and a hard place again. Do I talk to someone and tell them that he is crazy or keep quiet and wait until we reach land? Once there, I figured could separate myself from him and live my own life.

I chose the latter. My life had been crazy enough, and I just wanted to be free. I figured I could stay away from Frank once I got ashore. There are millions of women for him to go after, but I would not be one of them. I would stay as far away as possible. Each time we came near each other on the ship, I tried to make sure someone stayed between us or in hearing distance so that he could not stay the awful things he would whisper in my ear. I have to admit he was charming at times, and if I looked at things from the outside, he would seem like the perfect young man. He had a charm about him that I had not realized on the island. Now in the midst of others, he seemed to have a natural flow.

Four days and counting, and so far so good. Frank was busy hanging with the guys telling them about him and Rosa. He seemed to feed off their attention learning how to manipulate each one of them. I studied him as he studied them. Some enjoyed hearing sex stories, and he would tell them about him and Rosa in detail, adding more info than I needed to hear. Others wanted to know about survival, and he would adjust everything to fit their need. Everyone loved him, and although I was the only woman on the ship, I was pretty much left alone.

I watched him read books with a hunger and desire to learn. I watched as he talked to the captain. He was inquisitive and always asked questions. His desire to know was nearly the same as a child, always open and ready to grow. He learned quickly, and the captain even let him steer the ship once. Each night, I retreated to my room and read my Bible and thanked God for the opportunity to see my parents again.

I tried to pull the captain to the side once wanting to tell him about Frank but was stopped before I could start. He told me how great it was that Frank and I could have been on the island that whole time and that he was proud of me. He even hinted that Frank and I must have had some type of relation. I was disgusted at the thought, also the fact that he pictured me with Frank. Everything about men had become a turnoff. I was making peace with myself about living the rest of my life alone.

The Coast Guard ship arrived and took us aboard. Things went pretty much the same on this ship as it did with the other; everyone fell in love with Frank. I tried to keep to myself, but it was hard. We had become heroes, survivors; everyone wanted to know what it was like to live on the island. We even got a call from the president of the United States telling us what brave Americans we were. I could have laughed at that, *Mr. President, Frank is crazy and you just congratulated him.*

I noticed that with fame, you became a lot better looking. I was a black woman on an island for four years without a perm or makeup; I certainly wasn't the best-looking woman at the time. I had a huge matted 'fro with gray patches that I tried to do something with, but there was really no hope until I could make an appointment with a stylist. My teeth were yellow and in desperate need of a dentist, and my skin had been sunburned. The warm chocolate had now become a burnt coffee yet repeatedly I noticed several men giving me the eye. Maybe it was the thought of being next to fame or the feeling of conquering fame, whatever it was I did not want any part of it. Frank on the other hand absorbed all the attention as if he is a human sponge. Several women on duty teased and flirted with him like teenage girls on the prowl. I noticed that he paid particular attention to these women.

Me on the other hand would be happy to settle into oblivion. The Coast Guard captain told me that I should be receiving a call tomorrow; he was a kind man with gentle warm eyes and always treated me with absolute respect. His voice reminded me of Stan, the captain that died at sea along with us. I was saddened but overjoyed at his memory. I slept that night wondering what tomorrow would bring, hoping not to be let down again.

The next day I woke and hurried to find out who the surprise phone call was from. I figured it would be another person with political power trying to cash in on our newfound celebrity status. Walking into the communication room, several men stood around expressionless looking strangely at me as I walked over toward the captain. He had the same welcoming smile that I had grown accustomed to as he handed me the phone. I took it slowly first and then put it toward my ear. There were screams in the background and then the gentle and soft voice of my mom. It had been a long time since I cried, but hearing her voice made me cry like a baby.

"My baby," she said again between her sobs, "I prayed every night that you would be alive." Words choked up in my head as so many thoughts from my lonely nights flooded out at once. I could not truly hear her words but only the gentle kindness that I had longed for so many nights. "I love you, Sherry. I love you." I tried to regroup, knowing that I had made a fool of myself, but my dad then got on the other line. His voice still held the strength that I had in my memories for such a long time. He was also crying as he spoke with me. He told me how proud he was and how God was a mighty God. I almost felt guilty for all the times I cursed God and accused him of not caring or loving. Other members of the family yelled well wishes in the background and said they would be waiting for my return.

As I placed the receiver in its cradle, I felt as though I was floating on cloud nine, nothing would depress me, not even

Frank. As we passed each other in the hallway, I nodded to him and smiled. He returned my smile and then walked past me as if I did not exist.

Don't worry about it, crazy man. In a little while you will never have to see me again.

That dream didn't come true. When we landed, we became instance celebrities. The media was having a field day with us. Flashes from the cameras lights blinded me as I was getting off the ship. Reporters surrounded us from every direction shouting all sorts of question. "How did the others die? Did you two sleep together? We heard that one of the dead ladies was pregnant, did the baby have a name?" We were advised to say nothing, but Frank was eating up the publicity. The more he told his story, the more I felt I had to go along with his story.

We were rushed to the police station where things took a dramatic change. A detective, a goliath of a black man with a thick coarse mustache with a small scar on the side of his right eye, took the both of us into a simple room with stark white walls and sat us down. This was so surreal that it seemed like a scene out of old cop movie, but there we were, the two of us sitting down in a chairs with a gray metal table in front of us and a lamp without a shade and a glaring lightbulb in it. The detective and another younger white man in a blue blazer with tan pants and dark brown shoes sat across from us. The large detective introduced himself as Mr. Perkins and his partner as Mr. Quincy. He then informed us of our rights and then opened a file. I felt queasiness in my stomach and in a dry whisper asked for a glass of water. Their politeness was even more unnerving as I felt like a suspect in a murder trial rather than a survivor.

Mr. Perkins also took a sip of water from a cup in front of him. I notice that the cup said "World's Greatest Dad" on it so I assumed he was married and had kids. I quickly did a search and saw a small wedding ring. It was a simple gold band, which fitted into his simple if not scarred look. He started off by telling us that it must have been an ordeal for us to be on the island alone for all that time. He also said that this was a fact-finding mission. His partner flashed a smile to assure us that we were among friends. I assumed they had both rehearsed this maneuver before, but it did little to comfort me.

"Are we in trouble?" I asked, still nervous about the fact that I was in a police room. I had not seen my parents yet and yearn to see them. Mr. Quincy looked at us and told us that we had the right to have an attorney present if we wanted one. My heart began to beat faster, thinking several thoughts at once. Do I need an attorney? Why would he say that? If I ask for an attorney, would that make me look guilty? I looked over at Frank, feeling not sure what he was thinking.

He sat quiet looking at them, studying them and trying to get inside their heads. A brief silence for a moment and then he sprang to life. He flashed his smile, which worked on most women but did nothing for the detectives. "I completely understand, officers. I would imagine that it would seem strange finding a body in the middle of the ocean, my mom starving to death, me with a knife wound in my shoulder, and another body already buried on the island. Let me put you at ease, we do not need an attorney or at least I don't." He looked at me and continued, "The only reason I say that is because I did not wish to be bold and presume to speak for Sherry also." His voice was soothing and calmed almost hypnotic, both detectives loosened up a bit feeling at ease with his comment and the way he spoke. No doubt, they would review the tape later but for now he was winning them over as he did everyone else.

He began to explain how Rosa died from eating poison berries that she had mistaken for other berries on the island. He continued to say that I suffered some mental shock after accidentally stabbing him and went into hiding while his mother starved herself to death trying to keep him alive. He also mentioned that Cynthia's death was an accident and that she had fallen and hit her head on a rock and died. It was the same story that he had told everyone else, and after hearing it so often, I almost began to believe it myself. The only thing I had to agree on was that stabbing was an accident and that I was in a state of shock afterwards. In a way, it was true or at least I convinced myself that it was. I was in shock after I stabbed him and really don't remember much of what happened after that. He was an amazing liar, especially how he could throw it together so fast.

After another hour of questioning, both of the detectives seem to agree with what Frank was saying and at the older detective closed his notepad. "I believe we have all that we need," Mr. Perkins said, reaching over and shaking Frank's hand. Frank grabbed his hand and returned a firm handshake. He looked Detective Perkins in the eyes and told him that he would prefer that we took a lie detector test so that there would be no doubt what went on.

I nearly peed in my pants hearing the words come out of his mouth. *A lie detector test, has he gone crazy? The case was closed, and he wanted a lie detector test.* I wanted to slap him across the head. How could he be so stupid? I just wanted everything to be over and now this. The officers looked puzzled for a moment and tried to talk Frank out of it. They said there was no reason for something that drastic, but Frank insisted that it would be the best thing to put everyone's mind at ease.

Both men looked at each other, and after several minutes of trying talk Frank out of his suggestion, they agreed. They asked me whether I was OK with it also. I nodded feeling that I had to play along until the events played out. Any denial on my part would bring suspicion on my testimony.

Both officers got up from the table and walked out the room. They said they would try to arrange something, but until then, we were free to go. Once we left the police station, it was a media maze; everyone wanted us to be on their show. I was amazed at how many things have changed. I received an offer to be on talk shows, radio shows, to write book, and be in movies. I declined all offers hoping that the stardom would die down, but it didn't. Frank soaked it in, and thanks to him, it only grew stronger.

Chapter Eleven

M y mother planned a huge party for me. It wasn't enough to be a celebrity to the public, but now I was a star to my relatives. They showered me with gifts, hugs, and kisses. I didn't recognize most of them, but my parents introduced them to me and told me how we were related. It seemed that years away emptied my mind of those around me whom I once cared for. At the end of the day, I took many handshakes and well wishes from everyone but did not feel as though I were a part of the group. A few of my cousin offered to become my agent, but I respectfully declined. I wanted my days of stardom to end quickly. The only thing that mattered to me was seeing my parents. My mom Carolyn had aged a lot over the years; the worry lines etched deep into her face. An older lady who had lost a good amount of weight but still retained her spunk and kindness now replaced the memory I had of her. I worried about her and the sudden rush of people and fame that came along with realizing that I was still alive. I took a moment to look at her as she was walking around making sure everyone was taken care of before she would sit down to eat.

She looked back every once in a while at me to make sure I was OK and then continued to serve others. I guess she felt that as long as my father was by my side I would be well-taken care of. My father, Albert, hovered around me like an overprotective pit bull. He aged a little also and gained a few more pounds but underneath the wrinkles he still possessed the same kind eyes that I had always seen as a child. He often placed his hand on my shoulders and ask me whether I was OK. Although I was tired, I did not want to spoil their fun, and so I lied and agreed to all the hoopla.

After four or five hours of entertaining and answering questions, I was worn out, most of the people had left, but there still were a few hanging around. My mom came up to me and told me that she would throw everyone out if I wanted her to. I laughed and gave her a hug and told her that if she could keep going, then so could I. She gave me a quick hug and then had to return to the dining room to clean up a mess. *I never understood why people would bring kids to grown folk's events, let them make a mess, and not help to clean it up.*

I decided to take a walk outside for a moment feeling claustrophobic locked in the house. My dad moved in to make sure I was OK, and after I gave him a hug, he stepped back and gave me some room. "Don't be gone too long, dear, or I will come looking for you," he said. "I never want to lose you again." Although his words were meant to show his love they made me cringe. He sounded like Frank when he was trying to hunt me down. I tried to smile and hold everything in until I got outside. Once there, I began to sob silently by myself hoping that no one was around.

"You OK?" a deep voice said out of nowhere. I jumped, turning to face a tall black man holding a tissue. That was all

I needed to see at that moment, another man. I took the tissue and turned away from him. Starting to apologize for crying, I told him that I needed to be alone, but he spoke before I could get any more words out. "You don't remember me, do you?" I almost rolled my eyes. I had been hearing that line most of the night and now he expected me to remember him. What was he, a cousin or a friend of a friend? He told me that his name was Ray, like that was supposed to mean something. I tried to let him down as I did everyone saying that a lot has happened so forgive me if I don't recognize him.

He accepted that but then told me that we used to date in high school. I figured he was lying because I never had a boyfriend and then it hit me. Ray the little big-eyed kid who used to call himself my boyfriend. I started to laugh in his face, but then I realized he wasn't the same person. He had gotten a lot taller and had put on some weight. He also had gotten a lot better looking.

His face seemed to be relieved at the fact that I remembered him slightly. He flashed a great smile and then told me that my parents invited him. I hope he didn't think that he could put a move on me. I wasn't in the mood or ready for it. I thanked him for the tissue and told him that I just needed to be left alone for a moment. He excused himself and turned to leave. That was it, no second line, no trying to get my number? I took a look at him as he walked away; he had a nice walk and figured he may be someone I should remember, but now was not the time or place.

I stood against the hard brick wall of my house and looked around. Although it had been over four years since I had last been in the neighborhood, everything still seemed the same. The same large old oak tree still stood in the front of our home; its branches freshly cut yet it still gave shelter. My mom had always loved to plant flowers and evidence of her work lined the walkway up to the front door. Big bright sunflowers, daffodils, and magnolias led the way like military guards leading the way for the president.

I looked around remembering the moments I used to spend outside my parent's home. A feeling of loss overcame me as I thought about the time that had passed by, the time I could not get back. Looking out at the sun as it began to set, I couldn't help think about all the sunsets that were lost on the island. I tried to think positive, but each time crazy Frank came into the picture.

A shadow came over me, and I turned to swing. It was my dad who raised his hands up to defend himself. Although he was older, he still had some fighting skills. "Whoa, baby girl, I just wanted to check up on you. I saw Ray leave by himself, and I knew he said he was coming to talk to you." In a way, I had to smile. I always knew my dad wanted me to get married, but I at least thought he would have given me a little time.

Knowing his heart was in the right place, I told him I was OK. I took him by the hand and led him back to the house. Mom had already gotten rid of the rest of the guest and was now sitting in her favorite wooden rocking chair that my dad had built for her. I always admired the fact that even when she was a young lady she would sit and rock in it after all her work around the house and reflect on her day and pray. I noticed a newer one next to it that I assumed my father finally made for himself. She looked up at me and motioned for me to come and joined her. I started to hesitate but felt a gentle nudge pushing me toward her. My dad laughed and walked away.

I figured it was his way of allowing us to communicate woman to woman. As I sat in my father's chair, I felt the curves of the seat cushion formatted to fit his bottom. In a way, it felt as if I were still a little girl sitting on my daddy's lap.

For a moment, my mom and I just sat there looking out at the street in front of us. The silence was good in a way; I had grown accustomed to it. Mom placed her hand on mine, and without realizing it, we began to rock together in unison. She started out with an apology for inviting so many people over to the house. I tried to tell her that it was no problem, but she still saw through my disguise. It was not that I did not want to see my relatives, but that I had grown comfortable to being alone and now all of a sudden everyone wanted to see me.

Funny how I would dream of seeing everyone again and having a huge party but now the thing that I wanted the most turned out to be something that I wanted to get away from. She gave a quick smirk and asked how my talk with Ray went. I couldn't help but to laugh at the way she said it as to set up her best friend with a date. "It was OK, Mom," I said, hoping to avoid this conversation, but she started to move in for the kill. "He's cute," I said, finally giving her the answer she wanted. She went on to tell me that he was a single, God-fearing man.

"Is everything OK?" she asked, noticing the discomfort in my face. My emotions went back and forth thinking about a great man and then the image of Frank. Mom attempted to fish around as delicate as she could about what happened on the island, but she was never much for beating around the bush.

After a few moments of trying to be nice, she went straight to the point. "Baby, I know that you have been troubled since you've gotten back, and I don't know what happened on the island, but you know I am here to talk to and listen." I looked at her and smiled. She was the same person that I loved and the image of everything that kept me going while on the island.

I really didn't know where to start or what to say. I don't think I could take a lecture about telling the truth or about trusting God, so I tried to sculpt my words so that I would give only as much as I wanted to. "A lot happened on that island, Mom, some good and some bad. But I think that I am OK," I said.

She continued to look at me, studying my eyes and penetrating my soul. "Anything happened with you and that boy Frank?" It was a straightforward question, and I knew the best way to stop any more inquiries was to give a straightforward answer.

"No, Mom, nothing happened. It's just…" My words fell short, and I didn't take my own advice.

Like a good mom, she became concerned. "What's going on? I have been praying for you ever since I found out you were alive. Baby, whatever the issue, give it to God and he will take care of it."

Hearing those words made me cringe. *Trust God, give it to God!* What in the hell was that going to do for me? I started to get angry, angry with God and the mention of his name. It was his fault that I was in the situation I was in. Every time there was a problem, some Christian would just say pray on it or give it up to God. I guess I drifted away into my own world because when I came to, I saw my mother looking at me more concerned and calling my name.

"Baby, what's wrong?" Her voice was like ointment, calming me down again, but I had to a get my feelings off my chest.

"Why does everyone keep talking about giving it up to God? I tried that and what did it get me?" I paused and realized that I was yelling at the woman who loved me the most. She took it in and then told me that she understood but began to point out things.

"Baby, think about out of all the people on that boat, God chose to save you. Baby, there is a war between heaven and hell, and we are in it. I don't know what purpose God has for saving you, but it would be a shame to give up on him now. He hasn't given up on you." I tried to smile and accept the answer, but I figured it would be something that I would have to revisit later. Right now at this very moment, I wanted to talk to my mom about Frank. I told her everything that happened on the island. I told her about Cynthia, about Frank and his attempt to rape me, the reason why I stabbed him, everything. I could see a look of concern and anger toward Frank but perhaps even more fear of what my dad would do. I asked her not to say anything and to let me handle things. I just wanted to conclude the horror story of the island and then to be left alone. I even defended Frank in saying that maybe he only did what he was taught to do, learned what he was taught to learn. I convince her that things would change, perhaps once I took the lie detector test.

To my surprise, there was not reaction from my mom. I'm not sure if that was a good thing or not. She just seemed to sit there and take it all in. I waited until I felt I could wait no longer and asked her what she was thinking. She took a deep sip of her coffee and told me that she understood. Her words were simple, almost too simple. I wanted more; I wanted guidance and someone to tell me what the next step was.

I looked at her and then asked what she meant by saying she understood. Like always, her answer was strength from small words.

"Baby, I can't begin to say that I understand everything that went on at island, but I do trust you. You know right from wrong, and so I just want you to know that I am behind you all the way." Her words gave me comfort and I smiled. She was one of the best women in the world, and I loved her dearly. We settled into silence and then the stress of the day got to me. I was tired and wanted to go to sleep.

Morning came and it was the last day before we would take the lie detector test, and I wanted some fun. I felt as if a huge burden was lifted off my chest after talking to my mom, and now I wanted to see what the world had to offer. A lot had happened since I was away. Everything had changed so much, but still there was comfort about being back in DC.

I decided to go to some of the museums. It would be great chance for me to be like every other tourist and just walk around and take in the sites. My dad asked me whether I wanted his company, but I had to decline. This was going to be my day alone. I know it sounded selfish, but I've gotten used to being by myself and didn't want to feel as if I had to keep someone's company or my dad to feel as though he had to protect me.

My parents let me use their car, which felt strange since I had not driven in years. It took a minute to get used to thing; but after a few fast stops and aggressive turns, I was back to normal. Traffic was crazy, which was something that had not changed that much since I had left. It took nearly half an hour to get there and to find a decent parking spot. The good thing was that I found a spot right in front of the monument. Funny how you don't appreciate the things that are right in your backyard until it is gone. I stood there looking at it thinking about all that it meant. It was only a building, but it was also a symbol of all that America stood for. It stood alone, forever reaching toward the sky, reaching to be better.

That's kind of how I saw myself, alone and reaching. I stood in front of it in my daydreams until my thoughts were interrupted by a young boy about the age of ten. "What you looking at?" he said. His voice was high-pitched and sounded somewhat like the squeak of a mouse. I looked around for his parents and saw no one. I tried to ask him where they were, but he ignored me and proceeded ask more questions and to tell me everything about the history of the United States. He sounded like a parrot repeating information.

Every time he talked, he would smile and point to some imaginary place in the distance to prove he knew what he was talking about. I didn't want to stop his flow, but I had to find his parents. Things haven't changed that much that I didn't know there are crazy people still in the world and a child shouldn't be left alone. I heard a woman in the distance yelling for Frank, and my heart jumped. I crouched down as if I were a hunter preparing to defend myself from an attack. The little boy kept talking as though he was oblivious to anything other than impressing me with all the facts that he knew Washington.

How could you not fall in love with this cute black curly hair boy whose freckles blended in with his soft boyish face? The woman yelled out for Frank again, and the closer she came the more it disturbed me. I hoped deep down inside that wasn't the child's name. Of all the names in the world, what would be the odds of me running into a child named Frank?

Leaning over to become his height, I place his hand over his mouth for a moment to stop him from speaking. I asked him whether that was his name, and he nodded yes. Everything in me at that very moment wanted to hate him. I had to fight the urge to walk away and leave him where he stood. "Excuse me, miss," I yelled, trying to get her attention. I could tell that he must have been her son because the moment she saw him standing next to me, she rushed over nearly falling over herself.

She grabbed him by the arm and hugged him like she would never let go. I wondered how he escaped her for as long as he did before she came looking in the first place. I turned to walk away, but she grabbed me gently by the hand and said that she wanted to thank me. I tried to refuse, not wanting any undue attention, but it happened anyhow. I could tell by the look in her eyes that she recognized me.

"You're that lady from the island. Oh my god, you are. I must say you look a lot prettier in person than you do on TV. I always thought that if TV adds ten pounds to you, then I don't want to be on TV. I mean, look at me. I don't think I'm fat, but I would if I were on TV." She went on and on, and I now knew where the kid learned to speak so much from. I told her that I had to leave, but she started walking with me telling me all about her life and how she had to raise her son alone because her husband died in a car accident.

I felt sorry for her but even more so for me. The more she talked, the louder she became and then the child chimed in with more of his little tidbits about Washington. It was becoming somewhat of a circus because now people were looking and once they saw who I was they came up and wanted to speak with me about my life on the island. I wanted to run and hide, but they were everywhere by now. Some were even rude enough to block my path as I tried to make my way back to my car. Several flashes went off as people were taking pictures.

A policeman on horse came up to me and asked whether I was OK. I tried to put up a brave front, but he was smart enough to see through it. He told everyone to break it up and then proceeded to escort me to my car. After I unlocked the door, he handed me a homemade business card. "I am not sure if you know this or not, but you are a celebrity now. If you need security or something, call me. My name and numbers are on the card." He tipped his hat and then went away.

I got in my car and just sat there with my head down. So much for me taking in the sites. The only thing I wanted to do now was head back home. Home felt safe and at least there no one would bother me. I put the key in the ignition and drove away. In the rearview mirror, I saw the monument and all the people standing around it. I guess we are two of a kind: alone yet never truly alone.

Chapter Twelve

I went home seeking shelter in the comfort of being around the people I loved the most, at least there I could just be me. Pulling up to the house, I noticed a sleek black Mercedes Benz. I wasn't sure whose it was, but I had seen it at the house before. I stepped cautiously to the front door where I was greeted by Ray who happened to be leaving.

It was an awkward moment as we nearly kissed being so close as we passed each other. Our eye held each other for a moment and then we both looked away. He moved to the side to allow room for me to pass. I felt uneasiness as I figured his eyes would be on my butt. Mom, taking advantage of every chance to be the matchmaker, invited Ray to come back in now that I was home. He looked at me and sensed my discomfort and said that it would be better if he left. I had to give him credit; he was winning me over with his kindness.

He said that he would meet us at the police station tomorrow and then said a goodbye. I watched him as he walked out. There was something about him that I couldn't place, but whatever it was, I knew I was not ready, but he did have a small bit of my interest.

"What did he mean he'll meet us at the police station?" I asked my mother.

"Oh, by the way, Ray is the family attorney," my mother said with that same sly smile. My mouth dropped, and you could have knocked me over with a feather.

Mom looked at me concerned and asked why I was back so soon. I didn't want tell her everything, so I only mentioned that I just wanted to get ready for tomorrow. She could read right through me, but let it go for the moment. I knew the subject would come up later. I did have a lot on my mind about the test tomorrow. I knew all I had to do was to tell the truth, but it would be interesting to see how popular I become once the truth was told.

That night I had a frightful dream about Frank and me on the island. I woke several times with sweat dripping off my forehead. I even screamed once feeling Frank on top of me. My dad, God bless his heart, nearly broke his neck running into the room. It was funny to see him huffing and puffing as he threw open the door. There was also comfort in knowing that as long as he was around, I would be safe.

The morning came and everyone in house was quiet thinking about the big day. Mom went to work early fixing grits, bacon, sausage, waffles, orange juice, coffee, and scramble eggs. It was more food than I had seen in many years but all my favorites. Like always she only said that eating was good for the soul and that I would need my strength today.

I jumped at the sound of the doorbell. Several times during the week we had to call the police to keep the press off our yard, and I feared that today it would be a lot worse. Dad got up and looked out the window and breathed a sigh of relief. It was only Ray who had come over earlier to ride with us. My dad greeted him with a sturdy handshake and a hug. I took note on how friendly the two of them were as they walked toward Mom and me. He gave me a smile and went over to kiss Mom on the cheek. She also seemed to expect it as though the whole process had been done several times before.

He was offered a place at the table to eat, which he happily accepted. I could tell by the way he went to a certain chair and how comfortably he seated himself that he had been at the house before. After wolfing down some food, he said that he had a list of the question that they would ask. My eyes widened wondering what they were. Allowing me to simmer in my suspense, he waited for a few moments and then pulled them from his suit pocket.

We were all quiet as he slowly unfolded the sheet of paper. I asked how he got the questions, and he told me that since it was not for a crime and more for the press, as my representative he was allowed to view them in advance. Mom sat next to me and held my hand. My dad stood over us like a lion protecting his pride. Ray started off by saying that there were only four questions and began to read them.

First, did I kill Rosa? I felt myself becoming angry with the mere thought of being asked but tried to calm myself down. The next question was if Cynthia's death was really an accident. I laughed but was comfortable in the fact that it was. The next was if I had anything to do with the death of Kathy, the answer was no. I sighed, a little almost frustrated with the facts that things were so simple. The last question was if I stabbed Frank by accident?

Hell no, I didn't stab Frank by accident. It definitely was on purpose, and I was glad I did it. That is what I thought, but I said nothing. I smiled at Ray, and he returned my smile.

Mom squeezed my hand a little not really knowing what I was thinking.

"The questions are fine," I said. "I don't think there should be a problem." Ray gave a sideways glance trying to figure out why all of a sudden I went from scared to happy. He asked me whether there was anything that I needed to tell him. Part of me thought that I should say something, but the other half figured it was best left unsaid until I got to the police station.

We looked outside, and there was already a group of reporters waiting to snap pictures of me. The more I didn't want attention, the more it made them hungry to find out why. It was hard for their minds to understand that fame isn't always what it is cracked up to be and that not everyone wants it.

Ray shielded us as we made our way to his car. People were yelling out all sorts of things, both pertaining to the case and not. Some of them were rude in their search for the story. I was dressed in a pair of jeans and a light blue T-shirt and tennis shoes. I did not like confining clothes anymore and wanted to be able to run if I had to. After all, those years of wearing almost nothing on the island, I enjoyed the comfort of simple things.

We all jumped into Ray's car and sped off. Several reporters followed behind, but in his Benz, the whole world seemed to shut off. Trying to make himself a good host and trying to impress me, Ray asked whether we wanted to hear any music but primarily directed it at me. I told him he could put on whatever he wanted to; I did not care either way. I just wanted to get this day going. Mom and Dad stayed silently in the back just watching the two of us.

Ray pushed a button, and gospel music came on. It was good to hear some of the old music again. The things that they call music nowadays mixed old songs and plenty of rap while doing a fairly good job of disrespecting women. It was bit too much for me. I closed my eyes and just tried to take everything in. Ray started to hum with the music and did a good job. I could tell he had a good voice and so I listened. I found myself listening to his voice more than the music, which I didn't like. I wanted to keep my guards, but he was slowly knocking it down.

Passing the time, I imagined all the things that I would have done had I not gone on the cruise. I figured I would have had a high-paying job at some marketing company by now. I would have been married and possibly some kids. Life would have been good, but reality is reality; and so much for dreams, I was on my way to a police station.

The car pulled up in front of the station where there were other reporters. It wasn't as big of a zoo as I expected but still enough to be annoying. "Oh well here we go," I said as I readied myself. Ray jumped out the car and ran to my side to open the car door. His moments were smooth and easy as if he had done this type of thing before.

We were ushered in by two police officers and then we met the same two that had worked with us earlier. They both looked at Ray, not really trusting lawyers. Mr. Perkins led me to a small room where an elderly man was sitting next to a machine. In a way, it seemed frightening, but I have been through worse. Mr. Quincy offered me water or coffee, but I declined. I just wanted to get things rolling.

I was attached to a few straps and clips, which led back to the machine. The elderly man introduced himself as Mr.

Austin; he was an ex-FBI agent who often worked with the police department on giving the test. His voice was smooth and comforting putting my body at ease. I could see why they used him to administer the test. I was seated facing straight ahead trying to breathe as normally as possible. He began by asking me questions that I could answer correctly. It became nerve-racking as I saw him mark things on a paper out of the corner of my eye. Ray stood next to me giving me a reassuring smile.

My parents weren't allowed in the room, which I didn't like, but I understood. After asking a few questions, which he wanted me to lie about, he began to ask the questions that Ray had given me. It was exactly as he said they would be. I answered quick, precise, and to the point. I was getting excited for the final question, but it never came. Mr. Austin looked at me and told me that I could go. I sat there in shock for a moment. I could go? Maybe I wasn't hearing correctly. I asked whether he had any questions about Frank. He paused for a moment, and then as if it hit him, he nodded his head.

"Oh, I see. I guess no one told you. Frank told us about what happened on the island and the fact that he may have come on too strongly toward you. He said that you stabbed him in self-defense." I guess Mr. Austin saw the disappointing look come across my face. He told me that I could talk to my lawyer, and if I wanted to, I could try to press charges; but in his opinion, it wouldn't really be worth the time. The jury would side with Frank and the situation on the island, and if anything, they would just say that he was understandably crazy for the moment. Ray agreed as he was helping me up out of the chair.

I struggled to my feet feeling as though I was hit by a thousand rocks. Everything became blurry as I made my way out the door. Mom rushed to my side and asked whether everything was OK. My eyes started to water up, but I held everything back. "It's OK," I said. "I just want to go home." My dad gave Ray a look like if anything happened to his baby girl, he would have a price to pay. Ray moved close to my side asking whether he could get me anything. He was in the dark as much as everyone else.

Mom asked whether I got a chance to tell them everything. It was her way of not giving out too much info but asking me the question. I told her that Frank admitted that I stabbed him and if I wanted I could try to press charges against him. Dad immediately thought something happened between Frank and me and already plotted how he would kill him.

"Nothing happened, Dad," I said, calming him down. He tried to attack me, but I stabbed him. My dad's chest stuck out like a proud father. "I thought he was dead when I stabbed him on the island, but as you can tell, he is very much alive." My dad looked at Ray and asked whether there was anything that could be done. Ray pretty much told him the same thing that Mr. Austin told me. It felt like the life was sucked out of me and that Frank was winning, but I was tired and just wanted to go back home. I really didn't care anymore.

It seems like every time I tried to stick it to Frank; he stuck it to me. The next few months became worse and worse. He went on TV and took the test while also mentioning his huge book deal. The news spread like wildfire, every talk show had him on, and he charmed more and more fans. His face was posted all over town, causing me to want to shrink further into my world. The more press he received, the harder it was for me to disappear. I had become a recluse in my own home. It felt worse than being alone on the island.

I sat by myself one Saturday evening trying to watch TV. My parents had gone out to dinner, which was their normal dating schedule of once a week alone time with each other. I could only assume that was one of the reasons they stayed married for so long. They really took time to continue to know each other. Dad tried to convince me to go out with them, but I told them I would rather stay home.

Frank's book had become a top seller, and he was everywhere. Although he never went to school, he was tested and came out as a genius. I guess with all of us women teaching him, what better homeschooling could you have. I didn't have the courage to read the book yet, but from the few things I caught on TV and what others said to me, he only had nice things to say about me.

I settled back in my old faded blue pajamas and worn slippers with a cup of milk and a box of cookies. So far I had not put on weight, but I knew it was only a matter of time. I would either have to give up the cookies or start a workout routine. I thought about it and figured I would face that battle when it came.

Flicking through the different channels, I was still amazed at how many different stations there were. My favorite had become the Discovery Channel, which in a way always reminded me of the island. Maybe it was my way of escaping, but it felt good to see all the things I could have done or should have done.

My thoughts were interrupted by the phone ringing. I had long since given up answering the phone, but something told me to pick it up. Deep down inside I had hoped it was Ray calling looking for my parents. He asked me out on a date once, and I told him to back off using the excuse that I was not ready. He respected my wishes, and I had not heard from him since. Picking up the phone, there was only silence and then I heard him. Frank was on the other line; he didn't introduce himself, but I knew it was him.

Why was he calling? What did he want? My mind became flooded with questions and fear. He jumped right into telling me how much he missed me. I wasn't sure what to say and only kept quiet. He then went on to tell me how many women he had and the things he did with them and how he imagined it was me.

I was not sure where all this came from, maybe he was drunk but I was pissed. He had ruined my life so far and now he was invading my private space. I cursed him telling him how much I hated him. He laughed and said that he wanted me. He wanted to complete me and for me to complete him. I really didn't know what to say or to do, I was in a state of shock. The smart thing would have been to hang up the phone, but I couldn't just let it go. I had to fight back.

I told him to go to hell and that he was a devil. He laughed and asked whether I would be the devil's wife. I was burning up with anger but tried to stay calm. It seemed that the angrier I got, the more he enjoyed himself. "Listen," I said, "don't call my house ever again." He then became angry and said he would call whenever he wanted to. He said he could come over right now and have me if he wanted to. He then told me what I was wearing, what time my parents left, and what time they usually came back and then he hung up.

I dropped the phone in shock and horror. I ran to the front of the house and looked outside. There was nothing; the streets were empty. My mind began to swim. Where could he be? He was crazy, and now he wanted to torment me like he tried on the island. I fumbled back to the phone to call my parents. I don't know, maybe it was reaction, maybe I was still the little girl, but I wanted them back. I wanted them with me. Their phone rang, but I didn't answer. It went directly to their answering machine. I tried to sound calm and just told them I was checking on them. I didn't want them to panic, but I really wanted them here.

I didn't have a car and felt like a sitting duck. The police wouldn't do anything and would probably think that I was crazy. I started to panic and then I thought to call Ray. He was a lawyer and at the very least could tell me what I could do legally. I searched through the previous call on the phone and redialed his number. He picked it up on the third ring. His voice was a little groggy but perked up as soon as I spoke. I quickly told him what happened, and he said he would be right over. I didn't realize he lived so close. Time passed and no more phone calls from Frank. I begin to doubt myself and wondered if my mind was just playing tricks of me. Several more minutes passed when Ray pulled up.

I saw his sleek black Benz pull into the driveway as he jumped out and ran to the front door. I had picked up a knife and was still holding it. "You can put down the knife," he said cautiously, not wanting me to panic and accidentally stab him. I wasn't quite sure what he said. I was just so happy to see him. I dropped the knife and jumped into his arms. He held me like a protector.

We stayed like that for several moments with my head buried deep into his chest until he finally said that he thought it would be best if he came inside. I laughed nervously and somewhat embarrassed about how long I held him. Like a true hero, he grabbed a hold of my hand and began to walk around the house. "Do you think he is in the house?" I tried to whisper. Ray only said it was better to be safe than sorry. We went through the entire house and found nothing. Ray said that I should file a report just to have something on record, but I declined. I felt safe as long as he was there.

Ray looked at me and asked me to be honest and tell him everything that happened on the island. I was not sure if he were checking to see if his little princess had been violated or was he really concerned. I guess my cynicism was in full swing now. He softened my concerns by saying that he only wanted to know about Frank and why he would call. After telling him about everything, he shook his head. He said he wished that I had told him everything earlier. *I wish I would have also.*

There was really nothing he could do anymore. He said he would wait until my parents came home. I had dealt with Frank before, but now away from the island, I was afraid. Ray took me by the hand and sat me down. He looked in my eyes and told me that everything would be OK, he and God would protect me. And I had to admit, for the moment looking back into his eyes, I felt that it just might be.

Chapter Thirteen

I guess that's what they say about love. It comes at you when you least expected. You can do all you want to protect yourself from it, guard yourself from it, but somehow when it happens, it happens. I looked at Ray and although I saw him as my hero, he was much more. Maybe it was because I was comparing him to Frank or maybe because of the situation, I'm not sure but whatever it was, I felt something deep in my heart.

Embarrassed about how long I was looking at him, I turned away. He put his hand gently toward my face and turned me back to face him. There was no resistance on my part; I wanted him to touch me. He started to talk, and I put my finger against his lips. If there was one thing that I learned on the island was that people often messed up a moment with talk. Sometimes you just have to let it flow and talk later.

We began to move toward each other. I could feel his breath next to mine; my senses were heightened. Everything became clear. I could smell his cologne. I could hear his heart-beat; all thoughts of Frank or anyone else disappeared. It was only the two of us, and at that moment, we were becoming one.

I became the aggressor and pressed my lips against his. I wanted to keep that position forever, but he pulled away. Looking at me, he told me that it was not right. We should wait until another time. I started to protest, but then we saw the lights from a car pulling into the driveway. We both jumped to see who it was. Ray put me protectively behind him, and I felt safe as his hand went around my waist. This was what I had been dreaming about but not like this.

We both crouched down trying not to be seen and then we realized who it was. My parents had come home. I ran into both of their arms. Dad looked around shocked to see Ray at the house, not sure what was going on. He liked Ray but stood for no wrongdoing in his household. "What's going on here?" he said as he gave Ray a death looks and asked whether I was OK. I quickly told him everything that happened. He checked his cell phone and saw that I had left a message on it. He explained that he often turned his cell phone off and, out of habit, did it again for their date tonight.

After apologizing to Ray, we all gathered around to try to figure out how Frank could have been watching me. It was amazing to see Ray's lawyer mind at work. He began to systematically go down the list of every possible way he could think of. We did a redial but there was nothing.

After it was all said and done, we still had no better clue of how Frank saw what I was wearing and why now after all this time he was coming back for me. Dad and Mom convinced me to make a police report, and as I suspected, the police looked at me as if I were crazy. One even suggested that maybe I had been on the island too long, and the stress was causing me to imagine things. Ray quickly put him in his place and told him to do his job.

Nothing came of the report and nothing came of Frank. We took extra precautions in the house, installing new alarms and security cameras, and I even got a dog, but Frank never called back. It had over been six months and nothing. At the end, we all tried to sum it up that Frank must have been drunk. It still didn't explain how he knew what I was wearing but at least that gave me some peace.

There was one positive that came out of everything. Ray and I had become a lot closer. I couldn't help feel that at any moment this perfect man would do something to screw things up, but it never happened. He treated me like a queen and my parents even better. Often, we would spend late nights just talking on the phone. It was scary, but he was becoming my best friend. He almost made me forget about Frank but still deep in the back of my mind I wondered what he was doing.

The newspaper hit the front door and like every morning as I let my dog Spunky out for his morning duties while I picked it up and read the first page. On the front page was a picture of Frank. He just signed a huge deal to make a movie about his life. I didn't want to read it, but I had to. I opened it up and sat down at the kitchen table. The article listed everything that Frank had done since coming off the island and how much money he has made so far. To date, it was nearing 25 million. It didn't hurt that he was a very good-looking man and he knew how to parlay his celebrities into modeling for magazines, TV shows, endorsements, and now the movie deal. He was rolling in money, young, and crazy. In a way, I was glad all this was happening at least he would move on from me, and I could be free.

I had been thinking about moving out of the house with my parents anyway and really wanted to support myself. I had done a few appearances here and there and had stored up enough money to get a new place and survive until I could get a job; besides, it was getting hard to date Ray living at home with my parents with my dad's overprotective eye.

I decided to cook breakfast for my parents. They were shocked and suspicious about my efforts but enjoyed seeing me in a good mood. We hung out all day and later I had a date with Ray. Everything was perfect.

The day was pretty bland, and coming home after having a great time with my parents, I got ready for my date with Ray. I was in such a good mood that if he weren't careful, he would be able to have his way with me. My parents said they had some running around to do but waited until Ray picked me up before they left. Although I was in a good mood and we had not heard from Frank, they still were guarded. Frank may be off doing movies but like most parents, they still protected their baby girl.

Ray showed up on time as usual; he wanted to take me to a nice cozy steak restaurant in DC. Everything about the evening was great. The conversation was light and flowing. I often laughed out loud causing people to stare. I wanted a good time, and today was a good day. I was falling in love with Ray, Frank was out of my life, and I looked good in my outfit.

Everything was going well until Ray received a phone call. That was the one thing that annoyed me about the modern times. Everyone had a cell phone and every call was important. I was glad I hadn't given into the temptation yet to buy one for myself.

Ray answered the phone, which might have been his one fault. His face was rigid and his hand was shaking as he hung up. He looked at me and said that we had to go. I asked him whether everything was OK assuming that it was nothing more than an occasional problem that popped up at work, but he said no. My parents were in a drive-by shooting, and they have been rushed to the hospital

Ray drove like a crazy man and was able to get us to the hospital in less than ten minutes. We both jumped out the car like some cop movie. At the front desk was an elderly rotund white woman who by her worn appearance and glasses had been there for a while. I tried to ask her where my parents were, but my words came out in a garbled mess. She looked at me as though I was from another planet, telling me that I needed to calm down. I started to jump across the table and cram my foot in her throat, but Ray pulled me back.

He gave her my parent's name, and after she gave me a disgusted look for what she presumed was rudeness on my part, she pointed us in the direction of ICU. My heart was pounding a thousand miles a minute. I felt as if I couldn't breathe. Everything was spinning around me as we raced down the hallway. Bursting into the door, we asked the nurse on staff what was going on, where were my parents. She looked at her chart and then looked back up at us. Her eyes told the whole story before his lips began to move. In one moment, one second, my life had changed again—both my parents were dead.

I collapsed on the floor crying out to God. It was now official. I hated God for allowing anything to happen to the best people in the world. I wanted to die with them. I wanted to leave this world. Ray did some checking, and we found the doctor that treated them. He said that they had been gunned down in what appeared to be a random gang war. Mom had been shot twice and Dad trying to protect her had been shot at least five times. The doctor looked at us and said they were in the wrong place wrong time.

I went numb, my body went weak, and I just let go. I escaped into a small world that only I had the key to get into. Ray took me home and began to do due diligence finding out what happened. We got the name of the detective in charge. Ray wanted to call a couple of my friends to come watch me while he went down to the station, but I told him that I wanted to be with him. They were my parents, and I wanted to be there.

The detective handling the case was a woman in her late thirties. She was white, slightly slender, and a stern look about her. She spoke straight to the point and looked directly at us. There was a hint of compassion in her eyes but mostly business. She began to ask us where we were at the time of my parent's murder. We told her, trying not to get to upset with the question. She said that there was no witness, but they think it was the work of a Spanish gang that has been rising up lately.

She wrote down some notes, never looking up at the two of us. Ray grabbed my hand and gave a gentle squeeze. It was his way of seeing whether I was OK, but I wasn't. Both of my parents were dead and it could have been for no reason, just some stupid kids taking lives with no remorse. She asked us a few more question and then said that she would be in touch. By her tone, I was sure they weren't going to put that much effort into things.

It's hard to describe sadness; the ways I felt that night was the worst thing that any person should every have to experience. My whole body ached, and I was tired. Hell, this was not the island. Things were not supposed to be that way. I was too tired to cry, too tired to fight, and too tired to live. I didn't understand things and why I was alive. Why has everything around me died? I just wanted to join my parents and put my life behind me.

Ray drove me home, but I did not want to be there. Not now, not the home that held so many memories for me. I didn't know how to say it or ask him, but I didn't want to be alone. I needed him more than I needed anyone in my life. As much as I hated to admit it, I didn't want to be alone anymore. I wanted someone to hold me.

Ray continued to hold my hand, and I squeezed his as we pulled up to my home. "I can't stay here tonight. Can I stay with you?" I managed to say. His face didn't change and said I could use his extra bedroom.

In all our time dating, I had never been to his home. He quickly showed me the spare bedroom. It was spacious and painted a deep bronze color with neoclassical artwork hanging on the walls. A clear bowl with fresh cut flowers stood on a stand next to the edge of the bed. Ray brought out towels and soap and said that he would leave me alone. I took hold of his hand and told him I didn't want to be alone. I just needed him to hold me and that is what we did as I fell asleep in his arms.

That night I dreamt about my parents, I remember laughter and I remember us all holding hands, I remember fun, but then Frank showed up and ruined everything. I awakened to Ray gently shaking me. He said that I was cursing and yelling out Frank's name. I am not sure what the dream meant but deep down inside I felt that Frank had something to do with my parent's murder. I tried to explain what I felt to Ray, but I imagined the way it sounded. *Frank killed my parents.*

Outside of being a little crazy, why would he want to kill my parents? He has everything a person could want—money, fame—and besides, I'm not even sure he was in town.

Ray listened to everything and then to my surprise he said that if I really felt that way, we should wait until the police check things out and then if that did pan out to anything we would try something of our own.

As expected, the police came up with nothing. They put it down as another unsolved murder, and when we brought up the fact that Frank may have something to do with it, we got the usually rolled eyes and looked as if we may be crazy. Frank was living in another city and had an air-tight alibi when the murders happened, plus he had no motive or at least that is what the police believed. There was nothing to tie him with my parents' murder other than my gut feeling.

The death of my family made news but not too much. Another black family gunned down by a gang wasn't that much of an attention grabber. The fact that it was my family got more coverage than usual but that lasted only a small moment.

The day of the wake hurt the most. Seeing the two coffins simultaneously took my heart away. My parents had planned for when they would die and had everything spelled out in their will. They had a nice spot picked out next to each other under a large oak tree surrounded by the many flowers that my mom loved so much.

Ray had been like an angel to me, never asking for anything for himself and always helping in whatever way he could. Several nights I reminisced about my parents, and I could see tears well up in his eyes. They were truly like family to him. His parents had divorce when he was young and never really had contact with him other than to fight over where he should stay. When he was old enough, he moved back into the neighborhood, and my parents watched over him as if he were their only son. He had been there for them when they thought they lost me, and now he was here for me.

A large amount of people that showed up for the wake, and I was so blessed to see how many lives my parents had touched. Several people went up to say a word or two about both of them. Each time they spoke it made me realize more and more the loss I suffered. I had lost them before when I was stuck on the island, and now it happened again. When Ray got up to speak, there was a hush over the room. He was the type of man that demanded respect wherever he went even when he was not trying or asking for it. He began to speak and his voice trembled. He wiped his eyes for a moment and then stopped completely and began to sob. His tears brought an onslaught of other tears from men and women alike. I used to think that real man didn't cry, but now I understood that real men cried if something touched them enough.

Between my tears, I wondered if I should go up to the stage and help him recover, but I could not help myself and would be of little use to him. We all cried minutes before Ray was finally able to regroup. He spoke of the love he had for my parents and the good they did in the world. He talked about heaven and how they were resting now. He spoke with such love and such heart that it was hard for me to continue hating God. I did not know the answers, but somehow knowing that they had a place in heaven brought me a little peace.

After everyone spoke, the choir began to sing. I felt as though my body is floating above everyone, and I was just watching. I was watching the love and that my mom and dad had planted and like her precious flowers they were being watered by tears.

Ray was holding my hand, and I was holding his. I'm not sure who was supporting who but maybe that was the way it was supposed to be, maybe we were supposed to be supporting each other. Though my watery eyes, I scanned the room and looked around at all the flowers that had been delivered. It would have made my mom proud to see the different arrangements. I swallowed hard trying to hold back more tears, and then I saw something that caught my attention. At the right corner of the church, near the far wall was an arrangement of flowers that drew my attention.

Something about them kept brothering me and then it hit me; they were the same flowers that grew around Cynthia's grave when we buried her on the island. I didn't know who sent the flowers, but my heart began to race. It took everything in me to stay still and wait for the service to end. I must have been squeezing Ray's hand because he looked at me with a startled look. I could not form words in my mouth. I tried to imagine the best possible situation. *Maybe someone picked them by mistake. No one could have known what those flowers were.* No matter what I thought, the image of Frank kept popping into my mind.

The choir finished singing the last of their song selection and the pastor started his sermon. He began to quote the Bible, but his words became a muffled distance sound in the hollows of my brain. My focus was on the flowers, and until I found out who sent them, nothing else would matter.

Chapter Fourteen

M inutes seem like forever, and I was going through the motion. Several people came up to me telling me how sorry they were for the loss of my parents. I saw faces, but their words were foreign to me. My focus was on the flowers, and the sooner everyone could get out, the sooner I could see who sent them. I tried several times to position myself next to them, but Ray or someone else would inevitably pull me back toward the center of the church to offer their condolences.

It was sad in a way that in such a short time I met all my relatives from the celebration upon my return to civilization and now I am now reunited because of death. Several times people would come up to me and say to let it out, let the tears flow, but I couldn't anymore. I had to have at least one question answered. I made my escape and moved over to the flowers as everyone was leaving but did not see who they were sent from. I went and asked the person in charge of the church, and he did not know. He said that there were so many that it would be impossible to tell who sent them.

It was another dead end. Maybe I was imagining things. Maybe this had nothing to do with Frank, maybe in my own mind I wanted to blame someone. The flowers were unique but not impossible to get. I really didn't have any answers other than a burning feeling that somehow this all tied together.

Ray came back inside the church to get me. He asked what I was doing and seemed bothered that I was making the connection between Frank and the flowers. His pain was evident as he wore it on his sleeves, but I really didn't care; they were my parents, and I wanted answers and either he was with me or against me. He hinted that maybe I should go see a doctor, but I told him that maybe he was crazy. It was weird, but I lashed out at him as if he were Frank.

I continued to scream at him until I found myself buried in his chest again crying like a baby. "I'm not the enemy," he said. "We will get some answers. I promise you we will get some answers."

After the wake, everyone went to an aunt's house. I was not much for entertaining, but I did need to be there. It was my family and all my relatives, and as much as I hurt, they were hurting also. Driving over to my aunt's house didn't really help much. There were pictures around of my family, my dad when he was young, my mom when they first started dating, and pictures of places and times that past when I was lost on the island. I began to realize how much of our time together was missing and how much I had valued the little time I had gotten back on my return. My aunt Alice, a large black woman who wore her wig slightly off center believed that food was the great ointment to all pains. She offered me a plate of fried chicken, potato salad, greens, corn bread, black-eyed peas, and neck bones to help soothe my pain. Although her gesture was sweet, it was obvious by her size that she soothed her pain repeatedly. I politely declined, trying only to show my face for the moment until I could get somewhere and think things out.

The funeral was tomorrow and I didn't want to dishonor my parents, but my mind was a thousand miles away. Ray came over and pulled me to the side. "I know this has to be hard on you, and I don't blame you for not wanting to be here. But please, for the sake of everyone else, could you let the flowers thing go until after the funeral? Once it is done, we will track out who sent them. I have a friend who works undercover. I have him track things, and you can even see what Frank is doing."

Again, Ray had become my savior; he told me just want I needed to hear. I was on the verge of going crazy and knowing that something would be done at least gave me some peace and time to grieve for my loss.

That night we all talked about good memories of my parents and even the fact that if they had to go, what better way than to go together. There were some laughs and more tears, and for the moment, I let Frank and the flowers go.

At the end of the night when everyone was leaving, Alice offered me her place to stay. I declined hoping that I could stay with Ray again. She pushed the issue a little more saying that I should not be alone at a time like this and then it hit her. She smiled at Ray, giving a sign of approval. She patted him on the arm and said to take good care of me.

Ray drove me back to his place, and we talked for hours until I dozed off on the couch. Tomorrow would be a long day at the funeral, and I needed my rest. Ray being the perfect gentleman brought in a blanket and placed it over me as I slept. Somewhere between sleep and wishing, I dreamed he kissed me good night.

Morning came with the smell of coffee and pancakes. Ray obviously learned to cook from my mom. The smell brought back a flood of memories, but they were pleasant ones. Ray set up a nice table with pancakes, fresh cut cantaloupe, and bacon. Had it been any other time, it would have been a most romantic setting as we sat and ate outside on his deck watching the sun gently start to rise.

I didn't really have much of an appetite and neither did Ray. We basically went through the motion and sat quietly taking in the morning. It was going to be a long day, but somehow with Ray, I knew I would be OK. If there were one thing I took away from the island, it was the fact that I had gained an inner strength and to trust God even when things seem their worst. When all was said and done and the crying was over, you did what you had to do. Ray looked at his watch and sadness came over his face; he said it was time to get ready to go.

We arrived early and waited in the car. After a few minutes, several people began to show up. Some were old, some young, all dressed in black. So many people coming, each of their lives touched by my parents. If I die, my only wish is that I could touch as many people as my parents did. Ray squeezed my hand looked at me and then got out and walked to open my door.

Like everyone else, I wore black. A form-fitting black dress with large silver buttons, black belt with a matching silver buckle, dark black glasses, and high-heeled shoes. I am not sure if the ground was soft or my knees were wobbly, but I managed to walk to the front.

I was seated, and we were ready to start when we heard a commotion—the whine and click of several cameras and a lone person at the center of the ruckus. Peering beyond the hats of people sitting behind me, I saw who was at the center of the disturbance—Frank had shown up to my parent's funeral.

He looked around, and I assumed he was looking for me. He didn't have to worry much about that. I would be there in a heartbeat. I jumped up out of my seat ready to rip his head off or at least give him a kick to bring back memories. Ray had to hold me, which I was not going to make easy for him.

There was a mixture of surprise and excitement from my relatives when he showed up. He had become a big star and people sometimes act crazy around stars regardless of the circumstance. Some of the older ladies who had not known him only remarked that he was a good-looking man. I couldn't believe that he would show up and ruin my parent's funeral. Ray got up and walked toward him. Two large men stood in his way.

"You were not invited here, Frank," Ray shouted. Frank gave him a dismissive look and told him that he didn't even know who he was. He was there to see me. I rose up, stomping my feet into the soft ground with my high heels. I still had the veil over my face appearing like a linebacker moving in for the big hit.

Frank's bodyguards moved in to stop me, but Frank told them to let me through. As well-trained dogs, they moved to the side.

"Sherry, I am so, so sorry to hear about what happened to your parents. I received the news the other day and got on the next flight out here." His voice sounded sincere and truly regrettable. As much as I hated him right now, I hated the thought of ruining my parent's burial now.

"You were not invited, Frank," I told him as politely as I could without hitting him. "I really don't see what this has to do with you."

Taking a step closer to me, he leaned toward my face. "Regardless of what happened on the island, we were family. I just…" He paused and began to wipe his eyes. Looking up, I saw that his eyes had reddened as if he were trying to hold back tears.

"I know that I have hurt you in the past, and I wish I could take time back but I can't so I'll do whatever I can right now, in the present."

I felt like saying, "And the Oscar goes to…" But this was not the time or the place. My parents were in a holding point and needed to be put to rest.

I bit my lip, not really wanting to invite him to stay but not wanted to prolong things any more. Before I could say anything, he spoke again but this time louder so that others could hear. "If I am not welcomed, I will go, but you are my family and I will support you in any way that I can." Aunt Alice came toward me and said that he should stay. It would be the way her parents wanted it. I bet if she knew the truth she wouldn't be so God loving.

I figured that I would deal with him later; right now, I just wanted to allow my parents rest. I told him to stay but did not want any cameras. Frank made a loud speech again to the reporters asking them to respect the privacy of my loss. He would give a statement later on at the end of the day to each and every one of them.

He knew how to work the press, and each of them backed off. Finding his way up close, he sat near Ray and me. Ray clinched his jawbone trying not to swing at him. I tried to look straight ahead, feeling almost claustrophobic although we were outside.

Out the corner of my eye, I noticed Frank looking at me. It was a quick glance, the kind you give as though you have a crick in your neck and then try to straighten it out but just happen to look at the person simultaneously. He was watching me, I was watching him, and Ray was watching the both of us.

Crying ensued as the pastor said a few words from the Bible. I just wanted to focus on my parents. Like a child, I figured if I didn't see Frank, he wouldn't be there. *Ashes to ashes, dust to dust, amen.* It was over, and they lowered the coffins into the ground. In a way, it was beautiful seeing them both being lowered simultaneously. That is the way they led their lives, and it was only right that they should go that way.

Once it was over, I made a beeline to Frank as he was getting up to leave. "Frank, did you send flowers to my parents?" There was no denying it; he said he thought that it was fitting since those were the flowers that grew around Cynthia's grave also. He leaned in and whispered in my ear that he needed to apologize for the phone call a while back. He was drunk, and success had gone to his head. It had been bothering him, and he wanted to clear the air.

The worse feeling in the world is to wanting to hate someone, and they kill you with kindness. I know he had to have something to do with my parent's death. He asked me whether I needed anything. Whatever I wanted all I had to do was to ask, and it would be given to me. He then capped it off by saying that I had been the most like a mother figure to him on the island and if I could please see it in my heart to forgive him.

God I hated him. What am I to do now, he admitted to sending the flowers, apologized about his phone call and his behavior on the island, and offered to help in any way I wanted.

Ray must have figured that he had given us enough time and moved in to be my savior again. He looked at Frank, half snarling, and then told him it would be better if he left. To my surprise, Frank agreed, apologized, and walked away. I was not sure what was going on. That same voice that I had once heard a long time ago popped back up in my head. *Maybe I was wrong about Frank.*

That night, Ray and I talked. I would have to make a decision about what to do with my parent's possession, but for the moment, we talked about each other and about Frank. I asked him whether I could have been wrong about him. There was not a moment hesitation when he said no! Ray told me that he had been a lawyer for many years and that he could tell bull when he saw it. He said although Frank was good, he still was full of it.

I had to admit I was intrigued by Ray's manly aggressiveness and how he now protected me. I was alone, my parents were gone, and I really didn't know anyone else. He was my only lifeline to reality.

I studied him, feeling even more attracted to him as he spoke. His eyes were focused but caring, there was a sense of peace about him. I wanted to ask him what his secret was, but I figured I would have time for that later. A lot has happened, and I was just now starting to feel the effects of my grief. I just wanted to get away.

Ray suggested that we get away for a few weeks. My parents, if anything, were efficient and had everything in order.

Once I came back from the island, they redid their will and left everything to me and only asked that I tithe some to the church. They might not have been rich or at least they didn't act like it, but they had a nice little chunk stored away. Because my father made some great investments, I could live comfortably for the rest of my life and never have to work.

It seemed as if a lot were happening in a short amount of time, but I did need to get away and accepted Ray's invitation. I spent a few days trying to get the home in order not really sure if I wanted to live in my parents' house or sell the place, but I figured for now it would just sit as it held many joyous memories.

Several weeks have passed since my parent's funeral and can't say I did much but walk around looking at memories. Ray called and told me to be ready; he had something for me.

He picked me up at 7:30 on Saturday morning and said that we were going to the airport. He did not tell me where we were going but said that he would surprise me. He even went through the trouble of packing clothes for me. It felt good to trust someone other than myself, and I trusted him. A lot had changed since I was on the island. Security was tougher, and the lines were longer but still for my safety I would not have it any other way.

I was impressed that he had taken care of everything from the limo ride to the airport, to the flowers in the limo to the music playing as we made our way. Boarding the plane was a little frightening for me since the last time I had been on plane was coming back from the island. Ray, being ever attentive, held my hand as I made my way to my seat. First class, I guess I expected no less from him but even if we sat coach it would have been OK as long as we were together.

So far as I knew we were going to Florida, which I guess was OK, but I was not really that keen on being close to water. He assured me that I would have a good time and things would fun. I couldn't help trust him. He had a charming way that always made me smile.

We both made a pact not to speak of Frank while we were away. I agreed for the moment, but deep down I could not let things go. I still had this feeling about him and wanted to know whether I was just imagining things, good or bad I had to know.

The sun was shining, and it was a nice balmy 85 degrees outside. I had on a pair of blue jeans and T-shirt, which made me feel a little out of place sitting in first class, but still I was comfortable. My fame had died down a long time ago, and no one recognized me. Ray dressed the same way, making us look like school kids with a crush on each other.

We laughed often as we talked together. His conversation was smooth and knowledgeable, and even before the flight took off, I felt as if I were flying. This was something I often dreamed about on the island, but not under the circumstances.

The plane landed and after going through security again, we rented a car. Of course, Ray's taste was nice renting a dark blue Mercedes. We drove for about an hour and then pulled up to Orlando's Universal City. I was not sure how he knew, but it was where I had always wanted to go as a kid. Maybe my parents must have told him. We pulled into a Sheraton hotel, and like the perfect host, he opened the door for me.

I'm sure he could tell by my grin that I love the surprise, but still he asked me whether everything was OK. I jumped into his arms and gave him a big kiss on the cheek. I hoped that answered his question. "It's just what I needed," I told him. As we checked in, I noticed that he put us in two separate rooms, which was OK by me; although I would have preferred that we be together. No pressure or, better yet, no temptation.

I couldn't wait to be a kid again, so much had happened in my life and I just wanted to escape and that's what we did for the next few days. We laughed and played and acted like little kids, and I had to best time in the world. Every night we would stay up late and talk. Even when we went to our own separate room, we talked on the phone until late at night and then we woke early morning to repeat the process.

My attraction for him was growing more and more each moment. I knew he liked me also, but I was still guarded; I didn't want to stick my heart out there too much only to have it cruelly cut off. Deep down, I kept waiting for him to do something wrong, even at times trying to set him up so that he would say something wrong, but it never happened. He was perfect; the only thing that ruined the evening was passing the bookstore and seeing the number one bestselling book. It was written by Frank.

We tried to raise the perfect man. We tried to make him into what we thought perfection would be, and we were wrong. I often told them that even if we did our best there was a place for men to teach other young men. Cynthia was the biggest opponent saying that the world would be better off without them and that they should be used only to repopulate.

On the flight back home, the weight of the world came crashing back to me. Frank's book brought back all the memories of my past that I had wanted to forget. My fantasy had come to an end, and now it was time to work. Ray, sensing what I was thinking, moved close to me. "You think Frank is worrying what you are doing right now?" I was surprised at his candor. Trying to reply, I stumbled over my words, but he made a good point. I couldn't let Frank get the best of me. He was not even here, and I was allowing him to ruin the end of a great vacation.

Ray promised that as soon as we got back, he would call his friend in LA who was a detective and have him do a little research on Frank. At least it would put my mind to rest. I agreed, but I also gave him a deadline. I wanted to know info, and I gave him a month to get it done. He laughed, forcing me to smile back at him. It was a good match. If I was down, he always found a way to cheer me up, and I hoped that I could do the same for him. I leaned over and kissed him on the cheek.

The flight attendant came over and said that we made a nice couple. It was a risky move on her part assuming that we were a couple, but it was what I wanted to hear, what I needed to hear. Ray didn't say anything other than thanks, and that was good enough for me. The whole plane ride was just as fun going back as it was when we took off. Time flew by like mere seconds until we heard the captain telling us that we were approaching our landing. Ray mentioned that he would have to start working once he got back, all the time away was killing his practice; but if he had to die, it would be worth dying for me. It hit him for what he said and although he was trying to be romantic, the word *die* still stung as I thought of my parent's death.

He said that I could stay at his place, but we both knew that option was out of the picture. It took both our willpower to stay out of trouble on this trip, and staying with him, even if it were in separate rooms would be doing nothing but inviting trouble.

As before, a limo was waiting for us when we landed and took us back to our homes. My parent's house was the first stop, and as we drove, I found myself having to fight the tears from flowing. It was funny. While we were away and I was with Ray, I had tucked the pain deep down inside, but now it was returning with full force. Ray asked several times if there were anything he could do, but the best thing was for me just to fight through it. I would be OK.

The limo pulled up to my front steps. I looked at my parent's house noticing that the grass needed to be cut and all the flowers had died. I was glad in a way because it would give me something to do, some way of being a part of my parent's lives. I opened the door to leave, and Ray pulled me back. He squeezed his body next to mine and told me that I was the best thing that has ever happened to him and that he hoped he was not overstepping his boundaries but that he was falling in love with me. I laughed and wondered what took him so long. I had already fallen in love with him.

Sometimes in life you find a soul mate, someone that you are meant to be with and no matter how things turn out you always feel that somehow that person was put on this earth just for you. Ray was that person for me, and no matter what, I felt that we were supposed to be one.

I wanted so bad to reply and to tell him that I loved him also, but I couldn't get the words out of my mouth. Even though I had fallen in love with him, I could not say it. Not yet, not until Frank was out the picture. As long as he was there, it would always be a thorn in my side, and I knew I had to do something about it. Ray waited for a moment for me to say something and then his eyes showed he understood. Before departing, he started to dial his friend in LA and begun the research on Frank. They only came back with the same information that everyone else had. There was nothing new, but over the past months, a lot happened. Ray and I became more and more involved with each other, and I decided to sell my parent's home; the memories were too painful for me to hold on to. I also decided to go back to school to update my education. A lot had changed since I was a college, and I wanted to get into the flow. Life as I knew it is starting to fall into place for me, and in reality, Frank was being pushed to the recesses of my mind. I liked the way I felt; it was a feeling of being alive again. I couldn't help feel that my parents were watching over me and smiling.

Saturday night Ray gave me a call and told me that I needed to come over. The drive over was peaceful, but I did detect something strange about Ray's voice. It was something that most people couldn't tell, but I knew. I prided myself on knowing everything I could about him. I didn't want to be controlling, but if we weren't having sex, I figure it would be good to at least know the person.

I arrived at the house where he ran to the car like a love-sick puppy wagging its tail. I laughed at him as he opened the door and kissed my hand. Life was good but like always the good times don't last forever. After we went inside, Ray sat me down on the couch and then pulled out a manila envelope. His face went blank as he told me it was from some new detective he hired to investigate Frank and that some of the info may be a little shocking. As much as I wanted to know the info, I hesitated know. Ray, sensing what I was thinking, said that he didn't read it yet but the detectives had given him a quick brief. My heart started to beat rapidly, and I became short of breath not knowing what to expect, but I was ready. I had waited this long and had to know. Ray slid out what appeared to be four or five sheets of paper with several pictures.

Looking at me, he patted my hand and then began to read. The letter said that Frank was heavy into drugs and women, but noted that he especially enjoyed the company of black women or at least black prostitutes. From the outside to the media, he dated the average white Hollywood blond hair, blue-eyed Barbie doll, but under the cover of darkness he had a thing for black women. There were several pictures, and Ray hesitated to show them to me. He tried to forewarn me, but nothing could have prepared me for what I saw.

Each of the women in the picture looked like me, different shape and different sizes but nevertheless me. My stomach started to churn inside out as I flipped through one picture after the other. Ray tried to stop my hands from shaking, but there was no going back. I had seen it, and I was sick. I was not sure if it was fear or anger, but emptiness covered me like a cold chill.

I asked Ray what we could do, which he replied nothing. Having sex with a prostitute was wrong, and if caught it could look bad, but it had nothing to do with my parent's death or viewed as a threat to me.

We both looked at each other feeling somewhat helpless. Knowing the truth sometimes is not all it's cracked up to be. I began to shake thinking of what Frank would do with those women pretending they were me. His hatred of me was apparent, and Ray being Ray moved in to give me a hug to comfort me, but I pulled away. At that very moment I didn't want anything to do with men. A hurt look came across his face, a pleading look that said he was not Frank, but despite the fact and even though in my heart I loved him, he was still a man.

I rose to my feet with the file in my hand and started to walk away. I had to be alone; I had to think about what to do next. I tried to turn and smile at Ray hoping that it would be enough to let him know I was OK but as always he saw right through me. "What are you thinking?" he said. He voice was dripping with kindness and compassion.

"I really wish I knew what I was thinking," I said. I just knew I had to get away.

Ray apologizes several times saying that he didn't know what was in the folder. He said that he thought we should look at it together and kept blaming himself for not opening it before he called me over, his friend only gave him a briefing saying that Frank liked women and drugs but not too much more. In a way I am glad we both saw it. Isn't that the way it supposed to be? Love each other through sickness and health, love and pain. Well he was seeing the worse pain I could ever imagine. It felt as if Frank were raping me right in front of him, and I felt violated and ashamed.

Ray wanted to stop me from driving or at least to go with me, but I told him I needed time to think. My head was swimming with all types of thoughts and whispers. After few minutes of arguing on the dangers of driving in my condition, I told him that I would go and that he couldn't stop me. I blurted out that unless he was planning on becoming another Frank, I had a right to go and come as I pleased, and we weren't married. It was a low blow and the look on his face told the story. I know it hurt him, but I had walled off my emotions and focus on what I needed to do.

He swallowed hard trying to absorb the verbal punches that I threw at him and then he took my arm. "I can't stop you, and you are right we are not married. But I do love you, and we will be married one day. You can't fight this battle alone, so don't shut me out."

I kissed him on the cheek for being such a kind-hearted man but told him, "If you love me, then understand that I need my space." I crave to somehow find peace in everything and that I would be all right. He didn't like it but understood. Moving out of the way, he gave me room to pass but took the envelope back. It was OK with me; I had already remembered everything, including Frank's address and phone number. I would put an end to my demon.

I did the unthinkable; I started to call Frank. I wanted to give him a piece of my mind, but instead I found myself in the wee hours of the morning in an empty plane headed toward Hollywood. I am not really sure how it happened. First I was yelling at him on the phone and the next thing I knew he had invited me out to come visit him and to put an end to all this mess. He said he wanted to clear his name as well. I waged a private battle with myself wondering if I should have told Ray. Each time I thought I should, I convinced myself that it was better if I faced Frank by myself. I really didn't know what to say to him or why I had a right to say anything at all. He was a grown man and could have whomever he wants, but I just wanted him to let me go. Let me be free.

I guess deep down I knew I was an idiot for jumping on the plane, but I had to know for myself that Frank did not have anything to do with the death of my parents. I was already on the plane; there was no turning back. I had never drunk any-thing stronger than punch a day in my life, but I found myself asking the flight attendant for a glass of red wine. She asked me what kind would I like to drink, and I hadn't the slightest idea; I just wanted something to calm my nerves. She laughed and took the time to sit next to me and talk since the plane was mostly empty. She said that drinking was not the answer to whatever was worrying me. I would love to see her face if I told her whom I was going to meet and to ask him whether he had anything to do with killing my parents.

We talked for a while about who she was and about life. Her name was Pamela Johnson, and she looked every bit of the flight attendant. She stood about five feet eleven inches and had the perfect weight to fit her frame. I could have sworn she had her teeth whitened and straightened by how perfect they looked. Her voice was a mixture between a whisper and a high school teenage cheerleader. The thing that really made her stand out was the hazel green eyes that I am sure drove most of the male passenger crazy. A quick glance at her finger told me that she was not married. She looked as if she was destined to be a Hollywood star

I know it is kind of strange, but we really hit it off. She reminded me of a best friend that had been away from for a long time, but once together it seemed as if you never left. It was good to get my mind off what I was about to do

She told me that she had an overnight layover and asked me if I wanted to hang out. I guess my nerves were getting the best of me, and I wanted some company, so I said yes. I was supposed to meet Frank later that evening and now the fear of facing him was now creeping in. This was one of those moments that I wish I could use quantum leap and change things. I told her that I was meeting someone, but if she didn't mind waiting with me, I would love to have her company.

I figured this would be safe to have someone there with me when I met Frank.

I wondered if I were placing her in harm's way; but in the end, I figured that we could meet Frank in a public place, and she would be my excuse as to why I couldn't stay longer. She agreed, and I told her where I would be staying. She said that she would change hotels once we landed, and we could hang out together. She didn't mind being an escape goat for me to get away from someone. She said that she often used her friends the same way. We both laughed, but if she really knew me, she would have detected how nervous my laugher was.

The rest of the flight she went about doing her duties, stopping as much as she could along the way to speak with me. She seemed to lead a charmed life and indeed my suspicions were correct. She had tried to become a movie star but found that the industry was not all it was cracked up to be. Audition after audition and no money. That was at least a good sign that she had some values and that had to count for something. Maybe that is why we hit it off so well.

As we begun to land, I was having an imaginary conversation with myself and Frank. I could imagine him denying having anything to do with my parents and me trying to tell him that I thought he was lying. When it came time to prove it, I was at a loss and even saying that I hired a private detective and knew everything about his freaky sex life would have been wrong. Again, I kicked myself thinking that I shouldn't have been here.

That little voice that guided me on the island kept sending off alarms in my brain, but my stubbornness and pride kept shutting it down. My mind was focused on meeting Frank. I just hoped I am not making a huge mistake.

Pamela asked me whether I wouldn't mind waiting while she finished up a few items on the plane after everyone left. I didn't mind. It was the least I could do. She was going out of her way to help me, and I wanted to return the favor. It also gave me time to call Frank and tell him where I wanted to meet. I asked Pamela where was a good place to meet someone that was open and had lots of people. She laughed saying that whoever I was meeting must be a real bowwow of a dog. I agreed and then she gave me the name of a nice restaurant near the hotel but not close enough to connect the two together.

I called Frank and fortunately his answering machine picked up. I told him when and where to meet me and in a way felt good calling the shots. He was now on my terms and this face-to-face would happen. As I hung up the phone, I was startled as quickly ranged. I looked at the number, and it was Ray.

I had to face Frank myself. I knew Ray would worry and maybe even go over to the house, but this was my battle. I had to face it alone.

Pamela finished her work, and we both jumped into a cab. First, it felt strange to hook up with a stranger so easily, but it was fun. She seemed to enjoy life, and it helped that she knew her way around. We talked in the car, and I found myself talking mostly about Ray. I guess I loved him and wanted to close this chapter in my life. Pamela just nodded her head and smile, used to people talking on and on about someone.

We arrived at the hotel, and I looked at my watch. I had exactly two hours before I was supposed to meet Frank. Pamela asked whether I wanted to share rooms, but I only went so far with the friendly stuff. I wanted my own room so that I could just relax and think about what I would say. We both agreed to go to the restaurant together, and I told her that when Frank showed up I would talk to him for a while and then use her as an excuse to get away. It was a simple enough plan. What could go wrong?

The restaurant was nice but very hard to describe. It had a new-age modern look but the old dark cherrywood wall suggested it was once an older traditional building that had been remodeled. I appeared calm but kept looking at my watch every five minutes.

Pamela started to laugh at me; she didn't know half the story, but I imagine that a woman as beautiful as she was had to get rid of guys continually and so this was nothing new for her. A young waitress came to the table. She looked like the typical out-of-work actress, nice smile, underweight, bright, bubbly, and young. The whole time she spoke with us she couldn't stand still. After taking our drink order, she bounced her way to another table where she started the same process with another couple.

"So you want to give me more info on the loser you're going to meet?" Pamela said. Her question caught me in the middle of a daydream, and I blurted out his name.

"Frank," she returned the name. "He sounds kind of boring." I laughed a little and said that he was far from boring. That sparked up her interest a little, and she moved closer.

"Any sex?" she said it like talking about your sex life was not a big deal. I really didn't want to go down that path, but I could tell by the sparkle in her eyes that she wanted to know all the details. I told her that I did not believe in having sex before I got married, figuring that would cool her jets, but it only furthered her inquires.

"Wow," she said, looking at me as if I were some type of strange object. "You mean you've never had sex, not even a little?" I laughed again. How could a person have a little sex? For the next five minutes, she went on to explain the different types of sex and things to do to bring each other pleasure. I would have to remember her idea of abstinence.

We heard a commotion to the right of us near the front door. My stomach became immediately sick knowing that it was him. People were pointing and gasping, young women were trying to put on their sexiest look, and I knew Frank had just entered the building. The owner of the restaurant nearly broke his neck trying to run over and welcome the star in. I was amazed at all the commotion. I always believe that Hollywood was crawling with stars and figured that seeing one would be no big deal, but I guess I was wrong.

Pamela who saw him also was starstruck, and I regretted bringing her along. She looked and pointed at Frank like everyone else and then seeing my reaction she put two and two together. "Oh my god, that's who you're going to meet. Oh my god, oh my god," she said. It was like a broken record. I'm sure she didn't know who God was from our pervious conversations, but she said his name like a Baptist preacher. I got up from the table and excused myself. I wanted to meet Frank halfway.

The owner started to stop me from coming near his celebrity guest but realized that Frank was there to see me. He ushered us to an exclusive table near the back. He pointed to one waitress and told her that she was to stay with us the whole time, our own private waitress. Frank smiled at her, and she nearly melted on the spot. It was sickening and amazing simultaneously. I knew Frank had become somewhat of a star, but I never knew he was that famous. He took everything in stride as if it had been so much a part of his life that it was to be expected.

Seeing me, his eyes lit up and he gave me a big hug. I wanted to pull away, but his grip was strong and his hug was friendly. He gave the usual hello and said that I looked great. I only said hello to him not wanting to let my guard down. This was business. I told him I was here with a friend and that I couldn't stay long. He said the understood and extended his arm for me to walk to the table. I hurried to the table sitting down before he could pull open the chair for me.

"Where's your friend?" he said. I waved my hands in the general direction not wanting him to know exactly who I was with. He smiled and touched my hand on the table. I pulled away reflectively not wanting to touch him at all. His eyes soften and looked sad at my actions but then rebounded. Immediately, he began to apologize again for his behavior earlier and said that he was sorry for the loss of my parents.

I heard all this before and just wanted to get to the point. After seeing my determination, he began to tell me that his book was about his mother and how at the end she was crazy along with Cynthia but how they really loved each other.

His conversation has become somewhat of a plea for forgiveness and an explanation as to why he was so messed up. I didn't realize what we had done to his head. I had always tried to preach the Bible to him while we were on the island, but I guess it was hard for a kid to hear you preach about faith when it was not really in your life. I was beginning to feel sorry for him and everything we put him through. I even apologized for my part in everything that happened. Looking at him now, I was beginning to realize why he was who he was. We had gotten into his mind and messed his head up. He started to speak and stopped, almost in a crackling voice as he said that he wanted to apologize for his mother also. He said that she was crazy, and he listened to her poison. He also wanted to put everything behind him and would love for us to stay friends but understood if we didn't.

I didn't reply, I couldn't. How could I be friends with him? He seemed as if he were telling the truth, but I just couldn't shake this feeling of distrust and knowing what I did about the pictures did not help. I told him I forgave him and that I would not bother him anymore. I wished him the best of luck on all that he was doing and told him that I was glad that we met face-to-face. Just then Pamela walked up to our table. I had forgotten about her, but she didn't forget about me or at least Frank. She stood there for a second waiting to be introduced.

Pamela smiled as she stared at Frank; I didn't have to be a mind reader to tell that she wanted him to want her. She moved her head to the side and gave a big smile that would normally cause the average man to make a fool of himself. Frank, however, kept looking at me. Pamela opened her eyes a little wider and licked her lips. It was subtle yet seductive. I nearly laughed in her face as she kept trying to get his attention. She finally cleared her throat as a hint for me to make the introductions.

"Frank," I said, "I would like for you to meet Pamela." Frank smiled at her for a moment, and I honestly thought that she might pass out. She tried to act like meeting a movie star was no big deal, but trying to conceal it made her actions that much funnier. "So this is your friend that you were trying to get rid of," Pamela said trying to destroy anything that

I might have with Frank and opening up a window for herself. It was a backstabbing move, and I was a little disappointed that she tried to do such a thing without even knowing me that well. She seemed like a great lady, but her claws came out in a hurry.

Frank took my hand again and looked me in the eyes. Again he seemed hurt by my actions but then smiled. "Well, what's your verdict?" I had to be honest and say that he did not turn out to be the threat that I thought he would be, and so I just kept my verdict to myself for the moment. Pamela pulled up a chair and sat down, placing herself next to Frank. I could really care less except for what I knew of Frank's habits. I didn't want her to get hurt because of me, but after her sneaky comment, I figured she was a grown woman.

"Pamela, I was just getting ready to come get you," I said wanting her to understand that I didn't want her there. "Frank and I are about finished." I might as well have been talking to a brick wall, Pamela didn't hear a word I said and began small talk with Frank. He gave me a look of being sorry as if this type of thing happens continually. I slid my chair back to leave, but he stopped me, interrupting Pamela as she was talking. Almost pleading, he asked me to stay for a while longer; he said that he had a surprise for me. I wasn't looking for a surprise but said that I would stay. I know it was stupid, but he looked so sad and the least I could do was to help him get away from Pamela.

Sitting back down, he reached into his coat pocket and pulled out an envelope and handed it to me. At that moment he still looked like the little kid from the island waiting for approval. I opened it and looked inside. There was only a single slip of paper, which was a check. I didn't even look at the numbers but immediately said that I could not accept any-thing from him.

I tried pushing it to him, but he gave it back to me. He said that he knew I did not take any money from interviews or books and that I could have ruined him by talking about events on the island. The money was his way of saying thanks and to pay me back for being such a great person.

I tried to deny it again, but he said it wasn't that much and that I could give it to the church or something. As if a bright light came on in his mind, he then smiled and said that I could create a foundation in my parent's name. Thinking about my parents brought a lump in my throat, but I was also touched that he would do such a thing. Almost forgetting about Pamela, I heard her sigh as she thought about how good of a man Frank was.

She jumped in and said that he was so sweet. She also mentioned the few stars that she knew and how selfish and stuck-up they were. Frank looked at her and pouring on the charms asked her whether she might have been a movie star also. Pamela batted her eyelashes and said with a wanting gig-gle, "I did a few parts when I was younger, but now I work for the airlines." Frank told her that she looked too young to have given up acting. He said that he could get her a part right now if she wanted him to. The whole process was sickening, watching her throw herself at him and him feeding into her fantasy.

I couldn't take it anymore and said that I would leave. I thanked Frank for the money even trying to give it back to him again and then asked Pamela whether she was ready to go. I guess I shouldn't have been surprised, but she said that she would stay awhile longer if it were OK with Frank.

Frank said that he would enjoy her company, and although he would miss me, she would be a great substitute.

Saying goodbye, I got up, left, and headed back to my room. Pamela was old enough to take care of herself, and Frank didn't seem as bad as I thought.

Riding in the cab, I wondered how much Frank wrote on the check, whatever it was my parent's name would live on. They had done so much for the world, and maybe this is what I was called to do to continue their help and goodwill. I opened up the envelope and nearly passed out. Inside was a check for one million dollars.

I was shocked seeing the money that was written on the check. I didn't know what to think. This was way too much money to be given away. On the other hand, my church could use the money, and it could be done in my parent's name. I was torn for a minute thinking about all the possibilities, but I knew what I had to do. I asked the driver to turnaround.

He looked at me disgusted and then after grunting something in a foreign language turned around. It didn't matter what he thought, I had to do what was right. I had been gone for about thirty minutes and hoped that Frank would still be there. Either way I would have to give him his money back. A chilling thought came across my mind as I thought about what Ray would say when he knew what I was doing or what had been going on, but then even more what could he say if I showed up with a million dollars.

It was fun to let go for a minute thinking about what I would do with all the money, but then we pulled up at the restaurant. I got out the car and told him to wait for me. It wouldn't take long. I had it planned out in my mind what would happen. I would walk in, see Frank and tell him that the money was too much, put it on the table, and walk out. It would be that simple, but I knew I was just kidding myself. Still, it was fun to think.

Opening the door, I saw the manager of the place. He ran over to me and began to fuss over me as if I were someone important because I knew Frank. I asked for him for Frank, but he said that he left ten minutes ago with the young lady that I was with. Go figure. I knew Pamela was fast, but I didn't think she would be that fast. Guess that's Hollywood for you.

Now I ponder what would be my next move. I wanted to get him the money, but I was also getting tired. If he was with Pamela, then I am sure the both of them would be busy plus. I remembered his address. I could always send it to him in the mail. There was nothing else to do except go back to my room.

The cab driver took some pleasure in taking my money once we arrived at the hotel seeing how he left the meter running while I was inside the restaurant. I handed him the money and thought about giving him a tip but declined after seeing his cheesy grin. He had already gotten his fill for the day, and his service wasn't that good. He gave me another look of disgust and pulled away. I guess that rude cab drivers don't change no matter where you are at.

Walking back to my room, I suddenly felt lonely. I missed Ray and wanted to talk to him as I usually did most nights. I was feeling guilty about lying to him and didn't want that to be the foundation of our relationship. I made up in my mind that I would call him once I got back to my room and tell him the truth.

The same young woman who was at the front desk when I left was still there. She looked tired and ready to go home, but she still went out her way to say hello as I passed by. I gave her a wave and headed toward the elevator. Waiting on button, I looked around the hotel and noticed a bar nearby. It was tempting to get a drink before I went upstairs, but I decided against it. This was the second time I thought about having a drink and did not like the fact that I was training myself to resort to something other than God to take my mind off things. The bell rang, and the elevator door opened; I was almost to my room but as the doors began to close a hand reached in to pull them apart. It was an elderly white man in his fifties. He was well-dressed and clean shaven with a light tan. I noticed that he had a wedding ring on his finger and a gold chain around his neck. He had thinning hair, but it looked good on him.

He looked at me for a moment and then turned to face the door as it closed. I notice that he smelled like a mixture of smoke and cologne, which I hated but figured I would soon be to my room. He started whistling for a moment and then mentioned something about the weather. I replied not really wanting to converse but also not wanted to be rude. I guess my reply gave him a cue that it was OK to flirt with me because he turned around and asked what a beautiful girl like me was doing all alone and how any man that left a woman like me alone at night was a fool. It was a corny line but even more so that he was a married man trying to make a move on me.

I tried to be as polite as possible but wished the elevator moved faster. What's up with white men trying to get at black women? Maybe it was all the stuff they see on TV, or something left over from slavery days, either way I breathed a sigh of relief when my floor button rang. I said goodbye as politely as I could but then as if something possessed me I turned before the doors closed and asked him whether his wife would be proud of him trying to pick me up. It was priceless seeing his face as the door closed.

Walking into my room, I fell on the bed. It had been a long night, and I was tired. I rolled over and picked up the remote. Flicking on the TV and going through a few channels, I paused on a news station. It didn't matter what was on anyway, I needed to call Ray. It was a three-hour time difference and was almost 2:00 a.m. his time. I was tired and maybe my talking to him could wait, plus I tried to convince myself that it would be better if I saw him face-to-face. Slowly I drifted off thinking of Ray, but my slumber was interrupted by the sound of banging in the next room. It took me a moment to figure out what was going on, but then I remembered. I guess Pamela and Ray decided to come back to her hotel room instead of his place. She had the hotel room next to mine.

I was becoming sick to my stomach as Pamela was a screamer and had no bones about letting the world know how much of a good time she was having. I tried to turn the TV up full force, but the rooms weren't that big. It seemed that as the TV got louder, the louder she got as if she were trying to match and outdo it. I tried to wait it out but that didn't work either. It seemed they both were young and energetic and, so like the energizer bunny they, kept going and going and going.

I tried to call downstairs to get another room, but all the rooms were booked up. The bathroom became my only refuge away from the noise. I found myself taking a blanket, a pillow, and residing to sleeping in the tub. So much for a good night's rest. In my quiet time, I wondered why I didn't hear my phone ring anymore but remembered I had turned it off earlier and as expected he called. Even though it was late, I decided to call him.

The phone rang several times and then he picked up. I had never heard him angry before, but I could tell he was pissed. He was breathing hard and pausing as if trying to control himself as he spoke. "I've been trying to call you all day. I have been so worried about you," he said. I immediately wanted to get defensive but realized that he had every right to be mad at me. I tried to speak calmly at him, not wanting to anger him anymore. I tried to explain that I went to meet Frank but before I could get another word out before he went off.

He started to yell at me about how stupid I had been going out there to meet with Frank without telling him. I shot back that he was not married to me and that I was old enough to take care of myself. After a few more yelling sessions, he calmed down and got quiet on the other end. I tried to tell him how great Frank had turned out to be and the money that he gave me but that only brought on more silence. He finally asked what I had to do to earn the money Frank gave me. I didn't like what he was insinuating and certainly did not like his tone of voice.

I had to say a quick prayer to try to calm down. God versus the devil. I was fighting a battle and Satan was starting to win. I heard Ray sigh on the other line, and then he said that he was sorry. "I was worried about you and then to find out that you left out of town to meet Frank." He paused. "He could have been crazy. You saw the file."

"Yea, well he's not, and Frank turned out to be OK," I shot back. I couldn't believe my anger and the fact that I was defending him. Again, Frank was not even here, and he's ruining my relationship.

I told him that maybe we should talk tomorrow and that I would see him when I got back. Suddenly, I was tired and just wanted to go to sleep. Ray tried to talk some more, but I was finished. We both finished saying an uncomfortable goodbye. I felt my eyes water up and then I started to cry. I was alone in my bathtub, Frank and Pamela were in the other room, and I had a million dollars in my pocket. I cried like a baby. I wanted to call him back, but my pride wouldn't allow me to pick up my phone. I would just wait until tomorrow.

Sadness turned to fear at the thought of losing Ray, I know he was just worried about me, but I couldn't imagine my life without him. He was more than I ever expected in a man, and I feared my pride would cause me to lose him. I tried to call him again, but there was no answer; I guess he was really pissed. Trying to rationalize things in my mind, I figured that it would be better for him to let off some steam and then tomorrow we would be able to talk calmly. All couples fight and this was our first big one.

My neck started to hurt as I lie in the bathtub and then I became angry. This was my room, and I didn't shouldn't have to sleep in the tub. It had been an hour or so, and from what I have heard about sex, it should have been over with already. I opened the door and sure enough it was silent. I just wanted to crawl up into my bed and disappear under the soft comfort of my blanket.

The sheets felt cool against my body, the way a child search for the contrast of the cold outside world against its mother's warm body. I turned down the AC to as low as possible and then snuggled into my cocoon. Sleep would help me forget the night, and tomorrow I would be refreshed and could start again. I didn't realize how tired I was until I felt my eyelids pressing against themselves. I was somewhere between awake and sleep when I heard the sound of banging again. It was slow first and then rapid; screams from Pamela pressed through the walls I had made with blankets. They were at it again. I wanted to yell shut up, but I gave in and sleep took over and I thanked God. I dozed off to the sounds of moans and groans.

Chapter Fifteen

I slowly came to feeling as though my head was being split in half. Going to bed with noise and stress made me feel like hundreds of drummers drumming to the wrong beat. I wanted to curl up and just let time pass me by, but I was awake, and there was no going back. The good news was that all was quiet in the other room. I guess they got tired and dozed off and so did I.

Awaking after a long night, I pulled the covers off my head and looked at the time. It was 7:00 a.m., which wasn't late but late in my book. My body felt stiff after lying in the tub, but I expected as much. Reaching over, I picked up the phone and called room service. I needed some coffee in my system to get going. It would be a long day. My flight left at 1:00 p.m., which would put me back in Washington around 8:00 p.m. I had a few hours before I left to get my breakfast and freshen up, which I planned on doing by ordering room service and taking a shower.

I looked in the mirror and saw that my face was a mess. I looked tired, felt tired, and felt dirty. Ordering, I asked for scramble eggs, bacon, toast, orange juice, and some coffee.

It was a start and now all I had to do was to take care of the body. I figured the room services would take about thirty minutes, and so I had time to jump into the shower. A good thing the hotel had going for it was the large shower and bath-tub. Lord knows a hot shower would hit the spot. Turning the shower knob all the way to left, I let the water heat up. Amazing to me that in a matter of seconds steam was pouring out the room. Undressing, I looked in my little travel bag and found my shower cap. I really didn't want to spend the time doing my hair and figured I would give it a good wash when I got back.

The hot water felt good on my body. I could feel the tension in my neck and back being flushed away as the water flowed down the drain. I could have stayed there for hours, but I wanted to get going. Jumping out, I dried myself. I dressed and applied a small amount of makeup. I felt refreshed and ready to take on the world again. A knock on my door couldn't have been timed any better as the person on the other side announced that it was room service. A young Spanish woman entered with a big smile.

"Good morning," she said as if she were the bearer of good news. I returned the hello and pointed to a table at the corner of the room for her to set my meal down. She did so and returned with the bill. I was amazed how much a simple breakfast could cost not including the tip. I then chuckled to myself. What am I worried about, I got a million dollars. Laughing, I signed my name on the receipt and opened the door for her to leave. Before she left, she turned to me as if revealing some secret and said that there were rumors that big movie star was staying in the hotel last night. I quickly ush-ered her out the room.

I had lost my appetite and only wanted the coffee. Looking at my watch, I still had plenty of time and figured I would just spend the rest of my morning at the airport. I really didn't want to hear anything about Frank or run into Pamela, so I quickly downed my coffee and headed downstairs and started to pay for my bill. Again, the hotel lived up to what I expected. The front desk asked if I needed a cab to the airport, and within minutes, one pulled up to the front. A young man walked over to me and asked me whether I would like for him to carry my bag. I declined being that it was only an overnight bag. He smiled politely and then opened the door for me and led me to my cab.

I rolled the window down and let the wind blow into my face as we drove. It was another way to feel refreshed as we headed toward the airport. There was already traffic on the road, which made me feel smart for leaving early. Even if we were stuck in it for a while, I would have plenty of time.

So far so good. Everything was on schedule. I thought about Ray a few times but tried to put him out of my mind. It would be a long flight, and I would have plenty of time to think about him there. Although he was angry, I knew we would get beyond it.

God must have been smiling on me because there was no airport traffic. I jumped out, paid for my fare, and within thirty minutes I was at my gate waiting for the plane. All I had to do was wait. It felt good to just sit and people watch.

Some people rushed as though there was no time left on the earth, and if they didn't get to their place on time, the world would explode. Others dressed as if they had just come from a fashion show. It was a fun just to see people and just think, think about their lives, think about their problems, think about their success, it was probably what someone was doing with me; but so what, they could only guess, and no one really knew.

Time passed slowly as I watched and then one person passed by that I really didn't want to see. It was Pamela, and she looked a mess. Although makeup hid her appearance, I had seen her at her best and this was far from it. By all the noise she and Frank made last night, I am sure she didn't sleep much, but I didn't think it would show so much. She didn't see me first and I tried not to make myself noticed, but as fate would have it, she would be the flight attendant on my flight.

We gave a polite hello and then she hurried off past me as if she did not want to speak or ever see me again. Something was wrong and it involved Frank. I wasn't sure why, but now it also involved me.

Boarding the plane, I found my seat, which was in the middle of the plane next to the window. This flight had more passengers than when I flew the first time, which I didn't like. There was an older lady next to me who had a pleasant smile but kept staring. It bothered me because I would not be able to talk to Pamela. I noticed that every time she walked past me, she would lower her head as if in shame. That in itself was enough to intrigue me, but what really got me curious was that fact that I noticed scratches on her arm that had not been there before.

Midway through the flight, I caught up with her. It was between the bathroom and the kitchen galley of the plane. She tried to ignore me again, but I cornered her. I looked into her eyes and saw a sadness that replaced the beauty they held the day before, and I also noted under the heavy makeup some bruises. I tried to talk to her friendly, but it was hard when she wouldn't even look at me in my eyes. I cut straight to the point and asked her how her time with Frank was. Her sadness quickly became white-hot anger as she lifted her head and looked at me. "I hate that son of a bitch. Please don't ever mention his name to me." She tried to say something again and then she broke down and started to cry. It was a weird moment, the both of us flying high in the sky and her crying on my shoulders with the passengers looking at me. I really didn't know what to say or what to do other than to lend my shoulder as support.

One of the other attendants walked up to us and asked Pamela whether everything was OK. It was enough to snap Pamela out of her meltdown. She waved her friend away and then looked at me apologetically. Wiping tears away from her eyes and letting out a nervous chuckle, she said that she should have listened to me when I said that I was meeting a jerk. I gave a nervous laugh in return and then asked her what happened. Taking me by my arm, she moved me closer toward the galley.

"After you left, Frank and I talked for a while, and he promised to get me a role in his next movie. He asked me whether it would be OK if we went back to my place and talked some more about it.

"I kind of figured what he wanted, and he was good looking so I figured what the heck, maybe he would be good to his word. After we went up to the room, we started to make love or whatever you called what we did. He...he..." Tears filled her eyes again, and then she stopped. "I should have just stayed at the table and waited for you." The captain's button came on, and Pamela snapped to attention. No matter what her faults were, she was efficient. Before she returned to work, she turned and looked at me. "The whole time last night, while he was doing what he did to me, he kept calling me your name."

She walked past me as though she was a ghost and vanished in my mind. My heart started to beat hard as blood rushed to my head. I found my way back to my seat and the little lady that sat next to me asked me whether I was OK. I didn't reply; I just wanted this plane to land.

The rest of the flight Pamela wouldn't talk to me, and once we landed, she made herself busy and then disappeared through an employee door. She was gone, and I had only the memory of what she said on the plane. I was mad, confused, and lost. I really didn't know what to do. Frank was a twisted man and obviously did something to Pamela that was wrong, but like always, he was a star and from what she said the sex was consensual.

I was shaken, and the only person that I could think of was Ray. I needed a savior, or at least I needed him to lean on. Things were getting out of control, and I didn't know what to do. Turning my phone on, I called him and waited for him to pick up. He picked up after the first ring. "I've been waiting for you," he said. He didn't sound mad, which was good. I didn't want to spend any more time fighting. I just wanted him close to me. Before I could say anything else, he began to apologize saying that he was sorry for the way he spoke with me. "I love you," he blurted out as if it had been welding up within him. "You are not in this alone, and I want to be with you."

I wasn't sure what to think. Was he asking me to marry him? For a moment all my problems faded away as I tried to stay quiet and waited to see what else he would say. We both were silent for a few seconds, and I feared I was just hearing what I wanted to hear. Maybe he wasn't saying anything other than he was worried about me. I started to talk, but he told me to stay quietly for once. "I realized while you were gone that I could not live without you. We were meant for each other. This wasn't how I plan on asking you, but I guess it will have to do until I see you. Sherry Johnson, I am asking you on the phone, will you marry me?" I nearly dropped the phone. My hands started to shake so much that a young lady passing lent me her arm to lean against.

I stood there with my mouth open in shock. Funny how when things seem the worst, something good pops out of it like an exotic flower bursting through concrete. Ray waited a little longer and then asked me whether I heard what he said. I snapped to, closed my mouth, and said yes, yes, yes. Frank had disappeared from my mind, all his perversion and all his filth was but a memory for me now. Ray asked whether I wanted him to pick me up at the airport, but I had my own car and told him I would drive. He suggested that we meet at my house; he wanted to propose in person.

I really don't remember the rest of the trip back home. Somehow I got into my car and the next thing I knew I was pulling into my driveway. Ray's car was already there, and since he had a key to the house, I knew he was inside. I tried not to run to the front door but if I were clocked in the forty-yard dash it might have been a world record time. I wasn't sure what to expect other than possibly seeing him get on one knee, but as I opened the door, my wildest dreams couldn't have fit the picture of what I saw.

The room was filled with yellow, red, pink, and white roses followed by balloons of all shapes and sizes, each one had "I love you" written on them. Ray was dressed in a black tux with a shirt the color of pearl underneath and a black tie. The tux must have been tailor-made because of the way each cut accentuated the muscular tone of his body. I couldn't help notice the diamond cufflinks, which I thought was a nice touch to finish the picture. The lights were dim and the master of the love ballad Luther Vandross was playing in the background. He must have timed everything as to when I was pulling into the driveway.

He movements were fluent as floating, his body strong and confident. I stood there transfixed just watching him as he took me by the hand and moved me toward the center of the room and got down on a knee. My heart was beating out of control and sometimes stopping altogether. It was as if I was in another world watching everything as it was taking place.

Looking at me, he then bowed his head and closed his eyes and started to pray. "Dear Lord, I know that you took Sherry's parents away at your time, but I would ask of them permission to marry their beautiful daughter. I will assume that in heaven they can see into a person's heart and that they know that my heart is to love their daughter always. I would give my life for her and protect her with my soul and so I ask their blessing and your blessing over this night." I began to tremble holding back my tears; he continued as he opened his eyes and looked directly up at me.

"I know that you have been through a lot in your life, and I know that we have not been together for a very long, but I also know that I love you. You are my soul mate and you complete me. I've always known that I've been holding out for the right person and that God would bring her into my life. You are a miracle that washed up into my world, and I have been fulfilled. Sherry Johnson, will you marry me and make me complete?"

He then reached into his jacket and pulled out the largest diamond ring I had ever seen in my life. The size didn't matter, but if it did, he would have surely won me over by the carats it must have had. The ring had a platinum band and a large emerald cut solitaire surrounded by smaller solitaires and as he moved the ring even in the dim light it sparkled like rays of sunshine. He took my hand and placed the ring on my finger. I stood there like an idiot for a long time just staring at him. He looked in my eyes searching for something and then it hit me; he was waiting for me to say yes. I said it over and again, "YES, YES, AND YES, I will marry you." We both hugged each other and held each other and time stood still.

Ray took me by the arm as he stood up and we dance. Even though Frank tried to creep into my thoughts, I pushed him right back out. Frank would have to wait.

We kissed all night but stopped before anything else happened. We both could have easily gone all the way, but we didn't want to ruin anything. Everything was perfect, and I didn't want any regrets in the morning. He didn't either, which was one of the things I loved most about him.

That morning I watched him sleep, admiring him as he took breaths of life. I didn't want to disturb him, but soon I knew we would have to talk about Frank. Somehow we had to figure out what to do with him. How could I marry Ray and always have that monster in the background? I didn't know what could be done, but something had to be done. I thought to myself that maybe I could move to a different place, maybe Ray wouldn't mind relocating and we could both start over.

Without thinking, I began stroking the side of his face, feeling the strong contour of his jaw and thinking about our life together. He stirred and awoke, seeing me as I looked down at him. Even half-asleep he mentioned how I was the only thing he ever wanted to see the first thing in the morning. I kept waiting to wake up from my own fantasy and realized that Ray was a jerk; but the more he spoke, the more I realize that he was who he was. There is nothing fake about him.

Rubbing his eyes, he asked me how long I had been up. I told him only a few minutes. He stared at me for a moment and then asked what was wrong. I guess that was another thing I love about him. He could read me and know when my mind was on something else no appeared the opposite.

"It's Frank, isn't it?" he said. There was no denying that we were going to have this conversation and we're going to have it now. Last night was over. Quickly, I told him everything that happened on my trip. Although he tried to hide it, I could see the growing disgust on his face. I brought up the suggestion of us moving and starting over, but he stood ground. "We will not, I repeat, will not, run from this man. If I have to go out there and kick his butt myself, I will but you will be my wife, and he will not come between us."

He made his statement, and I had to admit it was kind of sexy. I wanted to yell out the window that he was my man. I wanted to let the whole world know whom I would marry, but instead I gave him a kiss. His anger went to passion, and we locked in a deep embrace and then he pulled away.

"We have to put an end to this," he said. "Frank has done nothing wrong legally despite being a jerk and so the only way is to just stay away from him and develop thick skin."

I gave him a smile, throwing him off for a moment. "What is that little smile about?" he asked. I told him that we still had Frank's check. We both laughed but knew it was only a joke; we tore up the check together. It's not often that a person gets to tear up one million dollars, but it felt as if I were ripping up Frank in my mind.

We laughed some more and then Ray said that he had to go to work. I asked him whether he really had to go, but he said that he had to make some money to pay for the wedding. That brought a smile to my face, and in some way, I felt that my parents would be smiling at us.

For the next month, I tried to put Frank out of my mind. Sometimes the thought of him resurfaced but mostly Ray took it upon himself to make every day of my engagement as much fun as possible. We spent many hours talking and laughing, simple things that bonded us closer and closer with each other. We both agreed that we would get married quickly. We loved each other to death and didn't think there was a big need to have a long engagement. The only thing we made sure of was that we took the pre-marriage classes at our church. I'm sure it was something that my parents would have wanted me to do.

Things seemed to be going pretty well until one evening when I received a phone call. The one phone call changed everything. A young man with a heavy Spanish accent was on the other line. He asked for me by name, and I nearly hung up on him. I thought he was a telemarketer being used to drum up business, but then he started to mention things about me that a telemarketer wouldn't know.

"Sherry Johnson," he said in a cool and efficient manner. "Be quiet and you will listen. I know where you live and what

KEN HARVEY

you are doing. Any time I want, I could kill you but I won't. You know why I won't? I won't because of my aunt." He was quiet; I imagined waiting for me say something. I had no idea what he was talking about or who his aunt was.

"Tell me," he said, "this Frank, was he an asshole on the island?"

I was floored, was he talking about Frank, the Frank I knew?

"I suggest you answer me," he said.

"He was a kid and we raised him. I guess we did kind of messed him up." I wasn't sure why I was defending him, but it was the truth.

I tried to push my luck and asked who he was again. The phone hung up. I listened to a dial tone nervously, not really knowing what to expect. I tried to figure out what just happened and who called. It wasn't Frank, but he knew a lot. Things were getting strange. I went to call Ray but the phone rang again.

I picked up the phone saying hello in a hurry. I was scared and wanted to know what was going on. "What do you want from me?" I yelled after a few moments of silence.

The heavy accented voice came on and asked me the same question. "What do you know about Frank?" I was getting frustrated but told him again what I knew about Frank, which I guess was enough to satisfy him.

"On the island, Rosa, how did she die?" I tried to repeat what was written in all the books, but he seemed to get angry. "Tell me how she died?" he yelled. His voice and tone frightened me, but I wasn't sure who he was. I didn't think he was a reporter, but I never told anyone about the truth on the island other than my parents.

222

"This is my last time," the voice said, calming back down. "I didn't like what I read about Rosa in the books, and it bothers me. Certain things have come to my attention and so I ask you again, what happened to Rosa on the island?"

I was frightened, but I began to tell him everything. I don't know why, but I told him how we were friends, the relationship between Frank and Rosa, her death and the baby.

He was quiet for a moment and then he spoke, "Rosa was my cousin. My name is not important, but what is important is the information I have."

I waited again in silence for him to continue. His voice stayed same calm and cool as he spoke. "It had always bothered me that Frank would get famous off writing about the island and the stuff that he wrote about my cousin, but what really got to me was that I had a dream. Do you believe in dreams?" I told him yes. "Good, I too believe in dreams and believe that sometimes they are a message. I received a message, and it was from Rosa. She told me to warn you. She was a great woman, did you know that?" I agreed with him and continued to listen. "Your parents, their death, it was from a street gang?" I am frustrated now and didn't like the fact that he brought up my parent's death.

"What do they have to do with this?" I screamed a little louder than I expected.

He sighed. "Their death...their death was not an accident. I am a businessman, and I like to know why people ask my people to kill someone." I stood there for a moment, eyes bugging out and nearly fainting. I could barely get the word out feeling sick and angry.

"What do you mean you like to know why people are being killed?"

He sighed as if it were a burden for him to repeat the information again. "My boys, how do you say? Got a call from your boy Frank to bump off your parents. They almost took the job, but I did not trust that white man. I guess my cousin must have taught him Spanish, and he came to us as if he were down with us because he could speak the language. He was throwing around much money, which was another thing I didn't like. Don't take that much money to pop someone unless you have other motives. Now I get the word that he wants to pop someone named Ray, and I traced that back to you."

My mind went into a whirlwind and I started to cry thinking of someone trying to kill Ray. I screamed, "You won't kill him, will you?" He laughed and told me that if he wanted to kill me or Ray, we already would be dead. He finished by saying that he has fulfilled the promise he made to Rosa in his dream. He also mentioned that we never had this conversation and to never try to contact him.

I dropped the phone and stared into space. I was in a state of shock. Twice Rosa had become an angel, and as if reflective, I started to thank God for her. Everything that happened was strange, but I needed to move. Ray's life was in danger. I picked up the phone to reach him, but he wasn't there. Quickly, I headed out the door to try to meet him at work. It was nearing time for him to leave, and I hadn't heard from him all day. A shiver went up my spine as I left thinking about Frank having my parents killed, and now he was after my baby.

I believe I broke speed records going from my house to Ray's office. It was amazing that I did not wreck the car driving so fast with tears flowing down my eyes and trying to reach him on the cell phone again. Turning the car into the parking space, I nearly hit his black Benz. I didn't care but was more relieved that I saw his car was still there. Running as if there was no tomorrow, I raced up the stairs, skipping over them two at a time. I looked around, and no one was there but his secretary.

Chapter Sixteen

Ray had his own private practice and was accountable to no one. His secretary was an elderly lady who, although was efficient, could sometimes be slow. I ran in his office and back out before she even got up. "Where's Ray?" I shouted at her. I must have looked a mess as she tried to remember where she last saw him. I began shaking her as if she were a rag doll or a wayward child.

She was frightened and I couldn't blame her; I was frightened. I needed to make sure he was OK. My heart was pounding as I tried to calm down and ask her again. "Where is Ray?" With her eyes wide with fear she said that she didn't know and that he left with a client. Trying to get information, I asked her what the client looked like, what was his name, but she couldn't answer any of the questions. She said it was someone Ray just met, and they talked downstairs. He said that he would go out to have lunch with him and then he would be back. I asked her for any information and the only things she could remember that she thought he sounded Spanish.

I wanted to slap her. She let my man go and didn't find out any more information than that. What kind of law practice was

Ray running? I know that he had won some big case a long time ago and was set for money, and this practice was more about the pro bono work than for financial gain anything, but I was pissed. Stroking my hand across my ring, I thought of him and an overwhelming feeling of despair cloaked me. I tried to rationalize all the information that had been deposited into my world today.

My parents had been killed by what was thought to be a drive-by killing. Maybe I was overreacting. Maxine, Ray's secretary, brought over tissue and asked whether she could do anything. I asked her whether she had any idea where Ray normally had lunch. She named a couple places, and I told her that if he called or came back to tell him that I needed to reach him right away. Confused by the whole process, she instinctively hugged me to let me know that it was OK and then I stormed out of the room.

Running to my car, I raced out into the street not really knowing where I was going. I knew of the places that Maxine spoke of and they were only a few minutes away, but I had a feeling he wouldn't be there.

Running through the list of restaurants like a madwoman, my fears were confirmed when he wasn't there. I sat there in the parking with my nerves frazzled, crying and praying to God for guidance. My cell phone rang, and I picked up; Frank's voice came on the line.

"You were going to marry him? How could you betray me? Why would you destroy us?" He was obviously crazy, and he somehow now had my baby.

"Where's Ray?" I screamed.

He gave a laugh and then started mocking me. "Where's Ray, where's Ray. Don't you worry about Ray right now. We need to talk," he said

He was silent knowing that he had my attention. "I know what you are thinking and you're wrong. They won't be able to trace anything to me. You would be amazed what money can buy, a little knowledge on how to do thing the right way, how to get by without having a record of your phone calls, disposable cells, what a marvelous invention." I knew he was right, he had money, and I had seen enough crime shows on TV to know that much was possible. His voice became eerily calm but the seething undertones of anger hid just below the surface.

"You think all that time on that island didn't screw up my mind? You think killing Cynthia and my mom didn't screw up my mind? How does it feel to lose a loved one?" I couldn't believe it, yet he was waiting for an answer. I couldn't give him one I just waited and allowed him to talk. He continued, "You know, I don't remember much about my childhood other than what was on the island. I remember Cynthia's beatings, I remember Rosa and me falling in love, or at least I think that's what it was, but more than anything I remembered you. You were always different from the others. You stood out. They all wanted to make me perfect, try to make me into this little perfect man. What does your precious Bible say, 'For all have sinned and fall short of the glory.' Well guess I fell a little bit short.

"When I was with Rosa, I thought of you. Through all my beating while you did nothing, I thought of you. When you thought you killed me, I stayed alive because I thought of you. So tell me, don't you think we need to be together?" In my fear for Ray and anger for Frank, I felt sadness for him. He was right; we did mess up his mind. I told them that there was no such thing as perfection. We couldn't make a perfect man, and now look at what we created. Frank was our own little Frankenstein monster.

"All I want is one night with you, just time to be alone. I will let your precious Ray go, and you two can get married but I need you first. I have to be the one to take your virginity just as you all took mine. How do you like that?" My stomach began to churn at the proposition he was making, yet I knew that if I ever wanted to see Ray again I would have to do what he said. A little voice was shouting that Frank can't be trusted, but I tuned out the voice. Ray's life depended on it.

Frank told me that I needed to go to the airport and purchase a ticket again to Los Angeles, which I imagine was a smart move on his part. Anything problematic, and it would look as though I wanted to come out to him. He said that his contact person would be waiting for me at airport. I pleaded with him to allow me to speak with Ray, but it only angered him. He said that Ray was alive and that I had to trust him. If I didn't, Ray would be dead for sure. Giving me no choice, I did what he asked.

He also said that he had people watching me as we spoke and would know everything that I did. That part I didn't believe until once again he gave me a description of what I was wearing. "Sherry, you are wearing black slacks with a crème-colored sweater with matching crème boots." This was too much detail to have been luck. I quickly looked around to see whether someone looked out of place, but there were people everywhere. A lot of them were on cell phones, some not. There was no way I could tell who was watching me. My thoughts focused back to Ray. I couldn't lose him. He was the only good thing left in my life. My mind began to spin out of control. Slowly I began to take deep breaths and exhale until a false calmness engulfed me

Frank told me to drive to the airport and buy my own ticket, which I did. I looked around to see whether Pamela was anywhere. Maybe if I could get her to tell me what Frank did to her it would be some evidence to use against him. I was desperate reaching for anything that may save Ray. Rushing through the security check, I handed my ticket to the flight attendant. I whisper to her is she knew where Pamela was. She looked at me surprised and saddened. She said that Pamela quit for no reason. She wanted to talk more, but another customer came to the counter. It was a short Spanish man with a thick mustache; his very presences sent chills down my spine.

Maybe he was one of Frank's men, maybe not. I hated that I was stereotyping a race but there was too much on line. I did not care about hurt feelings. Ray was in trouble, and I had to be obedient to save his life.

It was a long flight, the longest in my life. I kept thinking about Ray and praying that he would be OK. I tried to keep the thought of Frank being with me out of my mind. It was sickening enough thinking about what Frank had done with Pamela. Images of my mom and dad flickered in my head as I tried to think what they would say. I knew my mom would say that I needed to pray, seek out God's word, but I didn't know whether I could. We created this monster, not him. Praying to get out of trouble didn't seem as if it would do any good. Still, I said a quick prayer for Ray. He had nothing to do with this, and despite what happen to me, I wanted him safely.

We landed and I didn't know what to expect. I got off and noticed the same Spanish man that was at the ticket counter was leaving the plane also. I waited until he came toward me, I assumed that he would tell me the next step, but he walked past me as if I weren't there. I started to follow him thinking that it was a hint, but after a few moments he turned to ask me whether I needed anything and wondered why I was following him. I stood there frozen not sure of what to do, the only info that I had been to get on the plane and come to LA, and I would receive instructions from there.

I walked around for a few moments looking at folks hoping that someone would tell me what to do next. No one showed until a pretty young African American woman about twenty-one years of age with sassy blond dreadlocks twisted on her head walked up to me and asked me whom I was waiting for. I looked at her for a moment and didn't say anything. I didn't want to say more than I had to until I was sure she was there for me. "Are you Sherry?" she asked. I quickly said yes. She smiled and seemed pleasant enough. "Frank sent me to pick you up."

"Where are we going?" I said, wanting to know what was going on. She looked at me strange for a moment and then said to his house. "Of course, this must be your first time." I was puzzled.

I tried to quiz her, but she became quiet, almost fearful that she had said too much. Trying to pry information from that point on was like trying to push through a brick wall. She walked slightly ahead of me, not slowing down for a second until we reached outside. She opened the car door of a dark blue Lincoln limo and allowed me to get in. Then she got into the driver seat and began to pull away. She told me that she would not say anything but that Frank requested that she play a song for me. Pushing the button, the car went silent for a moment and then a song came on. At first I wondered what the song was but then it hit me; it was the same song that we all sang on the island.

"Could you please turn that off?" I said. It was repulsive to me as Frank knew it would be. She didn't say anything but only looked in the review mirror, the song continued until it ended. I started screaming at her to pull over and to let me out. She pushed a button and the wall came up, blocking me from seeing her.

We rode around for about an hour, and I noticed that there were fewer homes and more trees to give a sense of seclusion or perversion, depending on the buyer. It had already been fifteen minutes since I last saw a home, plenty of land but no homes except the large mansion that we pulled up to. I'm not sure how large it was, but it had to be at least ten thousand square feet. It was well groomed with beautiful flowers that lined the walkway up to the front door. Looking closer, I noticed that the flowers were the same ones that were on the island. The driver opened the door and extended her hand, pointing the way. As I started walking expecting her behind me, I turned to hear the car door closing and the car pulling off. The front door opened there stood my worst nightmare: Frank.

He looked at me and smiled. Wearing a pair of shorts, a multicolored shirt, and a pair of sandals, he opened the door wider and moved out of the way allowing me room to walk. Stepping in, I felt as if I were walking through hell's gates.

The house was cooler than the outside about twenty degrees, which felt good, but I wasn't there for the pleasure of getting out of the heat. I was there on a mission. He briefly moved his hands all over my body, taking his time around my breast making sure I wasn't caring anything and then took my purse. He had told me not to bring my cell phone and scanned, it to make sure I didn't. It didn't matter. I only wanted to make sure that Ray would be free. I looked at him sternly in the face and told him that I wanted Ray to be free before anything happened. Amazingly, he started laughing, "You're in no position to make orders of me. I will free Ray once we are done, and believe me once we are through, you may not want Ray anymore."

He was repulsive, but I didn't know what to do. I tried to reach a compromise and told him that I at least wanted to hear Ray's voice. I wanted to make sure that he was alive at least. He rubbed his face as though he was tired and walked over to a table that was in an office that sat at the right hand corner of the entrance. Sitting in a large soft leather chair, he pulled open the top desk drawer and pulled out a phone with some sort of attachment to it. I could only assume that it was the phone he used to call me and the contraption on it was to prevent its signal from being traced.

He spoke a few words in Spanish to the person on the other end and then laughed. I could only make out a few of the words I learned on the island with Rosa. He said, "No, don't kill him yet." My heart began racing trying to figure out how to free Ray and how to stop this from happening. He whistled for me as if I were a dog to come to the phone and then and told me to sit. I obeyed, and he handed me the phone. "Ray," I screamed trying to hear his voice.

There was silence for a while and then in a raspy tone Ray answered. Quickly, I asked him whether he was OK, if he had been harmed. He started to say something and then I heard a loud thud as they hit him. I screamed again for him, and he came back on.

"I'm OK," he said and then rushed out for me not to do what they said, don't give in. He was hit again and then the phone went silently. Frank grabbed the phone from my hands. He seemed angry that his instructions weren't followed to the letter. "I said he was not to be hurt unless I said so," he blurted out in English. Looking at me, he continued the rest in Spanish. The more he talked, the redder his face became until he noticed me watching him and then calmed down.

"When I tell people to do something, I expect them to do it right," he said. "I am sure you will have no problem with that." I was starting to get sick and scared. He was crazy, and worse because he could get away with it. I wondered how many women he brought up to his home and had his way with. I wondered about Pamela, and then after frightening myself, I tried to put the thoughts out of my mind.

Frank walked over to me and put his hand against my face. I started to pull away, but he said for me to remember that he likes people to do things the way he wants them to. There would be fewer problems in the long run, he said. I had no choice in the situation. I had to stand still while he caressed his hand along my face, each finger feeling like a thousand ants crawling over my body as he made his way toward my lips. I clinched my teeth, hating the feeling that I had no control of the situation.

He began to part my lips and everything in me wanted to bite his fingers off and spit them back in his face, but I could only pull away. He looked surprised and asked what was wrong. I thought about Ray and then I told him I was sorry, acknowledging him to be in control. He smiled and said maybe, maybe not, hinting that the night was still young and that I might be really sorry later. He then he switched back to what would be perceived as normal. "I made something for you to eat. I'm sure it was a long flight, and you need to keep your strength up. Please, join me in the kitchen." Making my way to the kitchen, I couldn't help see that everything was done with the most expensive taste. Two huge marble vases held large indoor palm trees with huge beautiful green palms line the pathway as you made your way down a long hallway. The ceiling had to be at least twenty feet high. The pathway was a smooth black marble, which led into a large oversize kitchen.

He walked me to a large brass table with a glass top. It was something that you would see in a five-star hotel, not someone's house. Continuing, he pulled an oversize chair out and offered me a seat. I sat quietly as he moved his arm across my back and then walked into the kitchen near the stove. "I'm a good cook you know," he said as if we were on our first date. There were several items on the countertop—fresh fruit, vegetables, breads, and spices. He went to the refrigerator and pulled out two large steaks and a bottle of wine. "I guess cooking is one of the true pleasures I have in life. I get to try different things, mix them up, and then sometimes when you least expect it, the perfect meal." He looked at me. "Have you ever had the perfect meal?" I didn't know what to say. What did he want me to say? I sat there quiet.

Slamming a large knife he had on the table, he started to shout. "This can be so much easier for you if you work with me. If not, it can be very rough." I tried to answer him, not because of his threat but because there was an opening. I wanted him to forget about the knives. He continued to talk to me as though we were on a date, and I tried to reply and smile as much as possible. The longer I could prolong him, the better my chances of getting the knives in my hand.

Once he finished talking and cooking, he brought two plates of food that any chef would have been proud to serve. He placed two sharp knives on the table, one for me and one for him. I stared at them thinking that I should take one and jam it into his throat, but he stopped me before I could start. "By the way, if anything happens to me, the same will happen to your man Ray. So go ahead and cut me. They have bigger knives, and I am sure it will hurt a lot more."

Smiling, he began to cut his steak. He motioned for me to do the same. Although I was hungry, I had no appetite for food, but I had to play the role. It was as if I were back on the island again, and we were playing the same cat-and-mouse game that we had played before. He cut a piece of his steak and placed it right to the edge of my lips. I refused to part them, not wanting to take anything from him. The sauce dripped onto the table as he swirled it around my mouth until I finally opened up. "See, it's not that bad," he said, knowing that it was good. He then offered me some wine, which I declined. If anything were going to happen to me, I needed all my senses about me.

He moved back in his seat and then took a sip of it for himself. Quick as a flash, he grabbed me by the arm and pulled me to him. He took the back of my head and pushed our mouths together where he forced the wine out of his mouth and into mine. I wanted to spit it out or at least back at him, but he put his hand over my mouth and pinched my nose until I swallowed. He then sat back into the chair and breathed in as he tasted the final and best part of the wine. He looked at me coldheartedly and said, "If I say drink, you drink. If I say sit, you sit. And if I say move, you move. Do

I make myself clear? Now that the rules of the game are clear, let us finish our dinner."

As we ate, Frank carried most of the conversation until finally he said something that sparked my interest. "Since you have been the perfect date so far, I have a surprise for you." He then tied a blindfold around my eyes and led me out of the kitchen through a door. Suddenly we stopped and he removed my blindfold. We were in a basement that had an outside entrance and in the room with a large flat screen TV. At first I thought there was a TV program on, but then I realize that the show was Ray. Somehow they were feeding the picture directly to from wherever Ray was. He was tied and gagged with a few bruises, but he was alive.

Chapter Seventeen

My eyes opened in horror as a masked man walk over and hit Ray in the face. His body jerked forward and then back as he tried to regain his balance. Frank looked at me searching for emotions, feeding off my hurt and fear. He smiled, stroking the back of my hair. "Guess what, I have another surprise." He said in a tone that caused my skin to crawl. I couldn't imagine anything worse. He pulled a small mic from on top of the TV and began to speak.

"Remove his blindfold," he said as the man in the mask walked over calmly and removed it from Ray's face. I wasn't sure how many men were around him, but I knew there were two for sure. One was taller and more muscular than the other and walked with a slight limp. They must have had a weapon to capture him because I knew he couldn't been taken by one man alone.

Ray's eyes quickly focus straight ahead. It was almost as if he were watching me. I sensed Frank getting some sort of perverse excitement as he pointed to a small camera also attached to the TV. Frank smiled knowing that Ray was also looking at me. I jumped to the camera and shouted to Ray that I loved him, hoping that he could hear me as well. My shouts were interrupted by a steel-like grip around my neck, pulling me back. Frank's grip was so tight that I began to see spots in front of my face. I staggered, not wanting Ray to see the pain, but his eyes said everything. He tried to move out of the seat but was hit in the back of the head.

Frank turned to me and looked me in the face. "You like my surprise?" I tried to slap his face, but he grabbed my arm and pulled me close to him. "I think before you go, we will give Ray a good old show, and then after I am done, he can have you. How do you like that?" I started to cry but that did nothing but get him excited. He moved in close to me and put his lips against mine. I tried to fight him, but he was strong. It was like the island again. I could smell him, the scent of his sweat, and the odor of his desire.

He tried to press his tongue in my mouth, causing me to nearly gag. I tried to bite it off, but he pushed me away and walked toward the camera. "Ray, you know she wants me, don't you? I think that you and she could make a good couple, but I get to have her first."

Ray was going crazy in his chair, his mouth was still gagged but he was yelling and moving around like crazy, both men had to use all their force to keep him still. I was frightened not really knowing what to do next. I didn't want Ray to see me like this; I didn't want him to see Frank with me. A feeling of despair started to come over me. I would have to give in and Ray would have to watch. I wondered if he would still love me. I wondered if he would still have anything to do with me. I tried to convince myself that after this I would let him go, not to have him feel as if he owed me anything by staying with me. As long as he was allowed to live, I would gladly sacrifice my body and soul.

My biggest worry was the thought of going through all of this for nothing and Frank killed us both. He had money, and the way things were planned out, anything was possible.

Frank switched things up again and spoke with me as a doctor would to a patient. "Please disrobe for me," he said. I looked at him in shock. I wasn't about to take my clothes off for him; and if he wanted them off, he would have to take them off. Unable to get the words out of my mouth, I shook my head defiantly. He said a few words into the mic and the men began hitting Ray. I wanted to resist, but I couldn't. I yelled for him to stop, which he yelled something back in Spanish into the mic and both men ceased what they were doing and moved away from Ray. For a moment his head was limp, but he continued to try to look up at me secretly, letting me know to keep fighting.

Frank looked at me as if waiting for me to do now what would be done later. He sighed and pointed to my outfit. I was stuck in a standstill not knowing what to do but then the voice that I long to hear from called out to me again. "Where is your faith, trust, and belief?" Everything in me fought against the faith that the voice was preaching. I could only see the facts that stood before me. Time itself seems to stand still as I looked at Frank who looked back at me with a smile on his face. I inhaled slowly, allowing time to catch up with my breathing and then I told Frank no.

He was taken back by the sudden strength in my voice. For a moment, we both stood looking at each other. It took him a second and then he tried to react, his reaction was to jump at me. I kneed him square between the legs. There was a great sense of relief as I watched his eyes roll up into his head. Someone needed to tell Frank that faith could be painful.

I froze, not knowing what to do. If I continued, he would kill Ray If I didn't do anything, I shuddered to think what he would do to me. The voice that had been in my head, the one that at one time had been a friend on the island suddenly came back to me; this time it was the voice of Rosa. I could hear her strong Spanish accident as she spoke, "Be strong and courageous. Do not be terrified. Do not be discouraged. After you have done everything to stand, stand firm then." Her voice was like the voice of an angel giving me peace. If Frank were to hurt me, if I were to die, I would die knowing that he did not get my soul.

Frank regained his senses and was on me in a flash as he punched me in the face. My lip began to swell and my tooth felt loose. He lifted me off the ground as if I wore nothing and dragged me in front of the TV. This was it; this was the moment he had been planning. I closed my eyes not wanting to see him. Just as I prepared myself for the worse, Rosa's voice came back to me again. "Open your eyes," she said. I couldn't believe what I was hearing. She was telling me to open my eyes to look at him. I don't know why, but I trusted her voice and open my eyes. I stared straight into his eyes not blinking. I peered deep in his soul and in doing so I found my strength. I was not him and he was not me. I would win this battle.

He froze not sure what was going on in my head, bewilderment etched into his face. He couldn't understand where my newfound strength came from. Trying to regain his edge, he made a move. His lust was stronger than the fear of what I was doing; my faith had become stronger than my fear. He reached for my blouse, wanting me to fight back, but I didn't. I just stood there looking at him. My mind was with God, and my body was a shell. The first button came off, and I readied myself for any type of violation and then out of the corner of my eyes I saw a scuffle on the TV. Something was going on in the room where Ray was.

Frank noticed it also and started to yell into his mic but froze. We both looked on as the two men in mask were being thrown around the room and then finally shot. I could tell that this was not part of Frank's plan as we both watched, forgetting the fight that we were embattled with. The new men also wore a mask and started to walk toward Ray. My heart was beating nearly out of control wondering if they were going to kill him also. I saw the gun in one of their hands as it was pointed toward him. The other man walked toward the camera and faced it. He slowly removed his mask, revealing that he was Spanish. There was something about him that looked familiar. He looked into the camera and mouthed the words, "Rosa." He then shot his middle finger straight up making an F U gesture for Frank.

My mouth dropped open, and Frank went pale as the blood drained from his face. There was no mistake what he said, and I could only assume that this was the person who had called me on the phone. He then put the mask back on and faced Ray. Taking a large knife out his back pocket, he freed Ray and then handed him a slip of paper and walked out the room with the other man. Ray sat there not sure what was going on and then read the paper. He looked up at the camera started yelling that he would kill Frank.

All his intelligence, handsome looks, and his planning couldn't help Frank now. My prayers had been answered, and now it was only me and him. He grabbed me quickly, not wanting to lose his advantage. He was scared, but he wanted to be in control. I wanted to hear the voice in my head again but knew it wouldn't come. This was now my battle, and I would win. I was still in good shape, and since Ray was out of danger, I could let loose. I clawed his face, drawing flesh and blood under my fingernails. He screamed out in pain. It would take an awfully good plastic surgeon to fix the damage that I did to his face.

There were three deep red groves across his face from his right temple to the bottom of his chin. He swung wildly and hit me with a backhand, causing me to fly over the couch. He moved quickly and pounced on top of me, hitting me in the face. Each blow brought stars to my eyes as I fought to keep my consciousness. Kneeing him was out as he straddled me above the waist. Placing his entire body weight on my chest, he started choking me as I struggled to gain my air. Black dots peppered my vision. I had to do something quick or it would be over. He leaned over and said that he would have me dead or alive, either way he would do what he should have done on the island. I spit in his face, which caused only him to laugh and spit back at me. Turning my head just enough, I bit his arm. The bite was strong enough to take a chuck of flesh out and spit it on the floor. He let go of his grip, and I pushed him off me.

I wobbled to stand, but he grabbed me again and put me in a choke hold, securing his forearm around my throat. I had to maneuver my head to the crease in his forearm to buy myself a few seconds more of air. I placed my hand on his forearm and lowered my center of gravity and then flipped him. It was something I had practiced a few times in a class I took after I got off the island, and it worked to perfection. He went over once again, releasing his grip. He was on the ground, and I now had to take advantage of it. I raised my foot and with the heel of my shoe stomped him in the throat. It was a solid shot that caused him to cough and grab his neck. Blood started trickling out of his mouth.

Now I was the hunter, and I was pissed. I moved to his midsection and then stomped him between the legs as hard as I could. He let out a yell that was both painful and hoarse because of the injury to his throat. I had him and wanted more blood. Every time he covered one part of his body, I stomped him in the other part, back and forth, back and forth until he no longer moved. I still wanted more blood; I still needed more. I had to put him behind me once and for all. I had to rid myself of him. Running to the kitchen, I searched for the knives that he used for dinner. I used to think that I could never kill anyone but that thought was gone. I would shove the knife down his throat as far as I could until I was sure he could never come back.

It was easy enough to find the knife. I'm sure Frank didn't expect this turn of events, but I was in control and I was mad. I grabbed it holding it tightly in my hand. The wooden handle felt cool, but I was hot. I knew if I didn't do it now it would never happen, but I was ready. I turned to go back down to the basement and completed what I started to do but caught my reflection in the mirror. I saw the crazed look in my eyes, I saw anger and pure hatred in my face, and I didn't like what I saw. I cursed myself for stopping and even more so for losing my edge. Now I had to ask myself if I really were going to become a killer. Did I really have what it took to kill a man? It's one thing to do it in self-defense, but to walk up to someone who is on the ground and place a knife in him was a different story.

I froze thinking that I should just call the police. I figured that they could sort things out when they got here. Reaching for his house phone, I picked it up listening for the dial tone but it was blank. I hit the tab several times but nothing. I guessed he planned for this. My heart was beating rapidly realizing how much time I had spent upstairs. I started to panic. I needed to go for the cell phone I saw him use earlier, but I also wanted to make sure he was still out on the floor. I had never been a person who took many chances, especially since the island, and wouldn't start now. I decided that I would check on him first and then go for the phone.

Racing back downstairs, I noticed things that I had not notice before. Although the house was massive, there was sparse furniture and very few windows. No pictures or art-work on the wall or anything that would make this place seem like a home away for home. This house apparently was being used for only one thing, and I wonder how many girls had been here before me.

The journey back to the spot where he laid seemed a lot longer, and my anger had subsided. Rounding the corner, I gripped the knife tighter holding my breath. I prayed that he would still be on the ground right where I left him. My worst thought became my reality; he was disappeared from the spot where I left him.

There were small spots of blood on the ground where he lay before. I franticly searched the room looking for him hoping that he would not jump out from some darken cor-ner. There were no windows below, but looking more closely, I noticed there were two other rooms and a bathroom. I had two choices, I could turn and run or search him out. I decided to get the hell out of dodge.

I gave a quick glance at the TV looking for Ray, but he was gone also. I wasn't sure where he had gone but at least he was safe. Now it was time for me to get safe. I wasn't sure where Frank was, but this was his territory. We were way out in the middle of nowhere with no phone, and it was already dark outside.

I ran back upstairs to the main house searching. The longer I stayed in the house, the more dangerous it would become. I froze suddenly. I wasn't sure but out of the corner of my eye I sensed something. I prayed it was not what I thought it was, but I had to check it out. Moving closer I saw a spot on the carpet and realized that it was blood, a fresh wet drop of blood.

He had been there in the room right next to me. I was starting to freak out. I had to get out of the house. Like a scared gazelle, I sprinted toward the door as fast as I could. Each heavy laden step made the entrance seemed like miles away, but I had to make my way outside. I had to get free from his home and his control. I just had to reach the door, and I would have some freedom.

I felt myself being pulled off my feet from my hair. On the ground I looked up to see Frank's hate etched in his face towering over me.

Chapter Eighteen

I wanted to kick myself for being so stupid. I should have known he would get up; I should have known that he would be able to do this to me. He kicked my hand hard and the knife went flying across the room. I could feel the blood rushing through my body as my hand began to swell. It felt as though it might be broken, but that was the least of my worries.

Blood dripped off his face as he began to laugh and shake his head as if to say that I should not have done that. I felt sick to my stomach. Somehow I had to find a way to fight back, somehow I had to survive. Without thinking, I yelled out Cynthia's name as if she were coming near him. He turned to look around in fear as he often did on the island when she would yell out his name to punish him. I got up and tried to crawl away, but he regained his senses and grabbed me by the legs. I kicked at him feeling his knee crunch against my foot. His body went down in pain, and I started to crawl away again. I would make it.

The knife was not more than ten feet in front of me, but it seemed like a mile. My body hurt, throbbing in places that

I did not even know existed, but I would get it. I had to get it. The question of whether to use it had vanished. If need be, I would kill him. Inching toward the knife, I felt as though victory was at hand. I tried to look back behind me to see whether he was near, but he just lay there holding his knee screaming out in pain and cursing my name. I knew I won, as quickly as all this had happened, I had won. I began to thank God and Rosa and those voices in my head.

I wondered what happened to Ray, but I stopped myself. I didn't have time to think about that. Reaching out a bit more, I reached the knife and held on to it for dear life. I turned to face Frank almost hoping that he tried to attack so that I could stab him without thinking. I was surprised to see him just sitting there. I knew I hurt him with the kick to the knee, but I did not think I hurt him that much.

"Get up," I yelled at him wanting to end this. I couldn't help the hate and rage that I felt for him. Still he said nothing; he just looked at me. I had to keep my distance between the two of us, at any moment I expected him to try something but instead he just sat there with a defeated look. "It's over Frank, it's over," I said, my anger still boiling over but subdued enough to speak. I looked at him almost as a mother would look at her child. Trying to act as fierce as possible, I told him to get up. He started to move but fell back on his butt grabbing his knee and howling in pain.

I began to inch my way toward the front door. I figured that if I hoofed it on foot, I stood a good chance of getting away. He was hurt and would have a hard time running after me. I kept the knife pointed at him, backing toward the door wondering why he wasn't trying anything. He kept a smile on his face, which began to unnerve me. Maybe he knew something that I didn't know.

A few more steps back, and I felt the door handle against my butt, I turned the knob and then paused. What the heck was I doing? Why try to walk when I could drive? "Give me the keys to your car," I yelled at him. He looked at me and smiled but said nothing. I tried to yell again and assert my demands, but he continued to give a sideways smirk. I wanted to walk up to him and kicked that stupid look off his face. I tried to think of every option other than killing him on the spot. The only thing left was to get outside and run. Maybe he was wounded enough to stay there for good.

Deep down I knew I was only fooling myself, but I had to try something. Turning the knob, I looked again at him and then ran outside. I was still in good shape, and so I kept a good pace. I remembered that there were no homes for miles, but there was a store about ten miles out. I hadn't run ten miles in years, but my life was in danger, and I had to do it. I also didn't want to stay on the main road because if he somehow got to his car, I didn't want to make it easy for him to find me.

I looked up and thanked God that there was a full moon. With the moon giving me some light, it made my run a little easier, but still it was dark and I was running through an area I knew nothing about. It seemed as if everything had come full circle again. I was running from him the same way it happened on the island.

I covered a good mile before I stopped to rest. I figured that I put good distance between both of us, and even if he were trying to find me, his knee would be giving him problems. I looked back in the direction that I came and was satisfied that I didn't create too much of a path for anyone to follow. The darkness was my friend here, and if I could stay the course, I should reach the store in a while. I only prayed that someone would be there.

I heard the sound of a branch break and jumped. I wasn't sure what it was and I was scared. I tried to convince myself that it was an animal. I stopped and held my breath hoping to pick up on the direction that the noise came from. Waiting, my eyes began to adjust to the darkness. I could make out things in front of me for about twenty yards. I decided to wait a few more seconds and heard nothing. My rest was over, and with a renewed energy of fear, I took off running again. I tried to pace myself this time instead of an all-out run as if I did before. I had learned a long time ago to play mental games with myself to make me keep going. Every time I got tired, I would picture Ray in front of me with his arms open calling me to come to him. That thought alone gave me strength to keep going.

Tiredness and pain started playing tricks on my mind. I saw little eyes everywhere looking at me, waiting for me to trip up. I wanted to stop again, bend over, and suck in deep breaths of air but I couldn't stop. Ray would want me to keep going. It wasn't that I depended on a man for my strength but that I chose to depend on a man for my strength. I learned a long time ago that strength is choosing to do something though you have to could do otherwise. I chose to believe in Ray, to use that as my focal point. Everything was going OK until I heard a snap and then pain shooting up my leg.

I buckled over in pain grabbing my ankle. Tears streamed out of my eyes as I cried out. I fell face-first on the ground, angered and frustrated by the turn of events. I think I stepped

into a hole, but was not sure, whatever it was changed everything for me, and I didn't know whether I could make it
anymore.

I tried to think between the flashes of pain. Each wave
made my body tremble and my stomach churn as I clenched
my teeth. I had to think what to do next. Now the same darkness that had become my friend quickly became my enemy.
I tried to plot out if I could defend myself if I had to. I limped
deeper into the woods, making myself the least visible as possible. I hadn't seen any animals, but I knew that they were there
waiting for a moment like this, waiting for me to become easy
pickings. Between the burst of pain, I had to think of what
to do. There wasn't much of a choice and at the end. I knew
I had to do what I had been fighting against all along; I had to
try to make it toward the road.

At least on a worn path I stood a better chance of getting help and being protected than staying in the woods all
night, but I also knew that Frank could be out there. I bit my
lip weighing the options and then redirected myself toward
the road. I tried to think of Ray as a source of light, but it
wasn't working this time. The pain was becoming unbearable.
I wanted to ball up and die, give in, but I knew I couldn't.
I had come too far, been blessed too much to give up now.
I have to fight my way through it.

Like on the island, I began to crawl over the ground
toward my destination. Slowly inch by inch it felt as if my leg
is hanging onto my body by strands of flesh. I started talking
to myself, telling myself not to give up. I couldn't give up.
I am a conqueror. I am a survivor. I said to myself. I knew
I had to believe I would make it or I wouldn't.

After about twenty minutes, I spotted the cleared out area. I had at least made it that far. No animals, thank God, and no Frank. I was where I hoped would lead to safety. Sweat poured off my body brought a salty smell to the air. That in itself pushed me on. I remembered the island, and I remembered surviving. I remember wanting to give up and to die near the sea but something kept pushing me. I knew this was my last stand; I had to find help and put a stop to all this. God help me I prayed

My mind started to spin from the pain and the over-exertion and then I blacked out. The next voice I heard was someone saying something to me. I wondered if it was God. Maybe it was him, maybe he'd come to relieve me of all my pain, maybe I would have peace in my life. "Are you OK, miss? Are you OK?" I struggled to figure out who the voice was from, it didn't sound like God but then again God can sound like anyone. I blinked a few times trying to regain my senses and then I saw him, a young white man in his late twenties, friendly eyes, and dark black hair. He was speaking to me. I wondered if this was another part of Frank's game, but as my vision became clearer, I noticed another thing—he was wearing a police uniform. I was saved; there was a police-man talking to me.

I wasn't sure how he found me or why he was way up here in the middle of nowhere. I tried to speak, but the pain in my leg returned to me as well my vision. I clench my teeth trying to fight it enough to ask who he was. He said that he was sent to this location because of a report of a distur-bance going on. Being the rookie of the squad, they sent him because they thought this was some sort of joke. He said they got a call from some man out in Washington who demanded that someone come out here to check things. Whoever the man was he knew the law and forced our hand.

It made sense now, the letter that the Spanish guys gave Ray. It was Frank's address. I began to cry into the policeman's shoulder, losing total control. He helped me up into his car and did the best he could to bandage my leg. He called for an ambulance to come help and began to ask me what happen. I tried to tell him everything, but my words came across like gibberish. I was shaking and frightened about everything that just happen. I tried to take a deep breath to calm down, but then I saw lights coming from up the road. For a moment, I admired how fast the ambulance had come but then realized it was coming from the other direction. It was Frank's car.

His car pulled up to a stop about ten yards ahead of us. He kept his high beam on and just sat there. The young cop didn't know what exactly to do. He told me to sit in the back of the car and stayed down. Putting his hand on his gun, he started to yell toward the car. "You in the car, come out with your hands up." There was only silence. It was hard to see anything, and Frank had the advantage. I tried to yell to the young cop to just wait and call for backup. We were dealing with Frank, and he was crazy.

I strained to see what was going on, but it was hard to make things out. One of the shadows made a quick move and then I heard a shot. I wasn't sure who shot who, but I was scared. The last standing shadow started moving back toward the car as the other one fell to the ground.

Fear overtook my body. I searched around trying to the knife that I had but the only thing available was a shotgun that was locked and the policeman had the key. I thought

253

about trying to run but that wouldn't get me too far. My leg was still killing me and any attempt to run would be stupid.

I did the only thing that I could do in the situation, the only thing that had gotten me this far. I closed my eyes and started to pray. I'm not sure what I was saying, but I just prayed until I felt a hand on my shoulder. I screamed figuring this was the end, but as I opened my eyes, I saw the young policeman. My heart leaped with joy, and I hugged him around the neck.

"What happened?" I asked him. He didn't say anything but reached for his radio. He called in for another ambulance and then turned to me. "Just stay here. I have to go check him out. I will be right back."

I tried to plea with him to stay, but it seemed to only bring about a cocky attitude. He turned to me almost insulted and yelled for me to say right where I was at. I told him that Frank could be tricky, but he moved ahead anyway. For a long moment there was silence, no sound, and then he came back.

I sat in the car puzzled not really sure what was going on. He started to ask me questions, which I couldn't understand. He asked me what my association with Frank was. I didn't answer right away, not sure where this was going. He then told me that he needed to show me something. He reached out his hand toward me, motioning for me to come with him. I was still in pain, but then my curiosity took over. I followed him to where Frank was and gasped.

Right in front of me by my feet laid Frank curled up like a baby and sucking his thumb. Blood was coming from one shoulder where he was shot. The young policeman looked at him and then looked at me. He leaned over and asked me whether that was Frank the movie star. I was speechless. This was not how I expected things to end. I thought things were going to end with a fight for the death but not like this. Frank turned to look up at me and began to cry and say that he was sorry. It was pathetic watching this grown man, this would be a killer had become this little child. Deep inside me, I felt pity for him but not that much. He was crazy and hurt, and I was free. After all this time, I was free. My victory was interrupted by the sound of the ambulances and other police cars. The whole thing was over. I was alive. I was the victor. I would no longer have to worry about Frank again.

Ray had jumped on the next flight coming out to LA and we met up at the police station. I limped into his arms and held him tightly. In the mist of criminals, policemen, and lawyer, we just held on to each other tightly as if no one were there.

I was safe, and the man I loved was in my arms.

I was free of my demon, or at least I hope I was….

End

About the Author

Ken Harvey
Former NFL linebacker,
businessman, father, friend.

Ken Harvey grew up in
Austin, Texas. Shortly after attend-
ing UC Berkeley, he was selected
for the first round, twelfth over-
all, of the 1988 NFL draft by the
Arizona Cardinals. There he played
six seasons until signing with the
Washington Redskins in 1994. He was selected to his fourth
straight NFL Pro Bowl in 1997 and ended his career with 89
sacks, averaging 8.6 per season. Ken retired just prior to the
start of the 1999 season.

In 2002, Ken received the prestigious honor of being nominated in the Washington Redskin's highest accolade as one of "80 Greatest Redskins." Shortly after receiving that honor, he was chosen and inducted into the "Redskins Ring of Fame at Fed Ex Field." He has been nominated for the Hall of Fame several times, but up to this point has never made it past the first round.

Ken currently works with Fellows Financial group where he is an advocate for companies and individuals.

Ken is married to Janice and has three sons, Nathaniel (deceased), Anthony, and Marcus.

CPSIA information can be obtained
at www.ICGtesting.com
Printed in the USA
FFOW04n1536050318
45439042-46153FF